Our Cursed Love

ALSO BY JULIE ABE

YOUNG ADULT
The Charmed List

YOUNG READERS
Eva Evergreen, Semi-Magical Witch
Eva Evergreen and the Cursed Witch
Alliana, Girl of Dragons
Tessa Miyata Is No Hero

Our Cursed Love

Julie Abe

WEDNESDAY BOOKS
NEW YORK

First published in the United States by Wednesday Books, an imprint of St. Martin's Publishing Group

OUR CURSED LOVE. Copyright © 2023 by Julie Abe. All rights reserved. Printed in the United States of America. For information, address St. Martin's Publishing Group, 120 Broadway, New York, NY 10271.

www.wednesdaybooks.com

The Library of Congress Cataloging-in-Publication Data is available upon request.

ISBN 978-1-250-85132-1 (hardcover)
ISBN 978-1-250-85131-4 (ebook)

Our books may be purchased in bulk for promotional, educational, or business use. Please contact your local bookseller or the Macmillan Corporate and Premium Sales Department at 1-800-221-7945, extension 5442, or by email at MacmillanSpecialMarkets@macmillan.com.

First Edition: 2023

10 9 8 7 6 5 4 3 2 1

For Chelsea—like so many of my books,
this story wouldn't exist without you.

And for May, with endless love.

Eight Days Until New Year's Eve

SATURDAY, DECEMBER 23

Remy

Through the train window, Tokyo's lights glimmer like birthday candles in the fading afternoon sun, and Remy feels like she's so, so close to having her wishes come true.

With a yawn, she rubs her eyes, shifting on her pillow for a better angle.

There are only two things she wishes for; one in particular that she's wished for every year, for as long as she can remember. Both might very well come true this winter break. If—*if*—she has more luck than she's ever had before. Knowing how things have been recently, though, this trip might be her last chance to make them come true.

The loudspeaker crackles overhead as the train conductor announces in Japanese, "We will arrive momentarily at Shibuya."

Remy freezes. She's not lying in her bedroom back in California, scrolling through travel blogs—the rocking train had lulled her into a jet-lagged daze on the ride from the airport to Shibuya Station. That's right. She's just arrived for a busy week, with an interview at her *dream* university, the potential answer to her first wish—and a full week with . . .

Her pillow. Who is *definitely* not a pillow.

Remy's eyes swing up and to the left and her breath hitches, in that involuntary way it does whenever she sees Cameron Yasuda these days. Her best friend is lanky and nearly a foot taller than her, his chest rising and falling gently as he sleeps—he can snooze through anything, even the train's loud conductor.

She knows almost all of Cam, her best friend throughout her entire life, even his soft, sleepy, quiet breaths. Dark eyes and light brown hair that's softer than clouds, and tanned skin from their days spent sitting in the park near home. He's a cinnamon roll, from outside to in; his kindness has melted even the coldest of hearts at their high school. And everything about him—all the little things, like his sweet smiles, his obsession with elixirs—feels like it's become a part of Remy, too.

Remy sits up, trying not to jostle him, but he rouses himself.

"Are we there yet?" Cam yawns. "A potion for your thoughts?" The city lights make his face glow.

"You'll whip one up here?" she murmurs back. "That's pretty smooth, even for you."

That's the second-biggest secret Remy keeps, but at least this one she happily shares with her best friend: magic. There's a whole enchanted side to the world, but it's kept hidden from "the general public." If he hadn't also come from a family sworn into magical society, Cam wouldn't be allowed to find out about magic because of past disasters where it's gotten into the wrong hands. By international magical society's laws, she would've had to marry him to share the world of magic . . . and she's not anywhere close to making that happen. After all, she hasn't even been able to confess her feelings yet.

He laughs. "I'll *try* to create whatever you want."

And he totally would, too, because Cam is *Cam*. He's always been a rock for Remy, whether she's bawling from a K-drama, burning yet another batch of cookies, or frantically studying for her finals. Cam always knows to bring tissues and a box of Goldsticks (their favorite magical snack) for their Netflix marathons, and he always knows just how to tutor her in chemistry so she can ace her tests.

But Remy can't ask him for one now, because the only potion she could ever imagine helping her would be a love potion—not that they exist, anymore. And this year, she made a different promise on her birthday candles, in late January. Her biggest secret, the one that she holds close to her heart, thrumming and beating with every breath, every wish: *This year, I'll tell Cam how I really feel about him.*

Except now it's December 23, and she only has *this* week before the year's up.

She stares out the window as the train slows. Somewhere, out in Tokyo, she has to find the perfect spot for her confession. The Spot where they'll potentially become a couple.

The doors purr open, and she hurriedly stands. Her arm shoots out right when Cam is also reaching out for her aqua-blue suitcase, and their hands collide.

Instantly, she turns into the mess she always becomes these days when Cam touches her, even accidentally. "Oh—I'm sorry—"

He withdraws his hand like her touch burns, and all her words dissolve into ash, dry in her throat.

"Um, no worries," Cam says, his eyes glued to the suitcase. "I'm just clumsy when I'm sleepy."

He's sweet as ever, trying to say anything to not make Remy feel bad, but the way he jerked back is enough of a sign.

If I tell him, Cam will be so sweet and nice, even as he rejects me. The lump in her throat grows, the lump that's been there for almost four full years. She's tried and *tried* to fall in love with someone else; she's kissed a lot of (human) frogs that definitely didn't end up sparking a feeling even close to the way she feels with Cam.

Remy grabs her suitcase and follows him out of the train and into Shibuya Station, wishing on birthday candles and this once-in-a-lifetime trip and shooting stars that Cam might be in love with her, too.

"We're meeting Ellie and Jack near that dog statue, right? Hachiko?" Cam asks.

She nods, squinting as she reads a sign, looking for the right exit among the five million possible exits. Cam and Remy have been learning how to speak Japanese at their Saturday classes for years, but it's bewildering that they're actually here.

"This way—I think." Remy points to their left. The train station is full of shiny white tiles, so pristine that they glimmer under the fluorescent lights. Before she knows it, they're exiting out of a ticket gate, and a winter breeze blasts them in the face.

"Oh," Cam breathes out with relief.

"That feels so good," Remy echoes. After a twelve-hour flight from San Jose Airport to Tokyo followed by the half-hour train ride, it's nice to feel something *real*.

Speaking of real . . .

Tokyo is truly *un*real.

A flood of business workers in black suits push them out like a tide; they're swept up and out of the station and deposited onto an expansive plaza, lined with buildings so tall that Remy is sure she'll fall over if she looks all the way up. Billboards flash with lights, and there are store names everywhere. She wants to drink in everything all at once: the chatter of people meeting friends, the blinking lights of advertisements from nearby stores, the sound of buses and cars whirring by on the road and filling the air with noise.

Remy and Cam gape at the edge of an intersection—*the* Shibuya Scramble, the most famous crossing in Japan, or maybe even in the world. The pedestrian light flashes green, and the floodgates open as people stride every which way, cozily dressed in thick coats.

Out here on the street, even without wearing rose-tinted charmed spectacles to check, Remy is sure that thick puffs of raw magical dust swirl from the passersby, shimmering with their joy and ready to be turned into a charm. The world can seem completely ordinary, but she knows: there is magic in it. She would bet a hundred yen that the coffee shop overlooking the crosswalk sells French press coffee tinged with enchantments for awe and excitement, and that Shibuya 109 is likely stuffed with cute, trendy clothes woven with spells for confidence.

"Wow," Cam says. "We're finally here."

It sounds silly, but she completely understands. Dedicating so many hours at their part-time jobs to scrape together money for the tickets, rummaging through their closets to sell off anything and everything that might add up to a few bucks, dipping into their savings . . . has led to *this*.

Remy's heart swells with joy. If they managed to make it all the way to Japan, surely they can do anything together, even *that* wish.

Cam drinks in the sights with a huge grin. "This is amazing, Remy. I'm so glad we're here, together."

He always knows the right thing to say, when Remy can't even decide when or how to confess her feelings for him. But she *has* to. Even if there's a chance she'll lose him, even if he rejects her . . . she *has* to get out her confession before they go their separate ways for college.

With Cam, there have been so many moments that feel like they've been stolen from someone else's life—like their movie nights lying out on her bedroom floor, or the school dance she asked him to as "just friends" where she was so close to blurting out, *I like you. Like, really like you.* But the thought of changing their relationship made her blabber about how the cheap decorations looked like a box of discount Goldsticks instead.

Remy has been searching for hints, for jars of good luck, for shooting stars that sparkle with the message *now-now-now.*

But what if there really is no perfect time?

She tugs at her hairband, and her stick-straight black hair falls out of its top-of-head messy bun, so her bangs and long hair frame her round face and owl-like wide eyes. Then she looks down at her black fleece leggings and the rumpled coat Cam had pulled out of his backpack for her, and groans. No amount of magic can fix this. She needs a fairy godmother—and those don't exist.

But this is the start of their trip. Maybe they'll be able to spend their winter break as a couple, instead of just as best friends.

Hesitantly, she turns toward Cam. "I've got something I've been meaning to tell you. I totally understand if you don't feel—"

"The bus is here! Over here!" A group of loud tourists plow through, and there are too many cameras and flag-wavers in her face. The moment they disappear, Remy looks around frantically.

Cam, her crush, the person she was just confessing her undying love to, is nowhere to be seen.

Remy

"Cam, where are you?" Remy wraps her jacket closer in the late December chill, wishing she'd remembered to bring a scarf.

A salaryman—that's what office workers are called here—dodges Remy's broken suitcase. One of the creaky wheels doesn't work right, and it keeps sliding away. She drags it back to her side as she rummages through her pockets.

"I swear, there's a vanishing charm on everything around me." Her phone screen is flickering with one bar of battery left, but that's enough to text. Cam had used her charger during the flight, because they'd been playing puzzle games on his phone. She unlocks her phone and it flashes to the background picture of her, her older sister Ellie, and their dog Mochi in front of their parents' tea shop in California.

Her phone blinks with a warning message: *No reception.*

"*Shoot.*" She hasn't set up her international phone plan yet. Because the general public doesn't know about magic, she isn't even able to use a charm to find her way, like that time she and Cam went hiking and ended up lost in the woodsy hills of Portola Valley. There are too many people around for her to open up her luggage and start pulling out enchanted charms, anyway. The Tokyo Magical Bureau would escort her straight back onto the plane.

"I'm totally not lost. I absolutely know where to go. Everything is fine. When I look around, I'm sure I'll find him . . ." She looks around at the bewilderingly bright billboards and fluidly moving, chattering crowds.

Remy and Cam would both willingly admit they're directionally challenged. Not to say that Cam isn't smart. His "for fun" hobby is recreating archaic potions. And together, he and Remy are whizzes at puzzles on paper, can get out of escape rooms in under forty-five minutes, and are one more train ride from completing level 5,518 of Candy Crush. But if either of them strolls into a store and walks straight out, they're completely unable to figure out which way they've come from.

Even if she *knows* she's bad at finding places, it doesn't help that nervous pit of anxiety roiling in her stomach. Because she hates not having Cam at her side, though she'd never admit it out loud.

Then—"*Oh.*" Remy spots him. Cameron Yasuda stands in the middle of the Shibuya intersection, scanning the crowds.

She thought she was ready to confess but, truthfully, she probably would've blurted out something completely unrelated again. Remy needs more courage than there is luck in the world in order to tell Cam she loves him. Something always gets in the way, like it's a big red stop sign that says, *No, don't confess now* or *He doesn't feel the same way.*

Just like those tourists.

The pedestrian signal is flickering out; Cam starts striding toward the other side of the intersection, and her heart jumps to her throat. Now. Now's her chance. She can run over to him, pull him out of the crowd, and finally have that conversation she's been avoiding all seventeen years of her life, ever since they were born at Stanford Hospital minutes apart from each other, their moms in next-door rooms.

There it is again—that feeling like she can't breathe. It's like when she swallowed the bagful of beans from that one time she and Cam mistakenly charmed the beans to make the two of them jump around instead of making them feel like jumping with joy. Or like when her parents ask what she sees herself doing as a career and she suddenly has the need to attempt a new coffee cake recipe, but this time it's a good kind of fluttery.

And what if Cam says he likes her, but not in that way?

She's too scared of the chance that their friendship might fall apart, even if it means a chance at more. It's senior year, and everything is changing way too fast. It started with her sister moving overseas to Japan so she could study at Tokyo Magical University, then college apps and that dreaded "What's your major going to be?" as if she knows her whole freaking life at age seventeen. And her upcoming interview—thinking of it makes her itch to dig up her notes again, and practice one more time.

TMU has been the dream school for her, ever since she heard about magical colleges from Ellie. If she gets in, she'd take their open degree program, and have the opportunity to explore different magical careers before having to figure out what she likes. If there's any place for someone as undecided as her, TMU is the right place, the one place where she'd belong, even if Cam's not at her side. She's even emailed with a few graduates from TMU to ask about their experience, and all of them have loved it.

Remy's always wanted a path that's custom-made for her, even the version of her that she tries to hide that's unsure about things. TMU, out of anywhere, is the place to figure it all out. She doesn't have a calling like Cam has his alchemy, Ellie has her art, Jack has his medicine . . . And she's longed for that. Remy has always wanted something that was all hers.

Five years from now, Cam will likely return from MIT or Stanford or Harvard—she's not the best at math, but she's 147 percent positive any of the top-tier universities would select him instantly for their Magical Alchemy programs—and he'll have a gorgeous, brainy, soon-to-be fiancée in tow. Remy will hate her completely and the new girl will be jealous of Remy, but MIT-girl will be so unintentionally charming that Remy won't be able to keep it up, and they'll end up best friends, too. The audience will sigh with delight, and after the credits roll, Remy will be no more than an extra in the crowd, as he gets married and has loads of beautiful and brainy kids.

And I'm his childhood best friend, the girl who's likable enough now, yet a complete secondary character in the movies. I'm the fun girl that people date before they find The One, so I go on dates with others to end up getting burned or realize I'm not in love with them, because they're not him. *I'm not brilliantly brainy like Cam, and I can't understand all that alchemy he's obsessed with. If I tell him I'm madly in love with him, we're going to lose that sense of comfortableness between us, the thing that makes us* us, *and he'll drift away from me faster than a missed shot on Candy Crush.*

Remy has to tell him *now*, before college, before it's too late . . .

MIT's early action results are already out, but he's been ignoring his phone reminders to check the admissions portal, for some reason. He keeps clicking *Remind me later*, like MIT's decision might change or he's nervous about whether or not he's gotten in.

But she wants things with Cam to be the same, at least for a little bit longer.

Because, even if he doesn't love her, being with him is home.

Like every time she's tried to tell Cam, she ends up shaking her head: *This wasn't the right time. I was totally going to get rejected. I'll find a better time later.*

But that sneaky thought burns at the back of her mind: *What if there's never a* right *time with Cam?*

"The girl stared at him with longing filling her soul," a voice narrates, and Remy nods emphatically. *True. Can't deny that.*

Then she freezes. "Ellie!" Her suitcase slides away from her, disappearing into the crowd as she barrels into her older sister, wrapping her in a huge hug. "I've missed you so much!"

They've only been away from each other for a month—when Ellie and Jack had visited for Thanksgiving—but it's been far too long.

Ellie Kobata grins. "Are you also going to say, 'Hi, dearest sister, you saved me from swooning'?"

"No way," Remy returns. Ellie smirks; she knows all too well that's a lie.

"Hey, Remy." Jack Yasuda, Ellie's boyfriend and Cam's older brother, materializes out of the crowd, his brows furrowed, pushing the aqua-blue suitcase. "Is this yours?"

It's jarring to see Jack when Remy is looking for Cam. Strangers comment all the time that the two brothers look similar, and *sure*, they have the same brown hair and coloring, and he's great for Remy's sister, and the way Jack's stony face lights up when he sees Ellie is cute and all. But Cam is *the* Yasuda boy for her. Cam's got this gentleness to his movements as he works out a puzzle; uncapturable laughter in his words when Remy and Cam argue nerdy things like the best anime of the season; and an infinite sweetness, like in the way—in the instant the plane hit turbulence—he gave her the anti-nausea meds that she thought she'd forgotten at home.

He's Cam, best friend, keeper of all of Remy's secrets, and the possible love-of-her-life-but-he-doesn't-know-it. And if things keep going the way they are, he'll never know. Everything else will change. At least they'll stay best friends. Forever and ever.

But nothing more than that.

Cam

Cameron Yasuda is doing absolutely great, thanks for asking. He's great at getting lost, great at avoiding his future decisions, and great at losing his best friend in a completely new city.

He squints up at the café he's loitering in front of as he waits for the pedestrian light to turn green again. Through the window, he can read the menu—he'll grudgingly thank his dad for years of Saturday Japanese school—and there's a tiramisu Mille Crêpe cake that Remy would love. Cam has read up on Japan's Magic Society; here, most magic-aware buildings are in plain sight—though their enchanted capabilities are still a secret to the general public. Those who aren't magic-aware might not realize charms and enchantments exist, but the most sensitive of people recognize it to a certain level. Like the genius kid that he babysits on weekends, who is obsessed with the stationery from CharmWorks, Cam's dad's shop—because he swears that using it to take notes helps him ace all his tests. Or the sweet couple who come by Remy's family's tea shop for a weekly date, saying that the cozy environment always fills them with contentment—because they don't realize that the matcha boba teas they guzzle up are charmed with joy.

Hopefully the pastries at this café are filled with bravery, because he could use some. It would be nice to take Remy here someday. Not a date, though, obviously, even though it'd totally sound like that if he asked.

His phone buzzes again. *Reminder: MIT early decision results out today! Check your email!*

That "today" was a few days ago. He's just not ready to look, yet. So, like a few too many times before, he hits *Remind me later.*

Cam applied to MIT for the right reasons. After his mom passed away from lung cancer, his older brother focused on a medical career, but Cam would rather be with his potions and Bunsen burner than having to see patient after patient. It would be too much like seeing his mother in the stark-white hospital bed all over again. With his affinity for magical alchemy, there are surely potions he can create that could change lives.

He's only applied to MIT so far because he can only apply early decision for one college. But for him, MIT is it. He doesn't have the money to apply to nearly all the schools in the U.S. like his richer class-mates, anyway. Besides, his application is so competitive, surely he's gotten in . . . And he needs that full ride.

But the thought of opening up the results gives him a strange twist in his stomach. He should enjoy this week, first. His last vacation with Remy, before they split up for college.

Speaking of his best friend . . .

Cam groans again, scanning the Shibuya intersection, looking for that bright smile or that aqua-blue broken suitcase that he wants to fix later, though Remy stubbornly told him not to worry about it. "Remy, how can you disappear so fast?"

If only they hadn't gotten separated when they'd burst out of the train station. The awe in her face as she drank in the huge overhead screens and the chattering crowds, the Hachiko statue, the way her eyelids had fluttered closed as she'd breathed in the breezy winter air, the tip of her nose turning instantly red—everything. He'd rattled off some nerdy fact about how the dog that inspired the Hachiko statue isn't a Shiba, like most people think, but an Akita, and she'd laughed.

"Only you would know facts like this, and I *love* it." Together, she's the Beauty (with brains) but he's just-the-Geek. Still, hearing that laugh, well, that's always *better* than magic.

But he doesn't have the slightest clue where she is. He doesn't even know where he is, to tell the truth. Other than the obvious: standing on the I-Need-to-Figure-Out-My-Life Street in Tokyo, Japan.

"Cam!" It sounds like Remy. He swivels around, though he can't see her.

Then a deeper voice that can only be one person. "*Yuji!*" Only Jack, Cam's older brother, calls him by his middle name.

There's a flash of light brown hair, the same color as Cam's, on the opposite side of the intersection. Jack's almost as tall as Cam, so he sticks out above the crowd. Ellie, his girlfriend and Remy's older sister, stands at his side, but—

Remy.

She's laughing with her sister, hugging Ellie tight. Then, her bright eyes meet his, and Cam doesn't even feel himself running once the light changes. In a flash, he's standing in front of her. "Remy! I'm sorry I didn't—"

"It's okay," Remy says instantly.

And thank goodness she cuts in, because Cam's wondering what he was going to say. *Sorry I didn't hold your hand?*

Brilliant idea. Better than the potion that he made the other day that vanished into thin air. That's *totally* what best friends do right before they have to leave each other for college.

Then, Cam turns to his brother. There's a pause; a long, measured look between them.

Cam can almost hear his father's shouts; Jack and their dad had gotten into a big fight over Thanksgiving last year, and things still haven't smoothed over yet. Before Cam had left, his dad was still grumbling about Cam leaving him to see Jack, even though Cam and Remy had started planning this three years ago, when she'd first mentioned her interest in applying to magical colleges in Japan.

"Hey," Cam says quietly.

"It's good to see you," Jack says. Cam's taut energy eases, just a bit. "How's Dad?"

Cam's shoulders hitch back up again. "The same." Mr. Yasuda is far from the easiest to deal with, but he's all they have after their mom passed away years ago.

Jack only nods; Cam knows he'd rather talk about anything other than their dad. "How'd you two get separated?"

Ellie laughs, quickly easing into the topic change. "Let me guess— you two were too directionally challenged to find your way back to each other?"

"Logistics, logistics. I'd just found him when you two found me," Remy claims. "Anyway, it's so good to see you. It's been too long!"

"Ellie's already made a list of places you need to go to," Jack says, nudging his girlfriend teasingly.

Remy laughs. "Typical." Ellie's a budding architect with a penchant for lists.

"C'mon," Jack says, nodding his head back toward the station. "The Tōyoko line train is going to be here in five minutes. If we hurry, we'll be able to get to Uncle David's before he finishes cutting up tonight's sashimi."

Seconds later, Jack and Cam walk side by side behind Remy and Ellie, who are already blazing their way to the next train. And there's a loaded silence.

"Truce?" Jack offers, quietly.

Cam pauses. "What?"

"I know there's a lot going on with Dad, and I'm sure he gave you an earful about coming here," his older brother says. "But while you're here, enjoy the trip. Don't worry about what's going on between Dad and me."

Cam wants to know if things are okay between Jack and *him*, not just between Jack and their dad. "Well—"

"It's okay. It's okay if Dad and I don't get along," Jack says. "But don't let that impact this trip. This is the last time you're free before college starts up. Next summer, you'll be taking that intro class for MIT, right?"

The phone feels even heavier in Cam's jacket. Maybe Jack just wants a truce for Ellie and Remy's sake. "Yeah, totally. Just a few months, and I'll be stuck on the East Coast. Who knows when I'll be able to come back here."

Student loans and scholarships won't pay for a vacation in Japan, that's for sure. And research opportunities between colleges are out there, but they have huge competition among undergrad and grad students. He'd be competing against scientists working on their PhDs.

His eyes catch on Remy, who has linked arms with her sister as they laugh and catch up. The sharp fluorescent lights would make anyone else look washed out, especially after a cross-Pacific flight, but she glows. As if she can sense his gaze, she looks over her shoulder, shooting him a grin, and Cam does his best to smile back.

Cam knew this already, but the reality of it is really sinking in. This is the last time he'll see Jack for a while, but it's his and Remy's last trip together for a long, long time.

Seven Days Until New Year's Eve

SUNDAY, DECEMBER 24

Remy

"Oh, shoot. Incoming!"

Remy ducks as something round and dark flies through the late-morning light. She's not fast enough, though, and it smacks against her cup. The magical jet-lag remedy in her mug sloshes dangerously, sparking with each swirl.

"Sorry," Jack calls, from the other end of the apartment.

"I can't believe you." Cam laughs. "Are you nineteen going on four?"

He takes the pair of fuzzy gloves from Remy's outstretched hand, and chucks it back at his older brother, but not before shooting Remy a grin that makes her stomach flip—and it's not the jet lag, this time.

Uncle David's apartment near Yūtenji Station is on the fifth story of an off-white building, simple and understated, with pale wood cabinets, sleek countertops, and a tiny, fairy-light-draped Christmas tree next to the windows that overlook the rest of the suburbs. The apartment looks like it's been featured on an interior design Instagram page, complete with tatami floors in the living room and the maplewood low table that Remy and Ellie are sitting at—except for Cam and Jack playfully lobbing their gloves at each other for an indoor version of a snowball fight as Remy tries to solve the latest level of Candy Crush (she's so close to beating level 5,519).

It's Christmas Eve, but nothing quite like the holidays that Remy celebrates at home, opening presents with her parents in the morning and baking cookies throughout the day with Cam for all their neighbors in Sorcerer Square. Here, for most, Christmas isn't a big thing other than the cheery decorations at stores and ads for snowy-white cakes. Staying true to local traditions, Remy and Cam's only plans are to get over their jet lag and catch up with Jack and Ellie. Though she *did* smuggle over a handmade Christmas tree of cookies in her suitcase to give to Cam today.

Next year—Remy's heart sinks at the thought—she and Cam will likely make cookies over a video call. Neither of them can afford to fly back home every holiday, not with flight prices being as much as they are, and they've both felt every dollar of that cost for the trip here, through each hour of their part-time jobs. But a video session just won't feel the same.

On the other side of the table, Ellie's wrapping up a gift for her friend who's meeting them in a few minutes. She'd been up late adding in the final touches on a postcard-sized sketch of a gorgeous, magic-aware girl with dark, luminous eyes, with her chin on her hands as she sits behind a desk filled with spell books, a few pairs of trendy rose-colored spectacles (way newer than the hand-me-down pair Remy got from her mom), and countless bubbling vials.

Uncle David and his wife, Aunt Kiyoko, both magic-aware, hurry out of their bedroom, dressed up in formal business suits, except for their shoes, which are at the doorway. They're both shorter than Remy, though Uncle David is like a serene stream, whereas Aunt Kiyoko is like a bird that flits in and out of the waters.

"Naomi should be here any minute now," Uncle David says, catching the balled-up gloves and tossing them cleanly at Cam, who darts in front of Remy to catch them. This time, there's no stomach-flipping grin, and Remy tips the mug to drink more of the enchanted brew. The gingery elixir tickles her throat, but it's not enough to distract her.

"Meet us at the izakaya down the street at six o'clock," Aunt Kiyoko says. "The owner is a friend and very much looking forward to hosting my American family for dinner!"

The excitable older woman, full of energy and light, has a way of uplifting every conversation, and Remy really wishes she were her aunt, rather than Jack and Cam's aunt. Aunt Kiyoko and Uncle David have taken the four of them in as their own. Even Jack and Ellie, who share a small apartment closer to Ikebukuro, stayed over for the night.

Aunt Kiyoko frowns at a vial on a hanging shelf near the door; the slightly pink hue of the glass reveals only a few floating specks. "I need some raw magical dust for my commute. David, do you—"

"Yeah, I should." Then he shakes his head as his pockets come up empty. "I used my last vial to set up the rooms for the kids."

"And that was very much appreciated," Ellie calls from the table, where she's bundled up in layers. Even though Remy's older sister has been in Japan for over a full year now, she's still not used to the December chill. "Want me to gather some?"

Uncle David had infused extra warmth into the blankets with a vial of magical dust and a charm from his favorite household spell book. Remy's usually not bad with cool weather. Back home in Palo Alto, Remy would be taking Mochi out for a walk in a light sweater, even in late December. Here, her wool peacoat and thick sweater are barely enough.

"You can finish up your art piece, I'll do it," Cam offers. He always volunteers back at home; his dad has no patience for anything related to happiness, unless it's in the form of money. Magic, though Mr. Yasuda will only grudgingly admit it, is strongest with emotions like joy.

Remy presses her thumb to the inside of her leather purse, and a hidden panel opens. She tosses over the pair of rose-tinted glasses; Cam catches them neatly. She loves when he wears the magic-gathering lenses. It gives him come-hither mysterious vibes like V from BTS, one of her favorite bands.

Cam frowns as he concentrates. Little creases wrinkle his brow, and Remy is reminded of when they were four years old and Cam had been told by Mr. Yasuda that there *wasn't* an ice cream buffet for lunch in elementary school, contrary to what Jack had led him to believe. Remy and Cam had gotten Jack back by creating a prank potion—thanks to the magical alchemy set Cam had gotten for his birthday—and swapped it with Jack's usual mouthwash; everyone in a one-block radius heard his scream the next morning when he'd seen his delightfully mossy-green teeth.

Even without the glasses, she knows what he sees: magical raw dust is everywhere that emotions spark. It's powdery and soft, like crystal snow. Especially in a multi-floor apartment building like where his aunt and uncle live, raw magic will be thickly layered and easy to collect.

To her, without the rose-colored glasses, it looks like Cam is simply gathering air—which is exactly what someone not magic-aware might think. But as he catches it in the rose-tinted jar, the charm-infused glass shows a steadily increasing pile of shimmering sand. "All the raw magical dust must be from our dinner last night."

Remy's stomach growls in remembrance of the decadent sashimi spread Uncle David had had ready for them. Between laughing at Ellie's charming stories about the kids she teaches part-time to Uncle David serving up bowls of homemade matcha ice cream—made with her parents' tea—she'd instantly understood why Ellie and Jack had moved here and never wanted to leave.

A clink of glass distracts her; Cam's trying to cap a vial and holding on to another two, though it looks like he's close to dropping all three.

"I'll do that," Remy offers, moving to his side.

They work in a steady silence; Cam focuses on capturing the dust and Remy tightly seals the vials so even a speck won't escape. It's just like the way Remy helps Cam out on his alchemy research projects, holed up in his room together. Aunt Kiyoko opens the door to peer out and an icy breeze swirls in, making her shiver.

"Hey, aren't you going to be cold when we go out?" Cam asks, as Remy finishes up another vial.

She waves him off. "It's not that cold." Remy was planning on wear-

ing her favorite pastel cardigan, anyway. Her friend Minami sometimes joked that Remy looks like she just stepped out of Taylor Swift's
Lover album; ever since, she's taken pastels and vintage pieces as her
fashion manifesto.

His fingers brush against the back of her hand. "You're freezing."

"I'm—"

Cam pulls his mittens out of his pocket and slides them onto her
hands, one at a time. His hands hold hers, briefly, and Remy's breath
catches.

Surely there's no more air in this apartment. The rest of the room
fades away, even Ellie and Jack joking about battling something out
in an art contest, Aunt Kiyoko chatting about the izakaya tonight . . .

"There." Cam grins down at her, taking his hands away. Thank
goodness, because Remy isn't going to be able to move after all. He
continues on, "Now you look a little warmer. I've got an extra scarf,
too."

"This is more than enough." Oh, god, with his proximity, with that
look on his face, she's burning up.

He takes care of her in a way that's as natural as breathing—
although she can never remember how to breathe when he does things
like that. A quiet, steady joy warms her more than Uncle David's spell.
Being around Cam always has that effect.

Wait. If he can see the raw dust . . .

"Oh, hey, can I borrow your glasses?" she asks quickly. Cam pulls
them off; he doesn't need them anymore.

Remy slides them on. The metal is still warm from his skin, though
that's not what makes her cheeks heat up like a full-on oven blast.
Sparks of raw magical dust shimmer around her, blinking into existence. The pure joy of being around Cam and his so-good-it's-deadly
laugh is way too obvious.

"Hey, you missed a bit." She gestures to where a few specks of the
pale, crystal-like dust cling to his cheekbone.

He tries rubbing at his face but totally misses. Remy reaches up,
and the traces of the raw magic dust tingle as she collects it on her

finger and stores it in the vial. Regardless of being near magical dust or not, touching him feels like it always does: the world is spinning around her when she hasn't moved a step.

"Thanks." His voice still has a bit of jet-lagged growl.

Remy takes off the glasses, sliding them back into her purse, her throat dry. Her hands feel like rubber as she grabs her mug and drains every last drop of the magical brew, just to try to concentrate on something.

The doorbell chimes and Aunt Kiyoko bustles over in her bright yellow slippers, a clashing mix with the serene interior. Remy has learned that the design is all thanks to Uncle David's artistic sense. "Ah, that must be Naomi-chan! I love all of Jack and Ellie's friends, but Naomi-chan especially so! She's excited to meet you both, Cam-kun and Remy-chan!"

The door swings open. Remy is facing away, but she can see Cam's reaction. Cam's eyes widen slightly as a cool breeze swirls through the warm apartment, prickling the back of Remy's neck. When she turns around, there's a girl framed in the entrance. Despite the freezing-cold weather, she's dressed in a thin gray puffer jacket, denim shorts, and black thigh socks that stretch up her perfect legs. Remy can almost hear Lia, Ellie's best friend back home, comment, "Wow. Smoking hot."

As if life isn't unfair enough, Remy reluctantly glances up at Naomi's face, and has to agree. The model-like girl that Ellie was drawing wasn't a reference picture from the internet. Her sister was actually drawing Naomi, with her heart-shaped face and artistically rumpled black hair grazing her cheeks and reaching to her shoulders. The beauty spot above her lip only further accentuates how gorgeous she is. She belongs on the cover of *ViVi*, the trendy Japanese fashion magazine.

"Ohayo!" Naomi waves to Jack and Ellie, and switches to perfect English. "Taka will meet us in Shimokita, he's searching for this awesome secret café for us."

Aunt Kiyoko almost drags Naomi over to introduce her to Cam. "Meet my nephew! Isn't he handsome?"

Cam bobs his head politely, but Remy can't miss the way Naomi looks up at him with her wide, doe-like eyes.

"Oh, hello!" Naomi says brightly. "It's a pleasure to finally meet you."

Remy ignores Ellie's smirk as she steps to Cam's side, playfully sliding her arm through his. "Hi, there!" Cam stiffens at her touch, and she swallows. Remy shouldn't be doing this, but she can't seem to loosen her grip.

"This is Remy," Aunt Kiyoko says. "Cam's best friend and—"

"Ellie's sister!" Naomi squeals and launches herself toward Remy. "Oh, your sister tells me so many wonderful things about you!"

Remy has to unloop herself from Cam as the petite girl locks her into a quick hug. If Remy were still wearing the rose-colored spectacles, Naomi would be positively sparkling.

The girl breaks away from Remy to grin at Cam again, with that bright, cover-model-worthy smile. "Shall we head over to Shimokita?"

———◆———

Shimokitazawa is a short walk away, through a maze of houses and narrow pavement streets. Ellie tugs Remy to her side, slightly behind Naomi happily chatting with the boys.

"So." Ellie's voice is a teasing undertone as she pulls her coat closer against the breezy chill. "How are things going between the two of you?"

Remy has half a mind to play dumb. *Two of you? Who?* But it's useless to hide from her big sister. "Things are great. Really great."

"*Really*? So you told him—"

"*Shh!*"

Cam, Jack, and Naomi are talking about the Good Luck Café— apparently their magical destination shows up in a new spot every day.

"I'll tell you later," Remy says, nodding up ahead. Ellie rolls her eyes.

"The first rule for those who find the tea shop is that they can't share exact coordinates; they can only hint at where it might be," Naomi is explaining.

"How's anyone know where it is, then?" Cam glances around like he might see it pop up between the small houses along this narrow road.

"There are clues on Mahine—that's Japan's top magic-aware social media app. Today's posts mention secondhand shops; a dead giveaway for Shimokita. Taka is already searching, so we'll meet up with him and keep looking. Hopefully I can find it first. I'd love to get my fortune told."

"A fortune?" Remy asks, despite herself.

Naomi turns around, beaming another one of those brighter-than-sunlight smiles. "Whoever finds the Good Luck Café gets their tea leaves interpreted by Mr. Yoshino, the owner. He's known in the magic community for his readings, because they're always spot-on. I'd love to get an idea of how I can better research the properties of magic dust. Or if I'll *ever* make a breakthrough on it."

They make a left turn past a gray stone wall and walk by a shrine covered by trees filled with leaves so thick that Remy can't see much inside, though Naomi has switched to telling Cam and Jack about its history, and how the Kitazawa Hachiman Shrine was built in the late fifteenth century, and all sorts of facts that Cam is likely soaking right up.

"Naomi's a magic alchemist," Ellie says. "One of the most brilliant at Tokyo Magical University's Faculty of Enchanted Sciences. I've been meaning to introduce her to you, Cam. She's the school's youngest teacher and PhD candidate."

"Wait." Cam stops still in the path. "You're . . . *you're* Professor N. Watanabe at TMU?"

She blinks. "I am. Who's asking?"

"Me. Cam Yasuda. I—I'm going to your research presentation at Tokyo Magical University. I emailed you a few months back . . ."

"Oh! You must've talked with my admin. He fields all the calls and manages my schedule. You must be something special if you got past his scrutiny."

Something special, indeed. Remy wishes her stomach wasn't twisted into a jealous mess. Even if she tried to drink some tea right now, she wouldn't be able to swallow a sip.

Remy had always thought that Professor Watanabe was an old, grizzly researcher, not, well, a prodigy only a few years older. Cam had even tried to look up a bio for the professor, but all photos and videos had been hidden from public view.

"Yeah," Cam says eagerly. "I know those academic reviews aren't usually public, but your admin allowed me access, after I shared some of my thoughts about your recent publications."

She laughs. "He's pretty good at sorting out the diehard fans."

"I mean, I've been the biggest fan of your expanded research into Takashi Ono's 1847 Soulmate Study. I hadn't heard of it before your article was published."

"Heard of what?" Jack asks.

Naomi grins. "Remember, that huge research project with all those magical tomes that crowded up my lab?"

"Tsukki thought you were making him a palace!" Ellie laughs. To Cam's questioning look, she clarifies, "Tsukki is Naomi's cat, and the protector of her lab. So, what was all of that for?"

"I published an article about it earlier this year, with more reference sources," Naomi explains. "Since no one had reviewed it since the early 1900s, I thought it would be interesting to look into it further. Basically, Dr. Ono proved that everyone has a soulmate, whether romantic or platonic in nature, and all the secondary sources and studies I've found have supported this."

Everyone has a soulmate. Remy perks up. This new girl might be the best bearer of news, ever.

"Do you think it could be disproved, though?" Cam asks. "Your conclusion led me to believe there may be room for error."

Naomi's eyes sparkle. "You read closely. I wouldn't be a researcher if I wasn't curious about whether it *could* be disproved . . . After all, the Soulmate Study isn't popular since it led to the banning of love potions, but still . . ."

Cam nods, eagerly. "That's true. Even if a theory is set into place, there is always room for new discoveries. That's something I've always admired about your research, Professor Watanabe. You always look at things with a fresh perspective."

"Just call me Naomi," she says, with a laugh. "It doesn't feel like a day off from my research when I get called 'Professor.'"

Remy has to tear her gaze away from Cam goggling at Naomi in awe. It's a relief when Jack pipes up to ask about the session Cam's attending, an hour-long thing about Naomi's current research projects. It's right when Remy is scheduled to have her first interview at Tokyo Magical University—the exciting start to her potential future in Japan, a step toward her dream university—but it wasn't supposed to feel like *this*.

Ellie leans in again. "So? How about I set you and Cam up on a date?"

The last time Ellie tried to set someone up, she convinced her best friend, Lia, to go on a date with Minami, Jack's semi-ex. It was a disaster. They'd met at the corner of University Avenue and Bryant Street, but by the time they'd made it to Kung Fu Tea—all of one hundred feet—they'd argued about twenty different things, most important being their attraction to each other. (Minami had firmly believed Lia had been head over heels for her since the beginning of time; Lia vehemently shot back that she was just doing Ellie a favor by showing up.) Minami has refused to speak to Lia ever since. Remy's sister meddling in her love life might ruin things completely.

"I've got it handled. I'm going to let Cam know how I really feel and ask him out—during this trip," Remy blurts out.

Ellie stops dead in her tracks.

Uh. Oh.

She latches onto Remy's arm. "Tell me *everything*."

Remy looks around frantically. They've reached the shopping district. Ellie and Remy are now standing in front of a secondhand shop bursting out onto the sidewalk with wire racks of oversized vintage band T-shirts on one side, and denim jeans on the other. The shop next to it is filled with pastel lace dresses that look like confections, with scores of floral-print and lace hair bows and accessories. Across the way, there's a tiny patisserie selling jiggly cheesecakes. At its side, a stairway leads to an underground vintage record store. Remy wants to inch into the music shop and bury herself in a pile of records, or hide forever in a jiggly cheesecake.

But Naomi and the boys are still walking, so Ellie tugs her to continue.

"Um . . ." Remy doesn't know the answers to the kinds of questions that her sister is probably thinking up. Her stomach recoils from memories of nightmares where Cam says, biting his lip, *Remy . . . I like you just as a friend . . .*

"Don't leave out a *single* detail," Ellie says. Remy can almost see her making a mental list of ways to help Remy and Cam get together.

"Well," Remy starts, continuing to look for an escape route. "Cam and I both want to see the illuminations at Yebisu Garden Place after we saw your drawing on Instagram. . . . I was thinking of telling him there."

Remy has spent sleepless nights staring at pictures of Yebisu Garden Place (and avoiding those nightmares of a life where Cam doesn't want to be friends with her or, just as bad, is dating the MIT-girl). There's something about its sparkling lights, the possibility of a chance of snow there, and the way it's named after Ebisu, the god of luck. It would be the perfect place to finally share her true feelings, and hope he doesn't "just friends" her.

Ellie nods eagerly. "That'll be perfect! Want to go tonight to scope it out?"

Remy swallows, glancing nervously at a curtained entranceway to a café they're passing by, squeezed in between a shop selling antique furniture and another clothing store. Tall bamboo stalks cover the front; she could've sworn it wasn't there a second ago, but Ellie is definitely distracting her. *Tonight?*

There's no magic big enough, but Remy wishes she could make her future flawless: Cam falling in love with her in an instant, the two of them embracing as snow swirls around them brighter than raw magical dust. If only she knew of a foolproof way to make him love her back.

Just friends . . .

Remy shudders. Then she takes another look at the curtains that flutter in another wintry breeze. It's some sort of tea shop. A hot mug of hojicha would be perfect right about now.

Remy blinks, pulling out memories of Saturday Japanese school as she reads the painted letters on the curtain.

福カフェ

"Hey." Remy stops. "Isn't that . . ."

"Stop trying to get out of this conversation," Ellie teases. "We've got to get the two of you dating, it's only been like seventeen years in the making."

Well, her sister isn't wrong. But Remy clears her throat, calling toward Cam, Jack, and Naomi, "I think I found the Good Luck Café."

Remy

The Good Luck Café is a haven amid the tall concrete buildings and endless stretches of pavement. Remy doesn't understand how she didn't notice it earlier. All she remembers is passing by a woman wheeling out a display to set up at her storefront, and the pinch of nervousness in her chest when Ellie had quizzed her about her love life. And then it was like a bamboo grove had sprouted out of nowhere, complete with the scarlet curtain fluttering at the entrance, stamped with white ink letters. The other shoppers wandering through Shimokitazawa pass right on by, their eyes flicking from the antique furniture store to the secondhand clothing shop, straight over the bamboo grove. This shop is definitely more magical than the rest.

Naomi steps forward, her voice hushed with awe. "Lucky you." Then she shoots a smile over her shoulder at Remy. "You'll get a reading from Mr. Yoshino. You can ask him about anything: college, your future, your love life—whatever is on your mind."

Love. Life. The conversation she was trying to get away from.

Her face burns. Hopefully she can just pretend the redness is from the cold.

"Are you Ellie's younger sister?" a smooth, rich voice asks in Japanese.

She looks up. A boy taller than Cam is dressed in a black leather jacket and dark-wash jeans. With his black stud earrings, slightly long hair swept perfectly into place, and a baseball cap tugged down low, he looks like he's just stepped away from a street fashion photographer. He shoots her a charismatic smile. "Remy, right? It's nice to finally meet you."

"Taka!" Naomi launches herself in the same, cheery way she'd hugged Remy earlier. She tugs him closer to the rest of them. "Meet Taka Suzuki, one of my best friends and classmates at TMU. He double majors in English and Magical International Relations."

"Ellie talks about you all the time!" Remy exclaims. "It's nice to finally meet you."

"Good things only, I hope." He laughs, leading them toward Good Luck Café. Cam and Remy linger at the gate, waiting for each other like they always do.

This would be the perfect chance to tell him how I feel. Before Cam goes off to some Ivy League, and I'm all the way here in Tokyo—if I get into TMU.

No. She's not ready. She needs a sign. Remy ducks through the scarlet curtain, and Cam follows.

"That's so cool you found this." Cam squints through the sun streaming down; it reminds her of impossibly perfect Saturday mornings, when he's chugging away at recreating one of Professor Watanabe's potions or completely absorbed in researching something of his own, and she bursts into his room, with a stack of pancakes delicately balanced on a plate or a basket filled with rice balls. And that way he looks up, lost in a haze of research and complex chemistry beyond anything she can even *try* to comprehend, with the light trickling through his window, pooling on that spot on his collarbone she wants to kiss and wrapping around his hands in the way she wants to lace her fingers into his . . . It's that moment when his eyes focus on hers when she breathes in sharply.

There's a phrase—*Koi no Yokan.* There's no direct translation, but it means that feeling of seeing someone and knowing you'll fall in love with them, someday. Remy hadn't been able to put a finger on what these feelings were, until she read about that. But even though it's supposed to be during that first sighting, she falls in love, every day, every moment she sees Cam. That slight intake of breath, the way her heart feels full when they talk; it's terrifying the way it's grown over these past years.

Then, there's a whirl of fresh air. It's like they're standing on the banks of the Katsura River in Kyoto, with the wind blowing off the flowing water. The faintly musty scent of the secondhand shops has disappeared; with the thick trees that surround them, she can't even see the rest of Tokyo now. The pebbled concrete path weaves through groves of bamboo and lush green trees that seem to have forgotten that it's the middle of winter.

The two of them walk in a steady, comfortable silence, drinking in the sights. Remy can't help but guess that the puffs of cedar-scented breeze are infused with a hint of magical wonder. Then again, with this view—and with Cam softly padding next to her—it feels particularly charmed.

They pause where the paths split apart. There are seven different options, each with faded wood signs next to them. Cam is busy reading the kanji, but she can't stop replaying that way Cam looked at Naomi this morning.

Koi no Yokan.

Did that just happen for him?

She chews on her lip. Hell, she can't match up to Naomi. She's no professor in the very subject that Cam's obsessed with; she has no research; she can't even figure out her college major. Ellie being in Japan had cemented her decision to apply to colleges here, but she'd only scored an interview with Tokyo Magical University because of being sisters with Ellie, who's a current student. How can she, a girl who doesn't have her future figured out, hold a candle to someone like Naomi?

Remy drifts closer to Cam, looping her arm into his. *Maybe* this *is the perfect chance.* His eyes catch hers and his lips part, like he's about to say something. Her throat burns tightly with the words she's never been able to get out. . . .

She blurts out, "I'm glad we're friends."

Acing things like usual, Remy. That's the perfect *way to start.* She could only be smoother if she'd stuck her foot into her mouth. *Can this magical forest swallow me up, please? Like,* now.

Cam tilts his head to the side; he's clearly puzzled. This has come out of nowhere, literally. Her cheeks burn. "This trip. I mean, we wouldn't be here, together, if we weren't best friends."

It's true; they'd signed up for shift after shift at the local bookstore (though, being surrounded by books didn't really feel like *work* to Remy), plus their parents' shops, counting up their tips and socking the money away. Setting up tons of price-tracker alerts to find the dirt-cheap airplane tickets; Remy discovering the charming suitcase that she loves from a garage sale for ten dollars, which Cam still says is nine dollars and ninety-nine cents too much. They'd worked for this, just the two of them, so she could interview at her dream college and they could explore Tokyo like they'd always dreamed about, too.

"I'd hate to be on this trip as enemies." Cam laughs. Then he gets quiet. "I'm glad to be here together, as best friends."

Best friends. Right. Remy grins like her heart isn't breaking as Cam nods to the path on the far right, where there's a sign for the Good Luck Café. "This way."

They follow the flat, black stone path as it widens to reveal a few empty waiting benches and then the Good Luck Café itself. The two-story dark gray building is far more modern than she'd expected, with shiny glass windows from ceiling to floor on the first floor. The wood sliding door, covered by a plank awning, is a nod to traditional Japanese architecture—something she's learned from Ellie—and Remy realizes that the café isn't just modern or old-fashioned. It's a perfect mix of both.

"Wow," Cam says. At his side, Remy nods. "It's gorgeous."

The door to the café is open, and the faint sound of chatter increases as they approach.

"Irasshaimase!" the waitstaff chimes, as they enter. The café is cozy and small, with beige walls and simple round wood tables, each with a tiny bonsai in the center. It seems that the café only takes up the first story; perhaps the owner lives on the second floor. Waitstaff hurry to and fro, carrying wood trays filled with clay cups and iron teapots and traditional Japanese sweets. The bitter, slightly floral scent of green tea fills the air, warm and welcoming.

"Hey, Remy."

She looks up.

Cam's back in that half-here, half-abstract thought land, the way he gets when he's trying to solve a complex problem. "There's been something I've been meaning to tell you—"

"Cam!" Naomi calls them over. "Remy!"

Remy shoots him a wry smile. "Maybe later? Looks like you're popular." She drops his arm as she pulls off her jacket. Despite the warmth inside, a soft, sad coldness brushes against her skin.

Then, she catches sight of the round table for six. There's only one seat each on opposite sides, and Naomi is waving Cam into the chair next to her, those gorgeously pretty eyes dead set on her best friend.

———◆———

Remy finds it difficult to look straight ahead. On the other side of the table, Naomi is leaning toward Cam, telling him something fascinating that she can't hear over Jack and Ellie laughing on her left or Taka—bless his heart—earnestly trying to keep up a conversation with her on the right.

She strains to hear her best friend's voice. "I've never seen an academic alchemy lab in person," Cam says.

"You *should* visit! Maybe after my presentation?" Naomi offers, and then shudders. "It'll be something to look forward to, at least. I always hate these presentations; it's just a bunch of foggy-brained old guys trying to find ways to knock me down."

Cam laughs. "I bet you don't let them."

"It's the principle of it!" Naomi protests. "I can't let them do that to the next girl who comes along, too."

Joke's on Remy. The brainiac beauty didn't wait until college to show up. She's already here.

At least Remy can drown her sorrows in delicious, endless green tea. Their waitress had mentioned that this is a gyokuro tea from Fukuoka Prefecture, made with leaves that were grown under shade for three and a half weeks; time out of the sun apparently gives it a sweeter flavor.

"Another cup?" Taka shifts in his chair. His model-worthy lips tug down with worry. "Are you sure you're all right?"

"Uh, super thirsty. Long walk, you know."

He flags over a waitress for a refill on their iron teapot just as the gentle piano music fades out, though Remy barely notices it. She frowns at her cup, willing it to magically fill up. The light traces of sediment swirl back and forth, like her feelings that won't stay hidden, no matter how much she tries to suppress them. *I should've said something on the way here! All I stupidly said was, "I'm glad we're friends."*

For all her previous relationships, they started like a blaze and went out just as quickly. She'd stopped dating after the homecoming dance earlier in the school year, because no one else compared to Cam.

Cam, who's leaving her soon.

She can't even imagine life without Cam right next to her side. What the hell do people do in long-distance relationships? Like, how can they go from being best friends and neighbors to people on the opposite ends of the world? There's only so much that video chats can let them experience together. Would that really be *love*?

Not for the first time, Remy wishes she'd applied to colleges in Boston. But the closest magical university was hours away in New York, and she'd only ever dreamed of going to Tokyo Magical University.

The curtain leading to the kitchen flips open, and a man in his thirties steps out. The waitstaff all pause to sweep into a bow, even though the man motions for them to move again.

Remy stops glaring at her tea. "What's going on?" she whispers to Taka.

"That's . . . um . . . Mr. Yoshino," Taka murmurs back, pulling his hat lower. His breath tickles on her cheek. "He does the readings."

The man stops at the table closest to the door. He's dressed in tailored black dress pants and a crisp white shirt, with a black half-apron tied at his waist. His skin is tanned, and his jet-black hair is parted neatly. The two women greet him effusively, and the woman with shorter hair gestures to her cup.

Mr. Yoshino nods, and in turn politely gestures her toward a small courtyard, visible through the windows. There are two chairs set around the small table. No fancy tablecloths, just two cups of tea and another iron teapot.

But, Remy has a feeling, if she were to put on a pair of rose-tinted glasses, she'd see that the tea there is absolutely glowing with magic.

Mr. Yoshino and the woman settle across from each other. The café is hushed; even the waitstaff, moving through the tables to refill tea or set down plates of sweets, are quiet. The glass muffles what the proprietor is saying, but the woman responds eagerly.

"I wonder what she's asking," Taka says. "Money, fame, love? What do you think?"

Remy glances over at the woman's companion, sitting alone at their table and watching her partner through the glass. "Maybe about where her love life is going? Maybe a job?"

Taka nods, smiling. "Yeah, don't you ever wonder where everyone's going?"

"All the time," Remy whispers. If only she knew the answers.

Mr. Yoshino picks up the woman's tea cup, shifts it to the side, and peers in. Remy finds herself longing for an answer to a question she hasn't even heard; what is it that Mr. Yoshino is foretelling?

Then, quietly, he murmurs to the woman, and she shoots her companion a quick nod and smile through the window. They beam at each other when they're finally seated back together, whispering happily.

"Looks like it was a good fortune," Taka says.

Remy gulps. "They're all . . . good, right? He wouldn't give bad fortunes. That'd scare away business."

Taka shakes his head. "That's what brings him customers. He doesn't sugarcoat his fortunes, and from everything I've heard, they all come true."

"*How*?"

"He's studied tea leaf fortune-telling his entire life; there's no one more dedicated to the craft in all of Japan. The tea leaves are specially charmed to show the truth—through a spell he won't even share with his own family. But you know how the non-magic-aware can't even see the entrance to this café, right? This *place* itself is magical, and I've got a feeling that helps with the readings. The Good Luck Café shows up in a different spot in Tokyo every day. There are some things about magic that we don't understand yet, and that's why researchers like Naomi study it all their lives. The Good Luck Café and Mr. Yoshino's one of those cases."

"Okay, but that doesn't mean his fortunes are real."

Taka laughs. "Fair. But I'm actually one of those people that he's told a fortune for. Three years back, I was wandering around Tokyo with a few friends, and I came across the Good Luck Café first, so I got my fortune read."

"And?"

"I asked about my future. He told me to keep studying and not to drop out, so that I could take my entrance exam for TMU."

"Anyone can say to study. My parents tell me all the time. If they could, they'd get my dog to tell me that, too."

Taka grins. "Except I hadn't told anyone—especially not my parents—that I was planning on dropping out. My parents would've disowned me—though they did, anyway, after I got in, because of some other stuff. Still, I never would've made it into TMU if it weren't for him."

Remy isn't convinced.

He leans over. "Naomi's older sister came to the café by herself; she was an aspiring author, but her professor had trashed her latest story. She was about to give up when she stumbled across this place. Mr. Yoshino read her fortune and told her that the next time she'd come by was when she was an award winner. Last year, she was awarded the Akutagawa Prize. Youngest winner ever."

Remy whistles, leaning back in her chair to think. "Damn. I hope he tells me I'll win the Nobel Prize. I guess I can ask about which colleges I'll get accepted into? Maybe . . . Ugh, I don't know what to ask."

Mr. Yoshino has stepped back inside; the entire room watches as he heads toward a table close to the kitchen, and Remy breathes out in relief.

Then Mr. Yoshino pivots. His dark eyes meet hers, and she nearly jumps out of her seat, almost dropping her tea. But, thankfully, he's simply stopping to talk to one of the waitstaff.

A pair of hands steady her cup. "Whoa, are you okay?"

She looks up into Taka's worried expression and squeezes out a nervous grin.

"I'm fine. Totally fine."

Everything's fine, except he isn't Cam, and it isn't his hands that are holding hers.

Then the question that she wants to ask pops up in her mind.

Taka glances over his shoulder. "I have to go make a call. Are you sure you're okay?"

Remy nods, and he disappears out the front door, quiet as a cat. She tries to take a sip of tea as she cranes to look for Mr. Yoshino—

Just as he steps up to the table and bows. They all bob their heads politely back—except for Remy, who's trying not to choke on her tea— and the man looks around the table. "Welcome to Good Luck Café. Who do I have the honor of reading a fortune for today?"

Everyone turns toward Remy, and Mr. Yoshino follows their gazes to look down at her.

Remy

A staff member guides her to the side door; Remy stumbles out behind Mr. Yoshino to the quiet, pebbled courtyard, shaded by leafy maples. Like the walk into the café, it should be petrifyingly cold, yet the breeze is somehow mild and temperate. There must be some expensive and magic-consuming warming charms around here, but no matter where she looks, all she can see are the pretty trees and—when she looks over her shoulder—everyone in the café staring at her.

Fun. She tries to wave cheerily at her friends, but she looks as smooth as the Tin Man from *The Wizard of Oz*. Ellie shoots her a thumbs-up, mouthing, *You've got this!*

Up close, she can see that Mr. Yoshino is middle-aged, maybe in his forties. He looks kind of like that guy who's in all the Japanese coffee ads: dependable yet with an air of elegance. He settles into his chair.

"If I may impose," he says politely, "may I ask you to pour your own cup? It's rather rude of me, but I'm afraid the magic doesn't read so well otherwise."

Remy takes the small iron teapot and pours a swirl of fragrant green tea into her cup; Mr. Yoshino inclines his head. "Now, let's wait a minute or so for it to cool down, then. When ready, you can drink, and then I'll take a look at the sediment at the bottom."

Nervously, Remy perches at the edge of her chair, staring at the white tea cup, with steam uncurling from the top. It's a pretty design, with gold merging where it looks like there were once cracks. It's a type of art called kintsugi, but she's never seen it used before in drinkware, only decorations.

"How do you make this kintsugi safe for drinks?" she asks.

Mr. Yoshino turns his head to the side, ever so carefully.

"My parents own a tea shop back in America," she explains. "We've never been able to use kintsugi because they've heard it isn't good to use for food."

"Usually, I don't reveal my secrets. But I want to assure you that this is safe; it's twenty-two-karat gold, so this cup itself is likely almost as expensive as the teas we offer," Mr. Yoshino says. "Though, I must say, our tea is quite pricey, too. It makes sense that your parents wouldn't want cups like these used regularly; they're too prone to someone walking off with them. Though, I am inclined to trust you, Miss Kobata."

Remy startles. "How did you know my name?"

The man smiles. "Ah, for that, it's none of *my* magic." He gestures toward his far left, where a small gray stone building peeks out from within the bamboo stalks. A silver sign dangles from the front, the words BENI'S APOTHECARY glowing with a silvery hue. "My sister told me the names of those who I'd read for today. She mentioned yours would be particularly interesting, and that you'd be with a big group. We usually only have single diners or couples. Are they your friends?"

It's true; Remy hadn't noticed it before, but theirs is the only big table in the room, the kind of round table that'd be normal back in California; not so much in Tokyo.

She can hear herself blabbering in her nervousness. "My sister, her boyfriend, my best friend, and two new people I've just met today. One's a professor at TMU, which is where I'm applying to, and the other is a student there—he studies Magical International Relations and English, which is neat because I didn't realize that I could double major."

Mr. Yoshino nods politely. Yeah, Remy definitely may be applying to TMU, but she gave him TMI. "So, do you have your question ready?"

How can I say that *question out loud, without being obvious?* Remy's throat is dry. *I should ask if I'll get into Tokyo Magical University. I've been dreaming about going there ever since I first heard about it, and I've got to get in. Or maybe ask what in the world I'm going to do with my life?* But, dammit, she already has her heart set on what she wants to know.

Remy's had plenty of dates. How can she ever know who is going to be *the* one?

The tea looks cool enough to drink; she knows from years of helping out at her parents' shop. Mr. Yoshino confirms it when he waves toward the cup.

"Keep your question in mind as you drink," he says. "And, when you are done drinking, please share the question with me."

She tips the cup up. When the liquid touches her lips, there's a spark, like electricity. Remy has heard of this before: it's the sensation of an extremely strong enchantment. But her earlier guess was wrong; it isn't the tea so much as it is the mug that prickles with a heavy concentration of magic.

It goes down smooth and hot; normally soothing to her soul, except she's too on edge to relax.

When she drains the last drop, she chances a glance at the bottom. There are no answers that she can see, just blobs of sediment, side by side. A strange pattern, sure, but it can't possibly mean anything. The gold lines on the cup glint as she speaks, her voice light and joking—the way she sounds on a first date, when nothing matters to her—but the strain of every word is pulling her apart. "I've been wondering, who is my soulmate?"

Remy's face burns. She wishes she could reel the words back into her mouth.

"Well." Mr. Yoshino nods slowly. "My sister was right. Today is an interesting day. I usually get questions about lost cats or if someone will be successful at a job or . . . Your tea, please?"

What did I just do? What did I just do . . . Remy offers up her mug. She's absolutely quiet when Mr. Yoshino nods, taking her cup to look inside.

Sweat dots the back of her neck. She sneaks a peek inside the café;

Taka is back from his call. Everyone stares out at her, Cam included. He smiles encouragingly, like he's trying to tell her, *It's going to be okay*, the same way he reassured her after the Chemistry midterm—she'd scraped a B-, even after all the tutoring he'd done for her.

Mr. Yoshino looks down at the cup, and then over to the table, at everyone watching them. Finally, he says, "The reading . . ."

He swallows.

If the fortune-teller says that Cam and I are soulmates, like everyone else says we are, then that'll be easy to confess! It'll mean he likes me, right? Or could come to like me, eventually. Then I wouldn't have to bring Cam to Yebisu Garden Place to tell him my feelings. We'd be going as a couple. It can even be our first date.

For some reason, though, the tea sloshes around in her stomach, unable to settle.

Mr. Yoshino clears his throat. "You should consider going next door." He gestures toward the apothecary he'd pointed out earlier. "Beni, my sister, mixes up great wish potions. I'm sure she'll have just the right thing. Her stock does wonders."

He's stalling. The man is trying to sell some magical tincture, when all Remy needs to know is the truth she's guessed at all along.

"Tell me the reading, please."

"Recently, I had a fortune that got even better results with one of Beni's elixirs. A couple wanted to find a better way to communicate, but they'd forgotten all the joy between each other. One of my sister's potions helped them spark memories of joy—"

"Please, my reading?" she asks. It can't be *that* bad.

Mr. Yoshino gives a long sigh. He picks up her cup one more time and stares at it; a shiver shoots down Remy's spine. Then his eyes drift back up to meet hers. "No. I'm sorry if you were expecting better news."

"No?" Remy echoes.

"No," the fortune-teller repeats, shaking his head. "I'm sorry, Miss Kobata, you *don't* have a soulmate."

Remy

Remy slides back into her seat, and Taka leans over. "How'd it go?" The rest of the café is already watching the next person get their fortune told; she's grateful for the lack of attention on her.

How did it go? I just found out I'm the only person in the world who doesn't have a soulmate. Remy would be the perfect experiment for Naomi and Cam to analyze. Something for them to bond over. She can already see their names, clustered at the top as coauthors of a ground-breaking article: *Takashi Ono's Soulmate Study Refuted.*

"Just . . . it's a lot," Remy responds, her throat dry.

Taka looks at her for a long moment; anyone can likely tell she's stunned.

"You don't have to tell us," Cam offers from the other side of the table. She shoots him a smile, even as her thoughts burn like wildfire in her heart. *I'd always hoped my soulmate would be* you.

Ellie, from her other side, nudges her. "Are you okay?"

Remy has to say something—though she can't wrap her mind around the fortune, yet. Everyone's leaning in to listen, including Cam.

"I asked about my college interview," Remy blurts out. "He told me that if I don't truly stun the team at Tokyo Magical University, I'm not getting in." She drops her gaze to the table; she can't bring herself to meet anyone's eyes after *that* lie.

"But your admission package is great!" Cam protests. "And you've practiced interviewing in Japanese and English for twelve months straight."

It's true; they've gone through so many questions she'd probably be able to jump into a presidential debate. Her heart swells at the way he defends her, looking so indignant on her behalf, like he's going to single-handedly convince all of Tokyo Magical University that she needs to be admitted.

You'll get in, we'll make sure of it, he'd said in January, when she'd revealed her dream college. It'd been the one New Year's resolution she'd told him. After that, they'd spent at least thirty minutes every day practicing for her interviews and polishing up her application.

"I think I know how to help you," Taka says.

"I'll take all the help I can get," she replies. "But what do you mean?"

Taka grins. "I'm a student ambassador for TMU. I can help make sure that you truly blow away the panelists."

"Wait—isn't that cheating?" Remy asks.

He laughs. "I've had candidates hunt me down while I'm at work just so they can talk. But, as an ambassador, I'm supposed to help."

"Don't worry about it, Remy," Naomi says. "The ambassadors are selected to represent the school. They're allowed to play favorites, if they so choose. Though you'll make quite a few people jealous if you're Taka's favorite."

Taka waves that away with such practice that Remy has a hint of an idea just how popular he is on campus. And with that, Remy's found a way to make her "fortune" work in her favor. Cam's eyes linger on her, though, almost like he can tell that she's told an absolute lie.

Six Days Until New Year's Eve

MONDAY, DECEMBER 25

Remy

I refuse to believe that's my future."

Remy stares back at the mirror in Uncle David and Aunt Kiyoko's minimalist bathroom, and wishes that someone would agree with her. But, like her reflection in the mirror, she's doomed to be forever alone.

I am not going to be a forever Second-to-Last Girl. There it is: the truth.

That was the rumor back at Palo Alto High. Back home, Remy was the Second-to-Last Girl. Everyone she'd dated ended up in a long-term relationship after her.

She hadn't wanted to be that for Cam. That was why she'd tried to push it off, laughed it off when anyone said they should try dating, tried to wait until their relationship was perfect, until everything was perfect, until—

Now, she won't even be second-to-last for him. She doesn't even have a *chance* to be his soulmate.

Sure, Mr. Yoshino has an absolutely accurate track record and all of that, but . . . can't she wish for more? Isn't there magic to fix this?

Surely, surely, she's kissed enough people to know that Cam matters to her. That, out of anyone, Cam should be her one true love, her soulmate.

A knock on the door pulls her out of her thoughts.

"Remy?"

The man of the hour. The man who will never be the center of her life, if fate has anything to do with it. Remy plasters on a smile as she cracks open the door.

"Are you okay?" Cam is dressed all in dark blues and black, like a perfect night sky that Remy wants to wrap herself inside. "You don't seem like yourself."

The warmth in his voice is sweet and her smile doesn't feel fake anymore. Today's busy enough, with a lot to look forward to: they're going to Tokyo Magical University. She has her interview and Cam has his magical alchemy meeting. "I've been looking forward to today."

It's true. Even if their futures aren't as entwined, she sure as hell will cherish every moment until they fall apart.

Cam

The entrance to Tokyo Magical University is definitely not where Cam expected, but at this rate, he'll never get there. Not with the way Remy looks so enthralled that she can't even move, though when he sees her huge grin, he doesn't even mind.

"A bookstore." Remy is positively drooling as they look up at the tall brick building, crammed into a narrow street in Shinjuku. "Eleven stories of books."

"Isn't your interview in"—he checks his phone—"less than an hour?"

Remy jolts. "Shoot. I don't know how to get in, either. The directions the school emailed me just said to go to the seventh floor of Kinokuniya Books, into the magical alcove, and to write down my destination."

"Maybe getting *to* the school is part of our entry test," Cam says. He got the same basic directions earlier today, along with the room information for Professor Watanabe's—Naomi's—presentation.

The shop is pretty empty at eight in the morning, and the clerks call over polite welcomes as Remy and Cam head to the elevator.

"Oh, wow," Remy whispers. "Even the magazines are so pretty and shiny. I should grab a few for Minami; she'd love them."

"Knowing Minami, she probably gets airmailed subscriptions," Cam says.

"It's impossible to get a souvenir for the richest girl I know." Then she gasps. "These magazines have *gifts* in them. That's so clever! Look at that makeup pouch!" She turns toward a set of books, laid out on a table. "And they have the latest Murakami novel. Damn. I need to pick up a Japanese copy."

"Don't you have enough books?" he asks, as they walk into the elevator.

The elevator dings as it shuts, but the noise is like static compared to her laugh; beautiful, heartfelt.

"No. Such. Thing," she responds. "Try me."

They stare at each other. *Try me.* Her lips are tipped up in a smile, so soft and gentle and so Remy. What would Cam try with Remy, if he had the chance?

All the air in the elevator has been swallowed right up. He tears his gaze away to look at the numbers. Right. Numbers. Numbers are like alchemy, solid and real. Fifth floor . . . sixth . . . *seventh.*

The elevator dings again. When they get out, there's a small alcove to the left. Cam blinks. A bronze emblem is set above the archway, made of a star and a cherry blossom. It's the insignia of the Japanese Magical Bureau that marks magic-aware entrances. They're in the right spot.

"That's incredible," Remy whispers.

"So," Cam says teasingly, "who's going to carry our luggage with all those books for the flight back?"

"You promised," she says.

"I never did." They definitely just switched off, whenever one of them got tired of pushing that obnoxiously misbehaving suitcase.

"You promise . . . *now!*" She reaches out to tickle him. "Promise you'll carry all five million of my books back!"

He laughs, even though she's tickling him over his thick down jacket, so it's not really that ticklish. It's her impish look; the way she's scrunching up her nose, intent on distracting him. It's the stray hair on her cheek, and that way he has to clench his hand to curb the urge to brush it away.

"Five million books?" he protests. "Can we compromise here? Like, maybe, three books and one magazine?"

"No compromises!" She laughs. "*Five million!*"

So, mature as he is, he gives in to that urge. He tickles her back. They fake-wrestle their way into the room, too busy laughing and trying to one-up each other to notice the room around them. But Remy's eyes widen as she's trying to dodge him, and she tips backward.

Cam grabs her, pulling her to him, but that sends them horribly off balance.

They careen down, and Cam grunts as the wind is knocked out of his lungs with a double punch: the hard tile floor on his back and a heavy weight on his chest.

Remy is on top of him.

The feel of her—even though they're separated by way too many clothes, damn his heavy jacket—is so good against him. The smell of her lotion—citrus and peonies—fills the air, and he knows the memory of this is going to be lingering on the edge of every waking moment, a reminder of a thirst he'll never be able to quench.

Remy groans, her forehead on his chest. "This is a nightmare. I have royally embarrassed myself beyond saving. Tell me this is just a bad dream."

She peeks at him, and he stops breathing. A little smile dances on her lips, and he wants to shift so that he can catch her mouth on his. It would feel like heaven to slide his hands up her back and pull her in as close as she can get so there's no more of this strange distance.

Because, what pulls him closer to her is how she *sees* him. She, out of anyone in the world, does understand *him*.

But he knows, just as much as he wants to lean closer—he *can't*.

Remy

This might be the pinnacle of Remy's life. Or the most embarrassing moment, ever.

She and Cam stare at each other, bare inches apart. This is the closest they've ever been since, like, first grade, where they had to draw self-portraits and Cam was intent on recording each and every one of her freckles. She was embarrassed, until he said, "They're like shooting stars. You're so pretty, Remy."

Thankfully, this room is small, and no one else is here. It's a simple area with the plain wood shelves and tables like the rest of Kinokuniya. Remy's not sure what makes this place magical . . . other than the sparks from Cam *underneath* her.

Remy gives him an *Oops, I messed up* grin. "Did I sweep you off of your feet or what?"

He laughs. "You blew me away. I heard there's going to be snow this week, but the weather forecasters didn't account for *you*."

His eyes trace her face. She wonders, like she's wondered a thousand times before—what would it be like to kiss Cam Yasuda? Would he spark like a potion, tipping over her lips and pulling Remy in?

Remy never had any problem being the first to kiss someone—but not Cam.

But now . . . with that way he's staring up at her . . .

What if this is her last chance?

She leans in, her heart in her throat, feeling his breath dance across her skin. *Oh, I'm going to regret this . . . but I'd regret not doing this more . . .*

A throat clears behind them. "Did I walk in on something?"

Remy yelps, elbowing Cam in the stomach, and scrambles off, face aflame.

"I'm so sorry," she apologizes profusely in Japanese. "I slipped and my friend tried to catch me—"

Taka leans on the doorway. He's in dark slacks and a buttoned-up shirt, looking professional, almost like he's ready for an interview.

Cam groans, sitting up with a dazed look.

She looks down at her outfit, the black blazer and skirt, her (once) crisp white shirt, the black heels she borrowed from Ellie. Hurriedly, she smooths out the front of her clothes.

Wait . . . the interview.

"Shoot!" Remy cries, pulling out her phone and checking the time. It's 8:45 A.M. "I'm going to be late."

Taka reaches out, adjusting her crumpled collar. Then he helps Cam back up to his feet. "Quite a fall. You sure you're okay?"

Cam, strangely, only grunts. "Remy, let's go."

"I can help. It's . . . unique getting into TMU, if you've never been." Taka steps toward the red shelves, motioning them closer. "Cam, you're going to see Naomi's presentation, right? You'll want to pick a book from the shelf over there. It'll get you to the right spot. Remy, here, we can share a book."

Taka picks up *The Girl Who Fell Beneath the Sea*. Cam hesitates. "I can go with you, Remy—"

She needs time to clear her head. *What* just happened between them? "I'm fine. You've been planning on seeing Naomi's presentation for ages, it's your highlight of this trip."

"Take my arm," Taka says. "I'd ask to hold your hand, but your best friend might throw his book at me if I do."

Remy laughs. "He wouldn't . . ."

Cam's glaring from where he's picked up the thriller *They're Watching You*. "So, how do we get in?"

"Open it up," Taka says.

Cam flips through the pages. "And? It's almost time for her interview."

"Tap the page once with your index finger," Taka says, "and write the kanji for the school and the department. Like, 'Tokyo Magical University, Magical Alchemy Department.'"

"Oh," Remy says. "I'm glad I'm going with you because I have to confess, I can't write kanji well. I can talk and read most things fine, but when it comes to writing kanji, my mind goes blank."

Cam has his forehead scrunched, like he's trying to remember the kanji. Then, his hand moves. One second, he's there. The next, he disappears into thin air, and the thriller falls back onto the shelf, closing with a soft flutter of pages.

"W-what?" Remy gasps. Books have always been a kind of written magic. When she rereads a longtime favorite, she sometimes finds new quotes that are filled with meaning, the words soothing her soul just at the perfect time. Remy can't count the number of breakups she's healed by reading a romance and knowing, *Hey, this is the date before The One. This is a sign that my soulmate is still out there, somewhere.*

But this takes that magic to a whole new level.

Taka taps on the page deftly, and his fingers trace the lines of the characters for *Tokyo Magical University, General Admissions Office.*

Remy looks around. "Is something supposed to change? Wait—"

For the second time today, Remy is falling. Pages flutter like wings, the sound echoing all around them.

This time, Remy falls into a *book.*

Remy

Not only is Tokyo Magical University her absolute dream school, but the Admissions Department itself is an absolute dream.

Remy breathes in. "Are *all* colleges like this?"

It's the grandest lobby ever. Two ironwork staircases lead up to a lounge area with a shimmering glass chandelier, where a few students in casual clothes are chatting. Frosted glass doors with metal plates show names of professors that Remy had studied on the TMU website. The ceiling is glowing with light streaming through frosted windows, arching above.

A man with heavy glasses comes in from behind them and bumps into Remy, with an annoyed grunt. Taka shoots the guy a look. "Hagiwara-san, are you all right there?"

"Apologies, apologies," the man says quickly, before disappearing through one of the doors.

"Are you okay?" Taka asks, but she's too in awe to care. After all, this place is *beautiful*.

"Totally fine. But, um, aren't we on the seventh floor? How's this all fit? How can we see windows in the *ceiling*?"

"We're now technically on the thirteenth—from outside, the top two floors are invisible, unless you're wearing rose-tinted glasses. Magic does some pretty amazing things," Taka says, trying to gently ease his arm out of her viselike grip. "I'm glad Hagiwara didn't hurt you; he's clumsy, among other things. But if you keep holding on like this, I might be the one that gets hurt."

"Sorry," Remy says, releasing her hand. "I got carried away. But *look* at this."

Taka laughs. "That's how I felt the first time I saw TMU, too, but I'd forgotten about that until now. You know sometimes how you don't *see* something for the longest time, even though it's right there in front of you?"

Remy's heart drops. That's her and Cam. For a long time, she hadn't noticed Cam in that way. But, around the beginning of high school, when she was dating the first guy that had asked her out, she realized that *he* wasn't Cam. After that, though, she'd gotten too scared to change things between her and Cam.

"You okay there?" Taka asks; he's noticed how she's dropped into a heavy silence.

"Just jittery about the interview that decides the next four years of my life, I guess?"

He gives her a wry smile. "Point taken. Let me get you checked in."

"I should do this on my own."

"I'm used to being used." There's a sadness to his words, but then he shrugs it off with a quick laugh. "Anyway, Ellie's been a good friend to me; I don't mind repaying the favor. It's not easy to get in, as you know."

Used. She'd never want to use anyone, and especially not one of her sister's close friends.

"You don't have much time," Taka says quickly. That sadness is gone so fast that she must've imagined it. "Are you sure you don't want me to help you?"

"I'm being stubborn," she says. "But this is for me, all right? I want this to be *my* future."

With that, Remy heads over to the desk to check in.

———— ◆ ————

t's a group interview consisting of Remy and five other potentials. It sounds like an awkward band name that'll never go mainstream. She hates this, having to compete against people who might be her classmates in the future, trying to show *I'm so special, I'm something you should look at.* Remy loves the quiet of hiding away with Cam, not being the center of attention.

Remy is the last one; she ducks her head as she slides into her seat. She and her fellow interviewees are in hard plastic chairs that face a desk with two interviewers, a man with black-rimmed glasses—the one who bumped into her—and a woman with long, flowing hair, both suited up like her. An empty chair sits to the woman's right.

"We don't accept tardiness at Tokyo Magical University," snaps the man. Remy *longs* to snap back with, *You walked straight into me earlier; you* saw *I was here.*

"It's not yet nine o'clock," says the woman. "We've still got three minutes. Besides, we're missing— Ah, there he is."

Another person slips inside. Remy gapes as Taka sits in the last interviewer's chair. Taka said he could put in a good word. She didn't think he'd be sitting across the table.

The other two interviewers greet Taka—the grouchy man is a little warmer in front of the other interviewer—and then the woman leans over the narrow table to look at Remy and the other hopefuls. "Welcome to Tokyo Magical University's admissions interview. You're one of the few to have been invited, so consider yourselves lucky. But understand that in every three groups, only one person makes it into our school."

The interviewers introduce themselves. Remy listens carefully when it's Taka's turn. Who the hell *is* he?

"I'm Taka Suzuki," he says, in that smooth-as-butter voice. "I'm a student ambassador for the Admissions Department. We're very excited to have you join us."

The dark-rimmed-glasses interviewer glares across the table the moment Taka finishes, like he can't wait to start scaring them. "So, tell me why you think you should get in." He flicks his eyes toward the interviewees' files, spread out in front of him. "You. Remy Kobata."

Remy flounders. All her words escape her, disappearing into ashes. Why . . . *why* did she want to go to TMU, especially when Cam is going to MIT, all the way in the US? When they won't even be on the same continent?

Taka clears his throat. He turns his head to ask, *Want my help?*

Remy sits up straighter and meets the old man's glare. She's not getting in because of Taka. She wants to believe in herself, even though this Hagiwara guy is trying to shake her confidence.

She has practiced this very question for hours and hours. With a deep breath, she responds, "Tokyo Magical University is my top college prospect. Through my research into potential schools, I learned that TMU was the first college created for the magic-aware, to help their students expand their talents to help the magic-aware as well as the general public. This is a mission I strive to follow in my own life—"

"Sounds practiced, but good enough," growls the interviewer, cutting her off. "Fine. You—to her left. Speak up, we're not a bunch of twittering birds."

As the next interviewee stammers and finds their words, Taka meets her eyes, giving her a small, subtle smile.

Cam

As Remy's best friend, Cam feels weird about someone having his arm around her like that. That's what he tells himself as he steps into the Magical Alchemy Department.

As the fluttering fades away, he finally puts a finger on that weird sensation making his stomach churn.

Jealousy. Right. *Totally* a best friend kind of attribute. Again, like a locked box without a key, he shoves his emotions away; out of sight and out of mind.

A clink of bottles makes him look around. He's in a maze of offices and laboratories, but each glass office is stacked upon the other, kind of like a thousand fishbowls. Instead of goldfish, scientists and researchers move around, looking sharp in their state-of-the-art rose-tinted glasses, studying billowing vials.

He's heard about this before, but seeing it for himself is on a whole other level. This is the highly confidential research area of TMU, the Magical Alchemy Department being one subset of it. And Naomi, who's a professor here, has full access to this, every day, including grants to get any of the resources she needs. Sure beats working at CharmWorks for some elixir cash.

Behind him, there's a bright red shelf filled with books. There's also a sign above a doorway: TRAVEL TO THE OTHER DEPARTMENTS IN THE NON-MAGICAL WAY.

He almost wants to head to the Admissions Department to see Remy again. She's having the interview that decides the course of her life. Surely he should be around for moral support? It's just sensible to stay by her side.

Sure, keep telling yourself that.

"What are you here for?" asks an automated voice. Cam yelps.

A floating book is face-to-face with him, a rich blue with yellow titling. "Hello, I'm Kino-chan, your guide. Ah, I recognize you. Welcome to the Magical Alchemy Department, Cameron Yuji Yasuda. I understand you are here for Professor N. Watanabe's presentation, beginning in approximately seven minutes and eighteen seconds. Please follow me."

Cam follows in awe as the book—a *book*, embossed spine and all—guides him through a series of narrow hallways leading to classrooms like his high school back home. He's heard about how the joy from Kinokuniya shoppers has increased magical dust—which made this the perfect spot for one of the top magical colleges of the world—to the point where the overflow gave a special power to books. The researchers of Tokyo Magical University took it to a whole new level by programming the books with artificial intelligence.

"We have arrived," the book intones. "Please enjoy the lecture."

Sliding doors open, and Cam steps into an auditorium. Hundreds of rows of seats are arranged theater-style around a stage. Naomi stands at a podium in a pale gray skirt suit with a lab coat, a small speck among a sea of murmuring, gossiping academics.

———•———

The presentation is interesting enough. It's an open door into the projects Naomi is working on, epitomizing the draw of magical alchemy: combining potions with spells to create truly magnificent work. But, Cam realizes, he's never heard of the other academics at

TMU having to display all their projects. Maybe they do at an internal meeting, but not to something of this extent.

A bell chimes; the Q&A time is up. Cam can't miss the way Naomi keeps her shoulders stiff, eyes alert for any last comments. One of the men up front waves his hand, showing, *We're done.* The rest of the academics mumble among themselves and start heading out.

Cam pushes through the crowd like a minnow swimming against the current, to get to the stage. "Naomi?"

She spins around sharply. "I am Professor Watanabe—"

The pinched look on her face softens when she sees Cam. "Oh, you made it. It's nice to know I had one ally here."

So he was right. That wasn't a normal academic review session.

"Come over to my lab?" Naomi asks. "It's just around the corner."

Cam can't believe he's actually going to visit *the* lab of Professor Watanabe.

"S-sure," he stammers. "Want me to carry your bag? It looks heavy."

She simply raises an eyebrow; she's not letting it out of her grasp.

A tall man strides up to them when they get to the doorway, giving her a nod. "You did well."

"I did my best not to bite off Yamaguchi's head," Naomi says tiredly.

The man runs his hand through his prematurely graying hair. "You fought." With a quick nod at Naomi, he disappears out the door.

"Our department head," Naomi says, and Cam has to reel in his mouth. Wasn't the leader of the Magical Alchemy Department one of the youngest winners of the Nobel Prize?

"This way," she says, hooking her thumb to the right, the opposite direction from where he came.

"You don't have a lab near the elevators?" he asks.

"One of the fishbowl offices? I don't need more people examining what I'm doing. Do you know why I don't share any pictures of what I look like online?"

Cam bites his lip. He hadn't thought of it before; he'd just figured

Professor Watanabe was really private, like Haruki Murakami or something. He makes a wild guess. "Because your research intimidates everyone?"

She looks at him with absolute disbelief, and lets out a laugh. "Well, that's what I get for asking. In TMU, I get judged by how I look before I even open my mouth. It's a double standard. If I didn't use a hair shine elixir and countless makeup potions and creams, I'd be called busaiku—ugly, in English—and an abomination to the department. When I dress nice and spend the women's tax of getting ready an extra hour every morning, I apparently made it into TMU just because of how I look."

"I'm sorry," he says. He never expected his professional idol to have had anything but a perfect path toward her fascinating research. It'd always seemed like Professor N. Watanabe knew just what to do, not that she was faced with hurdles like this.

He and Naomi have been walking through twists and turns of hallways. She stops at a plain wood door and unlocks it with a gigantic brass key. Then, she motions for Cam to step inside.

"Is a key enough?" Cam asks. "Isn't there better magic to keep your research safe?"

Naomi laughs. "Oh, yes, there is. But the key makes people linger at the door, and the keyhole takes note of those that try to get inside. For everything else, I have—"

There's a flash of black, and something pounces on Cam's shoulder. He yelps as a cat stares at him with yellow eyes, examining him from head to toe.

"Back when I started, someone tried to come in and mess with my files. Everyone heard about Tsukki," Naomi says.

"Good cat," Cam says. Tsukki meows, and massages his paws into Cam's shoulder.

"No claws!" Naomi calls over her shoulder, setting her bag onto a desk shoved into the corner. Tsukki yowls in disappointment as he hops down to curl up in a beat-up cardboard box by the door. Cam raises an eyebrow.

"Believe me," Naomi says, handing a lab coat to Cam. "I've tried plenty of fancy cat beds, and all he wants is that box. Remy's still going to be a while—those interviews take time. Want a quick tour?"

Damn. He glances out the window, where he can see the midday sun reflecting in the windows of the building across from them. He wants to go over to where Remy will be, and be there waiting for her when she finishes up.

But this is the lab of his dreams. Her space is huge, with three long benches filled with shiny tools and experiments. It's everything he's dreamed of, but even *more*. Cam wishes that TMU offered as generous scholarships as MIT; he'd apply in a heartbeat.

They walk through the aisles, Naomi pointing at her various works in progress. "That's something I'm working on: a pen that can only tell truths. Right now, though, it can only write out half-truths. Like, *I'm hungry, but all I want is ramen*, when I'm craving chocolate."

"Sounds like it'd be revealing *my* hidden desires. Most of the time, all I want is chocolate, too. But, wow. The cat, all these magical tools . . . I seriously think you're Sailor Moon reincarnated," Cam says, and Naomi laughs.

"One could only wish." She playfully mimics Sailor Moon's transformation routine. "Do you know that when I was little, I secretly believed I could become Sailor Pluto? That was one of the things that first propelled me to go to college."

"I think you're living my dream life," Cam says enviously.

Naomi laughs. "Why don't you apply to TMU, then?"

He sucks in a breath; the weight of his phone is about to tear a hole straight through his pocket. He still hasn't been able to look at his MIT email. Why *doesn't* he apply . . .

"It's complicated," he says, finally, to Naomi's curious look. "Family stuff."

"Ah. Family, the best and worst motivators in life," Naomi says, with a sigh. "Understandable. But think about it—I could always use a lab assistant."

Cam swallows; the idea of working in a lab like *this*—with Remy, at the same school, so they'll still be close to each other—

But he has obligations. Duties. Responsibilities.

It's all a dream that's nothing more than that: a dream. And once he's back on the plane, heading home to California, he'll be back in reality, again.

Remy

Ice cream." Cam grins with delight as they walk through a cheerful, shiny-tiled convenience store. The exhilaration of finishing her interview—*the* interview—hopefully well enough to get in is better than any sugar rush.

"I thought you wanted *hand warmers*." Remy laughs. Her post-interview plans are big. Like, Tokyo-level big. There's a central train line that goes in a loop around Tokyo, the Yamanote Line, so Cam and Remy have decided to go to all thirty stations in one day—or at least as many as they can squeeze in after their morning at TMU. Except, well, this is the third stop, and they keep getting distracted by all the food.

Cam lingers at the glass-paneled ice chest in the middle of the aisle. It's stuffed to the brim with ice cream bars, cups, and even cream puffs. "I shouldn't have bought that coffee earlier. My wallet's hurting. We saved up all we can, and my resolve melts at the sight of a convenience store."

Remy slides open the case. "Any epic trip isn't complete without ice cream. My treat."

He grins. "But that means I get to treat you at the next stop. It's an obligatory way to celebrate your interview." He picks up a cup of Häagen-Dazs—this one is made with hojicha, the roasted green tea that she loves, and it's studded with bits of mochi and crispy, cone-like wafers.

"Why do I feel like I just walked into a trap?" Remy laughs. "Game on, Cam. If you think either of us will get tired of ice cream, you're sorely mistaken."

Ten hours later, Remy and Cam half walk, half limp back toward Uncle David and Aunt Kiyoko's apartment. Today has seriously been the best day ever, but Remy has never walked so much in one day.

It was a blur, but a good kind of blur. She's going to have to scroll through their shared picture album later, to redigest and remember all the little moments where they were laughing their heads off. Because, in addition to the interview and their thirty-stations-in-a-day-no-big-deal race, and ice cream at almost every stop, they were also visiting all the game arcades in sight, taking pictures at the scenic spots, and of course eating their way through the circle. Those were the rules. Remy didn't make the rules, she just . . . well, okay, she and Cam did make the rules. And these rules—especially after seeing Cam grin like a kid even after the twelfth cone—were the best kind.

"I think my legs are going to fall off. Can we rest for a second?" she groans. They're next to a park, and Remy weaves her way through the trees to flop onto a bench. Even in her thick boots, the cold and all-day walk has gotten the better of her. She tries to rub life back into her calves, but they're 99 percent made up of the ramen noodles they scarfed up for dinner.

Cam gets down on one knee in front of her, and she freezes. They're not even dating, the fortune basically said her love life is doomed, why would he want to get married, but yes—

"A piggyback ride." Cam motions her closer. "C'mon."

"No way in hell." She cannot survive the idea of his hands wrapped around her legs right now.

He raises an eyebrow. "If my feet hurt, wouldn't you do the same?"

"Of course." Her answer is instantaneous. She wants to reel her words back in like the arcade games they were playing at Akihabara, some sort of fishing game that reminded her of Candy Crush.

"Then let me help you. Consider it a prepayment for that day in the future where you have to carry me, okay?"

With a laugh, Remy shakes her head, playfully inching away along the side of the bench. Cam unfurls himself and stands, thinking as he watches a light flickering on and off down the road. She should've taken the goddamn offer; she regrets it already.

Suddenly, Cam blurts out, "Chocolate butter caramel."

"What?" Then Remy gasps. "*No.*"

He nods dramatically. "*Yes.*" Slowly, with the care he usually gives the components for whatever elixir he's creating at the time, he pulls out a shiny gold box filled with little chocolate-covered biscuit sticks from his jacket pocket.

"*Butter* flavored? Chocolate, butter, and caramel? Mind *blown.*" It's Goldsticks, Remy's favorite magical snack. Japan is the birthplace of Goldsticks—known for their signature gold shimmer imbued with a hint of a mental focus charm (her go-to snack for studying). Apparently they have more than just Remy's standard milk chocolate or green tea. She takes a bite, and it lives up to all her expectations and more: a drizzle of caramel over a thin layer of milk chocolate around a golden, buttery biscuit stick, crunching ever so satisfyingly in her mouth.

"I went to a convenience store earlier," Cam says. "And *jackpot*. But this means . . ."

Remy laughs, offering the other end of the stick. He holds it gently, shooting her a grin that she just as quickly returns.

Their tradition started years ago, after Cam's mom passed away and he didn't have a turkey for Thanksgiving. He'd wanted a wishbone to wish that he'd always remember his mother. So, instead of a turkey, Remy offered to split a stick of Goldsticks. Ever since, it's become their way of making wishes and settling arguments. It's tough to get upset when you've got a mouthful of chocolate.

"What do you want?" she asks. First, of course, they have to bargain.

"I want to know your real fortune," he says.

Her heart completely leaps out of her chest.

Cam continues, his eyes steady on hers. "You've been avoiding talking about it, but I *know* you didn't ask about your college acceptance, Remy."

Oh, Cam. She wants to cry. Every time she's had a problem, whether it's a skinned knee from them playing tag in elementary school or a failing grade, he's always been there to stick on a bandage or guide her through remedial Chemistry.

"Maybe we can talk about it later?" Remy hedges, glancing away, blinking fast. She's just not ready to talk about the fortune.

She can feel the weight of his gaze, then he clears his throat. "Okay, a super-serious Goldsticks War. If I win, you get a piggyback ride. If you win, you get to give *me* a piggyback ride."

She laughs; he always knows how to lighten the heaviness in her mind. "Your ride will last all of one step, but sure. Three . . . two . . . one . . ."

"Split!" Cam shouts, and they snap the stick. A second later, he crows, "I won!"

Remy groans. Somehow, she's only holding an inch and Cam's already victoriously munching the rest of it.

He polishes it off and kneels back down. "Lady Remy, your ride awaits."

Her laugh evaporates the moment her fingers touch his shoulders. Then she squeezes her eyes shut, her heart thudding in her ears, as she wraps her arms around his neck. *I can't believe this is happening.* A second later, Cam stands up and starts back on the path toward his uncle and aunt's apartment.

The sidewalk is only lit with the occasional streetlamp shining like a trail of stars. If she looked around, she'd see the shops closed for the day or the brightly lit skyscrapers in the distance. But Remy doesn't notice the rest of Tokyo; she doesn't *want* to notice anything other than tiny, beautiful details. The wintry cold has impossibly melted away. Somewhere far away, she hears the hum of cars heading home. Cam's arms are wrapped around her thighs, his chest is sturdy between her legs, and his face is so close that if she leaned a little closer, they'd be cheek to cheek. In this moment, it's just the heat radiating from Cam, the faint white puffs of condensation as he breathes out, and the semi-darkness of the road.

A simple piggyback ride shouldn't feel so damn . . . *good*. It's supposedly below forty degrees, but it sure doesn't feel like it anymore.

Cam stops abruptly, and she wonders if she's said her thoughts out loud. But he points at a shop that Remy didn't really notice, not with this distraction that she's all wrapped around.

"Beni's Apothecary," he says softly. "Isn't that . . . isn't that Mr. Yoshino's sister's shop?"

She blinks. It is. Up ahead, there's a silver sign dangling from two sleek chains with a carving of a potion bottle. It's above a small door on the side of a nondescript brick building that seemingly popped out of nowhere, basically screaming magic.

"Naomi said it's like the nighttime version of the Good Luck Café," Cam says. "An adult version."

"Let's go." The words fall out instantaneously. "I have a question I need to ask Mr. Yoshino."

"But—"

"Goldsticks War." Remy rustles in her coat pocket and pulls out the unfinished box, dangling it in front of him. He laughs and reaches for the stick.

Snap.

Remy waves her larger half. He made this way too easy. "Hurry up, chariot."

Cam grabs her piece and steals it in a single mouthful. "Your wish is my command. Giddyup!" He lets out a neigh and fake-gallops to the entrance.

Remy bursts into giggles. They're still laughing as she pulls open the door for the two of them.

The bar is candlelit and demure, with a feel of alcohol-spiked chocolate-dipped strawberries: pretty, delicious, and way out of Remy's comfort zone. Cam stops short and she slides off, managing to land on her feet.

A short man in a black bow tie and sharply tailored vest and pants stops in front of them, slim menus in hand. "Hello. Are you here for a wish potion? Our elixirs will help even the most secret of your hopes to come true—as long as you know what it is, of course. Love, perhaps?"

Oh, hell. She can't tell Cam her fortune, nor that she likes him, not now and not here. Remy is *definitely* out of her comfort zone.

Remy

Cam clears his throat. "We're here to visit Mr. Yoshino. When we saw him yesterday, it seemed like your shops were connected?"

The host shakes his head. "Unfortunately, Mr. Yoshino's café is closed. At night, Beni's Apothecary opens up. Would you like to try one of our wish potions?"

Remy steps forward. "Yes, please."

Her voice is clearer than the tinkling glasses at the closest table, the older couple laughing gaily as they toast. Remy's cheeks burn as she slips her hand around Cam's wrist, tugging him with her. His skin is warm and soft under hers.

They weave through the tables; patrons are laughing happily, toasting each other. Cam guides Remy out of the way of a girl gesturing with another of those glasses, shaped like a potion bottle, her girlfriend nodding eagerly and hanging on to her every word. Finally, they slide into plush stools at the lacquered cedarwood bar next to shelves filled with cut-glass bottles twinkling in the light.

She's hit with déjà vu. Have they been here before? No way. The last time they were in Japan was nearly a decade ago, when Cam's mom was alive. Still, there's a strange sense of something settling in place. It's a good feeling, like she's getting closer to where she's supposed to be. It's the same feeling as when she picks up a good book and falls in love from the first line.

After all, she's next to Cam. And anywhere next to him is the right place.

Or, at least, for now.

"What would you like to drink?" The bartender slides over a pair of shibori, heated rolled towels, for them to wipe off their hands, and leans against the counter. Remy has to reel back in her jaw. A sense of power radiates from the older woman. There's an aura like she seems to know exactly who she is—she's probably never had to flounder around from an unfortunate fortune. Remy's eyes slide down to the woman's name tag, and her stomach flips.

"What did my brother foretell as your fate?" Beni Yoshino, the owner, looks between the two of them, and Remy has an odd sense that the woman can tell exactly what she wants. She's probably not the first forever-alone loser who has slunk into her bar, hoping for a solid drink to wash away her doomed future.

"Oh, it's nothing," Remy waves her hand airily.

"So it's bad." Beni shakes her head. A man in a black bow tie slides over a tray with an empty-looking potion bottle; she scans the glass and begins pulling out a few elixirs.

Remy breathes in with delight. The first bottle looks like captured ocean light; there is no other name Remy can find for the turquoise liquid, swirling with rays of gold and soft yellows. The second vial looks like fractured opals refracting with a rainbow of colors. And the last is a tincture in a wide-bottomed glass, with lush ruby-red ranunculus blossoms edged in black, steeped in water.

"Whoa. I've always wanted to visit a magical alchemy bar." Cam leans in. Back in suburban Palo Alto, they don't get the luxury of completely magical cafés and bars.

"For the good drinks?" Beni asks, pouring out some of the blossom elixir into a lacy gold cup. The clear water turns into a swirling glass of ruby liquid the moment it hits the gold. With a quick twist of her wrist, she pours it into another glass, and adds in two pieces of ice formed in the shape of a ranunculus, the ice petals sharply edged and beautiful. Beni grabs a yuzu on the side of her counter, and, with a channel knife, she twists off a section of the fruit, turning the peel into a perfect curl to lay on top of the glass. The citrus scent is bright and alluring in the air. Remy's throat is parched.

"I've always been more interested in the magic behind the drinks, but these don't look anything like my work," Cam says. "I've studied a little bit of magical alchemy, but this is a totally different level."

Remy shakes her head. "He's being modest. *Magical Times* listed him as one of their Top Youth Science Honorees this year." That was one of the things—along with his long list of experiments published in magical scientific journals—that had brought the top schools from around the nation calling.

"Oh, really now?" Beni asks.

His ears glow pink in the candlelight. "That was a fluke. When I'm bored, I experiment with different mixtures and that sometimes leads to interesting results." He clears his throat. "So, wish elixirs? How's that work?"

The older woman laughs. "There's no way I'm giving up my family's secrets to a researcher. So, what was that fortune?"

Cam's eyes cut to Remy, and Beni's gaze follows.

Remy flounders; Cam quickly says, "Mr. Yoshino said that she's going to have trouble getting into Tokyo Magical University. Can we use your wish potions to get her in?"

Beni stares at Remy like she can recognize Remy's lie from a kilometer away. Remy only smiles-grimaces back. She wishes she had Beni's expressive eyebrows; then she'd send, *I'm in love with this clueless guy. But I just got a fortune today saying I'm never going to find my soulmate—*

The bartender carefully pours out the opal-like elixir into a metal shaker; it almost looks like she's dosing out an extract of moonlight in shimmery rainbow hues. She adds in a few more pours from other vials, and shakes it up, pouring it into a delicate glass that, oddly, when Remy looks closer, has a piece of folded paper in it. A few seconds later, a waiter reappears to whisk the tray away. "Oh, god, you two have it bad."

Remy stiffens. "Really? I'm not going to make it into college? Are you a fortune-teller, too?"

Beni shoots her a grin, the words *You're so adorable* clear in a raised eyebrow. Remy guesses that Beni could tell entire stories with her perfect arches.

"I don't need a fortune-teller to know that's not your real fortune," Beni says, with a shake of her head. "A lot of people come in and out of here, you see? I can pin down liars real fast."

Cam protests, but Remy can't say anything in her own defense, because the fakeness of those words still coat her tongue, cloying and wrong.

"Think about whether you actually want to do something about that fortune," Beni advises, "before you make your wish."

Another waiter slides up to her with three empty glasses on a silver tray. This time, Remy looks closer. Each glass has a small piece of paper inside, no bigger than the stub of Remy's airplane ticket. Beni holds up two of the rose-tinted glasses—imbued with a strong magic, Remy realizes—and rapidly reads the paper, before moving on to the next.

"They've written their wish on edible rice paper with fruit dye," Beni explains. "Helps to absorb your own hopes—literally."

"So then you know what they want?" Remy would rather go streaking through the main streets of Shibuya than ask Cam out on a date, especially knowing from the fortune how doomed that would be.

"It doesn't help you if your wish is a secret," Beni says. "If you want something, you have to be able to fight for it. It has to be something you want badly enough, so much that you don't want it to be a secret. Look at them, for example. That group knew exactly what they wanted."

Remy and Cam follow the subtle nod of her chin toward the high top next to the bar, where three friends are laughing.

"Guess what they're celebrating," Beni says.

"A girls' night out?" Remy guesses.

"Breakups, all of them. One got cheated on, one realized she deserves better, and the last, well, the last realized she never was in love with her partner. They're celebrating a chance for real love."

Cam nods. "I'd never stay with someone I didn't love."

Remy's heart plummets, but she has to keep her mind focused. This wish potion is going to change things, she's sure of it. "How's writing out a wish help?"

"It'll help you bring to mind the feelings or memories to recapture that moment of joy, of bliss," Beni explains. "It's magic, but it takes more than just a drink. It takes *you*—your dreams and hopes. Without my patrons, my martinis would be just sloshing liquid that makes you tipsy."

She sets a rose-gold case no bigger than a jewelry box on the counter and flips the lid. Inside is a stack of small rectangles of rice paper. Then, she hands over a slim pen to each of them, the ink wafting with the scent of freshly picked strawberries, bright and sweet.

"So, what kind of wish potion do you want to make? Go on, write it out."

Cam begins to scribble something, too small and messy for her to read.

But the question burns its way through her throat and rests hot in Remy's belly. She glances over at Cam again and he meets her gaze. So, despite her misgivings, despite her worries, Remy writes out her wish and slides it across the counter, writing-side down.

Beni takes Remy's paper, scans it. Next is Cam's; he'd folded his. Remy can barely contain her curiosity, wishing she could read what he wrote.

"This isn't what you really want, is it?" Beni grabs two empty beakers, setting them in front of her. She dangles their papers from her fingertips. "You spat out some crap about college, and now you both just want to have an awesome trip?"

Remy and Cam exchange a glance. Okay, maybe "*I want to have the best trip in Japan ever*" was taking the easy way out. But it's true; her expectations and hopes for this vacation were higher than Mt. Fuji piled with snow.

"It's hard to find my bar, you know. Most people only find it once in a lifetime."

Oh, god. Remy is too damn scared of the truth. She's so damn scared of saying what would hurt the most, but speaking up might ruin everything. If she and Cam aren't meant to be, isn't it good that they'll still be friends? Isn't that why she didn't say anything in the first place?

But . . . that part of her that lives for their Saturday movie nights and spending parties off in a corner, working on puzzles together . . . that damn greedy part wants *more.*

"I want to be sure that the fortune from Mr. Yoshino is right," Remy blurts out.

The white lie is salt on her lips, sharp with wisps of wondering what it must be like to kiss Cam. To feel his arms around her, to feel like more than just friends.

To go against fate.

Best friends with Cam forever.

God, no. Hot MIT-girl comes to mind instantly. Remy tries to squash it down.

She clears her throat. "Mr. Yoshino read my fortune. But . . ." Her throat clams up. She tries again. "I asked . . . I mean . . . Mr. Yoshino . . . said . . ." Her words trail off into a mumble. "I asked if . . . if I had a soulmate."

Cam lets out a heavy breath. "Wait . . . what exactly did Mr. Yoshino say?"

"He said that I don't have a soulmate."

Cam is frozen in shock. "How . . . how can that be possible?"

Her heart leaps up with hope. What if he says *he's* her soulmate—

"This would be a fascinating study to continue Takashi Ono's soulmate research," he continues, and her stomach plummets. *What had he said about that? Everyone has a soulmate, whether romantic or platonic in nature. . . . And I have* no one. *Second-to-Last Girl status, forever.* "Scientifically speaking, I'm *sure* you have someone for you. This goes against all the research that I've studied."

Oh. This is Remy's love life, but it's science to Cam. Natural for a magical alchemy license holder, of course. Even if it's just a learner's license, he absorbs everything magical alchemy like a sponge. She wants to cry. She wanted Cam to— She's not even sure what, profess his never-ending love? Say that he'd already found a charm that shows they're soulmates?

Bone-deep want twists her breath, until she says what she's been thinking ever since she heard Mr. Yoshino's words. "I want to believe I have a soulmate. I don't want to live by that fortune."

Beni is quiet for a moment, then she says, "This isn't a simple request after all. You want to subvert fate?"

Is it even possible to go against destiny? Can *I change my future?*

For her, though, this isn't a science experiment to figure out whether the fortune is right. If this really is her fate, she has to do anything she can.

"Yes," she says, her heartbeat pounding in her ears. "I *need* to change my future."

Beni turns away with a snap of her black skirt. Out of the dim corner to the right, a sliding ladder rolls out, pushed by one of the waiters, or maybe an invisible hand of fate. It stops right in front of Beni and she clambers up—heels and all—without missing a beat. The hum from the tables behind them suddenly cuts out; laughter and easy conversations fade away. The entire apothecary is watching Beni.

"Madame," says the suited host, reappearing next to the counter and almost scaring Remy out of her seat. "Are you certain—"

"This girl is going against one of Michi's readings."

A heavy pause, then—"*Oh.*"

Remy swivels around in her chair. "Is it that bad?"

"It's not bad," the waiter says, like he's commenting on the weather. "It's *your* future. All of Mr. Yoshino's readings have come true in one way or another."

Her stomach sinks. The man says it like she has no choice, and maybe that's true.

But Remy didn't fall in love with Cam Yasuda randomly. Her love for him feels deeper and stronger than it has for anyone she's ever dated—and she's definitely tried to find someone else. There have been countless dates that she barely even cares to remember, where she pretended to laugh, even kissed and tried and tried to fall in love—but all she could think of was Cam.

And, true, it's taken her way too long to even think of admitting it to Cam—or to herself—but she'd really wanted to be sure Cam felt the same way.

So, yes, Remy is sure as hell that she wants to fight this.

The woman moves aside a panel and extracts the single bottle that it contains, bringing the glass down to set it in front of them. Then she puts her elbows on the bar and leans closer, with another of her devilish grins. "Are you ready for this?"

It's no bigger than Remy's hand, with a black-colored cork. The glass is so dusty it looks like the rose-gold liquid inside has been painted in soft hues as the light flows through. "This soulmate elixir is *potent*. In the Edo era, it was used for lovers who were in different social classes, and needed something magical to change their circumstances." Beni turns the label to face them.

"Damn. What level license do you have?" Cam asks. "After Dr. Ono's research and the Great Love Incident of 1850 in Kyoto, there was nearly a riot, and love potions around the globe were banned."

Only he would know the history of something like this.

The bartender smiles. "Selling them is banned. Creating them for your own use is banned. This one was made before that rule was set into place, but it's never been used. Besides, this isn't any one-size-fits-all love potion. It's an elixir to make your fate entwine with your soulmate within one week—or less. Though, since it hasn't been tested since it was made over two hundred years ago, who's to say it works?"

Remy rummages through her rusty reading skills to squint at the careful, beautiful calligraphy on the peeling label: *Soulmate Elixir—Forever with the Desire of Your Heart.*

"How does it work?" Cam asks, leaning forward.

"It's simple. Whomever you take this with becomes your soulmate." Beni glances between them. "So, do you two want to drink it?"

"Two?" Remy asks.

"I mean . . ." Beni gestures at her and then Cam. "Isn't the fortune about the two of you?"

"No!" Remy splutters.

At her side, Cam doesn't respond, and she's too terrified to see his reaction.

"There's just enough of this potion for two," Beni says. "Anyway, if you don't take this with someone, then you really *won't* have a soulmate."

Remy gulps. *I promised myself that I'd tell him. This is me, trying. This will only speed up the timeline—because he'll for sure be* the one *for me.*

She glances over at Cam; he's rubbing his chin thoughtfully. She can feel his curiosity about the potion nearly making his fingers twitch toward the glass. He's never been able to study a restricted potion before; the most he can get through his learner's license is highly flammable ones. Anything restricted is locked behind the glass case of the apothecary a few cities away.

"Can I take a sample of it?" Cam speaks up, finally. "I can study its impact, and—"

Beni snaps the glass out from under their noses; it disappears within her closed fist. "If you walk away now without drinking it, it'll be like this potion never existed. The Tokyo Magical Bureau wouldn't dare try to retrieve this potion from my bar. They know not to mess with the Yoshino family."

Cam frowns, his forehead wrinkling the way it does when he's trying to find a solution. Remy can almost hear his thoughts: *If he takes it, he'll be able to study a potion he may* never *see again.*

She asks, suspiciously, "Won't it cost like a million yen or something?"

Beni grins. "It's on the house. It's illegal to buy love potions, remember?" Then, she takes a long, curious look between the two of them, and Remy nearly explodes with embarrassment. Thankfully, Cam is distracted, staring at the potion with that focus he has when he's just starting to get consumed by another magical alchemy experiment.

"I can't take any responsibility for what might happen," Beni says. "With a potion this ancient—"

"It could have its effect negated due to time, or it could be more potent than ever," Cam finishes, nodding. "That's true. I didn't consider that it could have side effects other than its intended use. Have you tested its viability?"

Beni laughs. "I wouldn't want to waste a drop of it. And once you crack open this cork, you'd have to drink up fast. You can't seal this one again."

"The potency of a potion like this would have to be absorbed immediately for its full effect." Cam mutters something about the max life of potions under his breath.

"Besides," Beni says. "It's convenient that you came with a friend, isn't it? Your future will be sealed with a kiss, just minutes after drinking up."

Remy almost falls off her stool. She peeks over at Cam, who is still resolutely staring at the potion like *the bottle* is his soulmate. But, then, his eyes shift over to her.

"Wouldn't it be fascinating to see if this ancient potion works?" he asks, eagerly.

"But . . . you want to take it with me?" Remy squeaks out. "With your learner's license . . . I thought you weren't supposed to touch banned materials."

"This will be a once-in-a-lifetime opportunity," he responds, instantly. "I'll never get a chance to even *see* a love potion like this again. I can be a live test subject, recording the results from start to finish. Anyway, it's practical, right? To be soulmates with you. We know each other so well already."

Her heart clenches. *Of course. Cam is only taking a potion to become my soulmate because of his academic curiosity. Because it's practical.* Remy should've expected this from one of the top youth magical alchemy researchers in the world, but it still hurts. Well, maybe this elixir will help Cam realize that Remy can be someone he can love, too. Not just be infatuated with potions.

The bartender lets out a short laugh. "This *will* be interesting, that's for sure." Beni's smirk shows that she likely realizes that Remy truly wants Cam to be her soulmate, even though his love right now is only alchemy.

"If it does work, though, you have to report back and tell me how it went." The woman leans on the bar, dangling the glass in her fingers; the pale pink liquid swirls around mesmerizingly. "So, do you want it? Going once, going twice—"

Remy grabs the love potion, staring at the sparkling liquid, and ignores the bartender's grin as she drifts away to take care of another order, because if Remy looks at her too closely, she's going to drop the bottle.

There's no way she'll ever lose her one and only chance for winning Cam's heart.

Remy

There's no way this will work." Remy laughs, nervously. "Not if I've gotten that fortune."

"But that's where magic comes in," Cam says. "It's a loophole, in a way. If you apply magic, you *can* solve things that normally might not work."

So, in a nutshell, her destiny, as foretold by Mr. Yoshino, is to be forever alone. But with this potion, she *will* have a soulmate.

If this potion works.

Cam and Remy's eyes meet; she can almost feel that electrical spark between the two of them. But he grabs his water cup, and takes a deep drink, breaking their gaze.

Remy stares at him over the water glass. Damn, that mouth.

It's pressed against the rim, showing how impossibly full his lower lip is. He doesn't have to color his lips for the perfect sunset red, looking soft as clouds that Remy wants to sink into. She can imagine what he tastes like, like she's imagined a thousand times late at night, all alone, staring at her dark ceiling. Back home, Cam lives across the alleyway in his family's apartment; did he also stare up at the ceiling, thinking of her? And what she would do to him and his lips?

Love definitely *looks* delicious.

"Remy."

She pulls her head back into the conversation. "Yeah?"

"Are you sure?"

Am I sure I like you? Am I sure that, when I see you, my heart lightens because I can tell you anything, anything, *but the fact that I love you, because that will change everything? Even if I'm a mess, even if I'm never positive of anything, wasn't I sure—up until that moment Mr. Yoshino told me my future—that I loved you, and that I'd find the courage to tell you, someday?*

Screw hot MIT-girl. Remy had, deep down inside, always hoped it would be her.

She leans over, her voice casual and cool, so, so light. "This might not even work." Her words are laced with a dare. "But I guess I won't know until I try it."

Cam grins and Remy's heart flips. It's the same dangerous grin before they snuck into their high school pool in the middle of the night and the security guard almost caught them. A few years back, Remy's older sister had been on a mission to check off her bucket list, and that had spurred them to try some new things themselves. It's the moment that Remy's heart swooped and Cam's laugh was uncontained and free, and Remy realized, her feet pounding on pavement as they'd fled campus on foot: Yeah, she'd always had a crush on Cam, but what if she *did* something about it? What if she asked him out?

Maybe it's only when she's on the edge of something strange and scary and new that things actually change. Because, to take a step forward, that means leaving everything in the past behind.

"It might not work," Cam echoes, that kissable smirk pulling up his lips. He adds, "But it could change everything. It could—"

Then his phone rings loudly in his pocket and, belatedly, when the people nearby turn to look, Remy remembers that in Japan, no one leaves their ringer volume on. Cam scrambles to silence his phone, and grimaces. "Jack's wondering where we are; they're heading back to the apartment."

It's past time for them to leave. Remy has missed messages on her phone from Ellie. Even one look around at the bar shows that most of the groups are layering jackets over their shoulders, laughing as they pick up their bags. Remy took too long staring at Cam's lips, but she can't fault herself for that. Even Beni's finishing up tidying her row of highball glasses.

"We should head out," she says hesitantly. Her fingers move to slide the potion back over the counter but—

"Dammit," she swears, so loud that Beni looks over with a grin, but Remy doesn't have time to apologize.

The cork pops under Remy's fingertips. The scent of yuzu, bright and fragrant, wafts toward Remy and Cam, surprisingly refreshing.

With steady hands, Remy pours the drink, beaming a smile at Cam like this is nothing, it's totally nothing. This is for fun and not her heart on the line. This is just so Cam can test it out.

Before she can pour herself a glass, he gently eases the bottle out of her hands and pours hers. Remy's eyes sting; she has to look away.

Because this is the Cam she's fallen in love with. The one who does all these little things for her. Not because he doesn't think she's capable, but because he wholeheartedly *cares*. He cares; even if he doesn't love her that way.

Before she can think twice, she blinks away the tears and slides her hand around the cup he's poured. The pale rose-gold liquid swirls on the ice, magic sparking bright like champagne.

Cam, I sure as hell hope that this potion will help us find out that my soulmate is you. *Then I'll finally be brave enough to let* us *change and say my feelings out loud: I love you. I want to be with* you *forever, never someone else. I want you to be mine.*

But those words are far more permanent than a glowing pink potion.

So, instead, she grins and holds out her glass. "Cheers."

His brown eyes meet hers in a dare, a promise. *We're in this together.*

"Cheers," he says, and then they're both tipping back their cups, the potion sliding cold and bubbly down their throats. This burns. Not the drink, but this hope, this wonder that they can be more.

They look at each other and burst into laughter. They're both examining each other like one of them might jump onto the bar and start belting out love songs.

"You're okay, soulmate?" He laughs.

Remy smiles back. "I'm okay, soulmate."

Her belly is filled with a warm buzz. It's like the drink was made of absinthe, because Remy's on autopilot as they gather their coats, laughing when she accidentally punches Cam (lightly, she says; *ouch*, he replies) in the side as he helps her into her coat.

Then—hell, it *is* working, because Cam only pulls her in closer when Remy dares to loop her arm into his, as they stumble out of the apothecary into the cold winter air, the fizz smoothing into a sweet-honey feel in her stomach.

Out on the sidewalk, they look left and right. Where do they go from here?

Cam's got his phone—or, at least until he drops it, and Remy giggles.

"That drink was nonalcoholic."

"I swear, though, that magic is stronger than your grandma's Christmas punch," Cam says. Then, he adds, in an undertone, "Though not as strong as your real punch."

Remy laughs again, air-punching him, and he pretends to fend her off, but suddenly he wraps his arms around her—she thinks it started off as a way to stop her Olympic-worthy punches but, snug in his arms and face upturned to his, she's not sure anymore.

They stare at each other, their breaths stolen air, soft and gentle, their faces only inches apart. Remy can see every little detail, the way his lashes are boyishly sharp, the slight stubble going up his cheeks, and the way his lips part, ever so slightly.

The love potion—or this intoxicating embrace—is making her heart thump. Cam, only Cam, has seen her at her weakest times, and at her best. He is the protector of her secrets; he's taken her as she is, every time, and been her friend for *exactly* who she is. If that isn't worthy of her love, she doesn't know anyone else who would be.

She can almost taste the sweetness, that delicious softness of his lips. *Yuzu. It'll taste like yuzu, like the potion. A bit salty yet so, so sweet.*

The streetlight flickers out overhead, throwing them into stuttered, temporary darkness. When the light returns, Remy tells herself, she can lift herself up on her toes, and their lips will meet—

The light seems to understand her plan and blinks on, warm and bright.

But something has changed.

Cam loosens his grip, his face blank like he's drank in those shadows, or maybe something worse.

"Cam? Are you okay?"

When his eyes finally focus on her, Cam tilts his head to the side and asks, "Who are you?"

Cam

You know when you have a feeling that you're forgetting something important, but you don't know what that is?

That's the only thought rolling around in Cam's head, because it feels like he's flatlining as he stumbles backward from the girl in his arms. *Beep . . . beep . . . beeeep.*

He remembers the apothecary and the long wood bar. He remembers Beni, with her sly-cat smile. Then the luminous soulmate elixir, a once-in-a-lifetime opportunity, something he's been wanting to study forever. True, it was a banned potion, but he had a solid, flawless reason for taking it—though he can't recall the reason right now. He remembers taking it with someone, someone important.

Then he blinked, and that someone was in his arms, and he has no idea who she is.

Cam stares at the girl standing in front of him, her soft bangs a little messy and her head turned slightly to the side. A breeze blows through, and the shoulders of her pastel-pink jacket inch up against the cold, and he has to push down the immediate urge to offer his coat—*why would he do that for a stranger he might never see again?* Her cheeks are red with the cold, but her eyes shine bright and pretty, like he just told a joke and she wants to laugh, but she can tell there's something off, though she's definitely not as confused as him.

It's kind of like this: Cam could try to recreate elixirs invented by the best magical alchemists in the world, but if he has just an ingredients list and not the true directions, he would never be able to understand the nuances it took to get to the final vial. He doesn't know if the magical dust needs to be infused into moonlight or boiled together, or if adding shadow-seeped coriander might make it simply burst into flames.

Now, he's pretty sure there's been thousands of days and interactions between the two of them, but he has no idea what it really was like.

He and the girl stare at each other. The panic running through his veins is making his thoughts frazzled and cold and is emptying his brain all at once. He examines her in the way he's been examining his life recently: from a distance, trying to pick out what went wrong.

Did he hit on her at the bar and try to take her home? And that's why he was holding her, and she was gazing up at him like that? No, hell no, he wouldn't do that to a stranger, because his heart belongs to—

Cam's brain buffers like a spinning wheel of death, but he can't find an answer.

His heart belongs to *who*?

"You're joking, right?" the girl is saying, as his thoughts spin in meaningless circles. *Dammit, Cam. Why are you so damn useless?*

"Cam?" the girl asks. There's a familiarity to the way she says his name, and it *feels* right.

He shakes his head. "I . . . I don't know who you are."

Remy

In the grand scheme of things, her best friend forgetting her existence was something Remy had never considered. Sure, in ten or twenty years from now, when MIT-girl steals Cam forever and they start traveling the world due to her successful job as a global social justice entrepreneur, saving lives and inspiring entire cities into new levels of growth. But there are still years before that horrible, happy-for-everyone-but-Remy ending.

She says, with a laugh, "Hello, I'm Remy? Protector of your secrets and the story of how you and I both landed in detention in first grade—by the way, sneaking a bunch of butterfly cocoons into our classroom supply closet was, as I had said, a *horrible* idea—"

"It wasn't a horrible idea," Cam says. "But I did that on my own. I put in the milkweed and set up the lighting, and I was stuck in detention all by myself."

She knows the Cam that's telling a joke, because he always grins too early, before the punch line. She knows the Cam that watches over her, but only when he thinks she isn't aware of what he's doing, because she's his best friend, and he's hers.

She doesn't know this Cam who stares at her the way he looked over at Taka and Naomi yesterday, polite but blank-eyed and quiet.

Her heart thuds in her chest. This has to be a joke. There is no way at all that her best friend of seventeen years could have possibly forgotten her. The cold air swirling around them reaches deep into her bones, freezing her words out of her mouth.

Remy gestures at his phone. "Check your camera reel."

Cam pulls up his photo gallery, and frowns. "This is from today, that could mean—"

"Scroll further, Cam." There's a sharpness to her voice that she can't hide. He can't almost—almost, what had that been, a *kiss*? He can't almost kiss her and then make up some elaborate, ridiculous joke to try to pretend that moment didn't happen. This is so unlike Cam that Remy doesn't know what to think.

He goes past the airplane pics, the two of them with their heads together as they tried to beat level 5,471 of Candy Crush. He pauses on a close-up of Goldsticks. "Hey, those are my favorite. Isn't there some sort of game people do—"

Remy leans over and swipes quickly. It's a video of Remy and Cam having a Goldsticks War at that garage sale, over the ugly blue suitcase Remy loves so much.

"You . . . you remember this, right?" She searches his face, waiting for a laugh, for his wide grin as he says, *Got you!*

"Oh," is all he manages to say.

He starts skimming through their history together: bright spring days picnicking at Heritage Park, lunches at Oren's Hummus, and lying out on the grassy clearing at Palo Alto High School. His forehead wrinkles in a frown.

He goes to their life as four-year-olds, their field trip to the firehouse when they were at Bing Preschool.

He even goes to the beginning, the first time that Cam and Remy met each other, wailing babies held in their mothers' arms, born minutes apart. They were in matching onesies; his said *Boba*, hers said *Tea*.

Then he looks at her again, down at the screen, and back up. His voice is soft and apologetic, and that's what aches the most. "What . . . what did you say your name was?"

Then it sinks in, the cold spreading throughout her body, like she's standing coatless in the freezing winter night.

This isn't a prank. Cam seriously doesn't remember her.

Remy spins around to look for Beni's shop, but the lights are off and the sign is gone. "No, no, no . . ."

"Wait, I swear I was hanging out in an apothecary here a moment ago," Cam says.

"We were there," Remy responds, her voice sharp with the ice-like panic freezing her senses. "We were there, *together*."

She yanks at the door handle and it flies open to reveal a dark hallway. Dull lights flicker on, illuminating a set of closed stores.

The apothecary is gone, and Cam's memory of her with it.

Remy

"The expert has arrived." Naomi strides into the apartment, bringing in a swirl of cold late-night air along with a cheeky wink and a wine-red handbag slung over her shoulder.

"I assumed a Magic Reversal team would've been alerted?" Remy says, closing the door behind her. They seriously need all the help they can get, even if it means reaching out to the Tokyo Magical Bureau. Ellie and Jack are still on their way over; it'd been her and Cam, wallowing in an empty silence in the kitchen. Aunt Kiyoko and Uncle David are asleep, and there's no way in hell she's waking up Cam's relatives to let them know the two of them have majorly screwed up.

"Ah," Naomi says, setting her handbag on the dining table with a *clank!* Remy puts away the towel that she was using to wipe down the already-sparkling wood—she cleans when she's nervous—and moves the tiny Christmas tree centerpiece onto the counter. "*I* am the first responder for the Tokyo Magic Reversal team, especially when their main office is closed."

"Wow," Cam says. "How'd you get into that?"

"I was offered a spot due to my research." She opens her handbag; there are several pockets and slots, and zippered bags within zippered bags. Clearly, Naomi's used some sort of expansion charm. She pulls out an extremely large bag—bigger than the handbag itself. When she unzips the case, the thick padding is holding only a small circular tin. "The reversal team needed an alchemist for potions that are circulated on the black market or sometimes made at home that don't work the way they're supposed to after steeping for loads of years, so they hired me. Anyway, what'd you take?"

"A restricted potion," Cam says. "I think it made me forget Remy, because I've seen the pics of me and her."

Naomi's eyes narrow. "And you don't remember her at all?"

"Not even my name," Remy whispers.

Cam reluctantly nods. "The only reason I'd ever believe I used to know you is this weird, weird sensation. Like déjà vu."

"What's déjà vu is this feeling that we're all going to get in trouble," grumbles Jack as he and Ellie come inside with another burst of cold air.

They settle into the chairs, and Ellie leans into him, a fondness in her eyes. "Kind of reminds me of a few years ago. All that mess turned into something good, I'd say." Stoic Jack breaks into a sweet smile. Ellie always tells Remy how amazing Jack is, but honestly, most of the time it seems like he's one hell of a lucky guy. The way that Jack carefully helps Ellie take off her coat makes Remy have a feeling that he knows how lucky he is, too.

Jack nods at Naomi. "Thanks for coming over, unofficially."

Remy frowns. "Why unofficially?"

Naomi opens another one of her pockets, and a rose-gold badge shines under the light. "You got a Magic Reversal team member without the red tape. The bureau would've sent me and then kicked you both out of Japan immediately. At least with an unofficial visit, I don't have to send in a report until things open up again in the New Year."

Remy freezes. She needs to get *into* TMU, not get kicked *out* of Japan.

Naomi's eyes cut to Cam. "In particular, we don't usually allow people who mess around, illegally, with potions to keep their license." There's an edge to her voice. "It's one of the fundamentals of being a researcher. Test in a closed environment, where you can reduce variables and keep things replicable for future studies. There's no value in going rogue if you're going to ruin things—especially at a cost like this. You have a magical alchemy learner's license, right? Can you show it to me?"

Cam opens his blue leather wallet and digs out the rose-gold card—

Naomi snaps it up, sliding it into her bag. "That's going to be a suspended license, unfortunately."

Cam is pale. "Uh-oh."

"Quote of the day, idiot," Jack mutters. "You're always so careful. What the hell were you thinking?"

"I . . ." Cam sinks his head into his hands. "I don't know. But—I can't do any alchemy without my license—my learner's set won't even open—"

"That's the point of the suspension," Naomi says, though she looks a little sad for him. "Unless you can give me a solid reason you had to take that potion."

"I told the truth," Cam protests. "I remember I wanted to take the potion more than *anything* I've ever wanted before. That I *needed* it. I just don't remember *her.*"

Everyone turns to glance at Remy. She lifts up her phone to show a picture from when they'd started eating Goldsticks on the bench. "I'll share what I know."

Using photos, Remy pieces together their day—from the interview at TMU to even the silly parts, like eating ice cream all around Tokyo or their Goldsticks War—and stumbling upon Beni's Apothecary. All the way to both of them drinking the soulmate potion—after agreeing to try it together—up until when Cam had forgotten about her.

Minus their almost kiss, of course.

"It closed for the day," Remy explains, finally, with a groan. "We couldn't get back in."

"This all sounds vaguely familiar," Cam says. "And I saw the pictures of me and Remy."

"And you remember him?" Naomi casts her gaze toward Remy.

"Of course." There is no way she'd ever forget her best friend—even if he doesn't remember her.

"But, if you took the same potion, shouldn't the side effects be the same?" Jack asks.

"A potion that ancient—and powerful—is bound to be volatile, with different side effects based on the person," Naomi says.

"I'm guessing it's like the way I can't stand heights, but you could be dropped onto the summit of Mt. Fuji and not break a sweat," Ellie tells her boyfriend. "Different people, different reactions."

Naomi nods. "It could be working in ways we don't understand to get the final result it was made for . . ."

The final result . . . Remy hopes that's the truth: that, somehow, she and Cam *will* end up together. Even though things look pretty bleak right now.

Then, Naomi shakes her head with frustration. "Those Yoshinos."

"Beni Yoshino is descended from one of the ancient families of Tokyo," Ellie explains for Cam and Remy's sake. "Ordinary magic families like us, we're not allowed in their circles. Which means we don't have access to their magic, but that's why the places that they open up to the general magical society, like their café, are so appealing."

"A two-hundred-year-old love potion," Naomi is repeating to herself, sounding more and more frustrated. "The ways I could analyze that . . ."

"See?" Cam protests. "If you had the chance to research a once-in-a-lifetime potion, you'd want to test it out, too!"

"Did that potion knock out your common sense?" Naomi asks. "You could have pretended to drink it and then swiped the bottle. You could've cast a tiny charm to seal it away. There are a million things you could've done instead of *drinking* something that's banned."

"There wasn't any way to get to it other than drinking it, I swear," Cam says. "I couldn't pass up this chance." His forehead furrows. "I *know* the reason I took it was solid, better than any theory I've ever read. Other than for research, though, I can't remember what exactly that was."

"Well, let's hope you were right about this." Naomi gestures him to the seat in front of her. "Time for a checkup. Let's see what we find."

Ugh. Remy doesn't want to watch Naomi's pretty hands all over Cam. Naomi unzips a few more compartments, revealing layers of magical, rose-tinted tools and vials. With Cam's consent, Naomi begins to hold his hand, using the magnifying glass to examine his wrist. Remy can barely stomach Naomi's graceful fingers fluttering along his arm.

Then Jack heads to the front door to let someone in, and Remy welcomes the opportunity to look at something—*anything*—else. Taka slips inside as the kitchen clock strikes eleven, and takes the last empty chair next to Remy.

That's totally normal and all, except he's also weighed down by ten bags of Kentucky Fried Chicken, the greasy scent wafting out.

"You must really like chicken," Remy says.

"It's Christmas," Taka says, as if that explains everything. Then he grins. "Oh—"

Cam clears his throat. "It's a thing in Japan to celebrate Christmas with KFC."

Naomi says, in that pretty-as-chimes voice, "Okay, pick up the square meter on the table, and hold it with both hands. Right, like that. In a minute, it'll give us a reading to show any magical foreign substances in your system."

More quietly, only so Remy can hear, Taka explains, "Christmas is a couple's holiday here. If you're single, then you get together with a bunch of your other single friends, eat loads of KFC, cut a Christmas cake, and hope that you'll all find someone next year."

Remy had completely forgotten about Christmas after Cam's lost memories. It's cruel that this is a couple's holiday, and the guy she loves has completely forgotten about her. She's still holding on to his present, too—a star cookie tower shaped into a Christmas tree. The worst part is that he won't even understand why she'd give him something like that, because he's probably forgotten all of her haphazard bakes or the mountain of sweets they've devoured together. No matter even if she gives him the present, Christmas is all but over.

Cam

Seeing the tool kit of an internationally recognized researcher should feel exhilarating. Spread out on the table, there's a bronze scale that keeps shifting, even though there's nothing on any of the three platforms. A set of seven vials, in a rainbow of colors, is suspended in a glass case and barely visible through a swirling, black mist. Everything gleams; it's the best of alchemy tools that money can buy.

But Cam feels empty.

"Okay, that's the first set of tests, complete," Naomi says. "Let me set some other stuff up, so hold on for a minute."

While he waits, he shifts closer to check out the bronze scale—maybe something he'll learn will be useful—but Jack gives him a pointed glare. "Do you want to have your license completely revoked? Stay away until Naomi says otherwise."

Cam steps back toward the wall, near the stranger that he's supposed to know.

Standing just inches away, his stomach flips strangely. How can he have forgotten his supposed best friend? No matter how he tries to think of her, no matter how much he tries to remember what they used to talk about, what they did together, nothing comes to mind. Only today's memories of looking through his phone at thousands of photos of them together.

Nothing makes sense, and he's the one to blame.

"Do you recognize this stuff?" Remy asks.

He shakes his head. "I've seen that set of vials. They're used to track poisons, and determine a proper antidote. But I don't know what that three-arm scale is."

"Yeah, your equipment doesn't look anything like this," Remy says.

How— My *equipment?* Not to be rude, but he doesn't allow *anyone* near his equipment. He locks it up the moment he's done with an experiment, just in case his dad comes in and breaks something, in another of his arm-waving soliloquies about how Cam should live his life, and how much he has bragged to the other store owners about Cam's future in the Ivy Leagues.

"That glass syringe and needle set looks sort of like that thing we used back when we had to extract that ounce of ultra-refined magical dust," Remy continues, pointing to a case opened out on the table, with a set of needles featuring sharp, rose-gold tinted tips. "It gives me such a headache to use my crappy set of rose-tinted glasses, I seriously hope you get a new set when you have to do those projects in college."

He used to run experiments with Remy? "Are you interested in becoming an alchemist, too?"

She laughs; it's a joyful sound, something that makes Cam feel warmer inside. "Me? A magical alchemist? I save that for the pros like you. I'd like to work with something related to magic but I haven't figured out exactly what yet, so that's why I'm applying to TMU."

Something clicks into place. *That's very Remy.* Of course she would want to try out a few intro courses to different majors before committing.

His brain nearly stops.

Very Remy? How would he even know that?

A hand tugs at his sleeve. "Cam? Earth to Cam?"

His thoughts clear; Remy is still standing next to him, her eyes wide.

"Sorry, you were lost in your own world. I—I thought the aftereffects of the potion were getting worse, or something."

"What's up?" he asks.

"*You're* up," Naomi calls, patting the chair next to the table. "The initial diagnostics didn't tell me much. But I've got a few more tricks. It's time to see what's really going on."

He swallows, his heart beginning to pound, as he steps forward.

———◆———

Cam never thought *he* would be the experiment. His head is spinning—and not all from the blood loss—after Naomi extracts his blood, smears it on a few glass slides, and distributes a few ruby-red droplets into bubbling vials.

She unlocks the tiny box that was in the gigantic, padded case, and lifts out a spiral notebook, no bigger than her palm. With a quick flip of the cover, she tears out a page, setting it carefully on the table.

"This paper shows how long the potion will last in your system," Naomi explains. "In essence, it's a half-life litmus test; but in this case, it works on potions. I had to strip your blood's essence to isolate the potion on its own for a strong enough concentration, and put it into an amplifying elixir for an extra boost. It's not going to be enough to figure out the contents or, say, how to remake it, but at least it can show us this potion's duration."

Damn. This is a level of magical alchemy he's never seen; it makes his afternoons of experiments look like child's play. This is neat. It's almost enough to ease the edge of his anxious, worried thoughts.

"Why's it locked away?" Remy asks.

"You'd be surprised how many people would want to steal this out from under my nose," Naomi says. "I'm in the process of filing a patent. Until that's done, I'm not going to let the prototype out of this lockbox."

"Is that why this wasn't part of your seminar earlier?" Cam asks.

"So you remember that—interesting. And yes, it's not something I'm ready to share with those hawks at TMU." Naomi nods at the paper. "Hold this with both hands. That'll help it recognize that it's based on your body and system; people tend to absorb potions differently, so this helps me eliminate variables."

He holds it carefully with the understanding, according to what Naomi's saying, that her notepad and this piece of paper are probably worth more than everything in his dad's shop.

It's smooth and slippery, kind of the same size as the origami bookmarks that Remy makes . . . Wait—how'd he know that?

Cam looks over at Remy. She's standing next to her sister, her wide, owl-like eyes focused on him. When their gazes meet, she straightens slightly. She's undeniably pretty, with those bangs that are rumpled from the hat she was wearing earlier, and her long hair swirling over her shoulders. But someone looking nice doesn't make Cam fall in love; he knows that deep in his core. Maybe his heart already belongs to someone else, but he's not sure what's the truth without his memories, and he's not going to go out on a limb and guess about his past. He believes in pure, solid facts, not fiction.

Naomi swirls one of the vials that looks like sparkling, liquid diamonds; the colors intensify to a pale red; she pours in a vial of seemingly clear liquid, though Cam has a suspicion it's glowing with magical dust.

A burst of smoke puffs out, concealing her hand. Within a few seconds, it disappears. Cam blinks. There's only a small, pale gold droplet at the bottom of the vial. At first, he thought the contents had vanished into smoke.

"Where'd it all go?" Remy asks.

Jack frowns. "Doesn't the Law of Conservation of Energy exist? Like, basic thermodynamics?"

"It doesn't apply to magical alchemy—or at least, that's what we thought, originally," Naomi explains. "Then, we realized that magic, invisible to the naked eye, is what it turns into after alchemy interactions such as these."

That's what Cam loves about magical alchemy: an elixir may look like nothing, it can even *disappear* into nothing, but it sure as hell is something awesome.

Naomi tips the vial over Cam's outstretched hands, and the droplet slides out.

The moment it hits the paper, energy crackles at his fingers, like a live wire. Then, that sensation vanishes as the paper absorbs the droplet, turning it into the same rose gold of the original potion. Colored ink swirls into:

一月一日から

"From January first?" Cam reads.

"So, after that, the effects will lift?" Remy asks. "That's not long at all!"

Naomi shakes her head. "This is a *banned* potion. It's pulling the date that it'll be fully effective, when it'll truly become a part of his system. From the moment the clock hits January first, Cam will never remember you again."

Remy

The horror on Jack and Ellie's faces matches the shock reverberating through her body. Taka seems worried . . . but Cam . . . Cam and Naomi are discussing it scientifically, with all emotions cleaved out of their conversation.

She wishes he would frown, wishes there was a hint of a Cam that misses her, but he simply says, "Permanent, huh? That's interesting that the potion isn't instantaneous."

Naomi nods. "It's like if you eat this chicken." She waves her hand at the bags on the kitchen counter, long forgotten. "You eat it, but it doesn't absorb into your bloodstream immediately. Similar to alchemy. This potion, because of the magic infused into it, has an especially long absorption time within your blood, which was what I was testing with that paper."

"And how do I revert things, scientifically speaking?" Cam asks. There's a shine to his eyes that Remy usually loves, when he's stuck in an experiment and he catches a glimpse of an idea to fix things. But it's usually things like a laughing potion when Remy's had a bad day, or a reading elixir that can help Remy find the book that she's looking for in her wall-to-wall bookshelves.

"Well, you can survive without your memories, even though they're of your best friend," Naomi says. "But I'll research how to get things back to normal."

Cam nods, as if that makes sense to him, even though it'll never, *ever* be sensible to Remy. Then he turns pink. "And my license? I need that. I can't be a magical alchemy major without it."

Jack growls, "Cam, be grateful you still have some of your memories. I don't think you realize how close of a call you've had."

Cam shakes his head. "You don't understand how rare that was! Like, shooting-star kind of rare to find a love potion this well maintained—"

"Well maintained?" Jack shoots back. The two brothers bicker back and forth. Remy and Ellie exchange a knowing look; this is their way of hashing their emotions out.

Taka snags a box of biscuits, and offers it to Remy. She shakes her head; she can't stomach a single bite.

But, then he says, softly, only for the two of them to hear, "Remy, I'm sorry. I know Cam was your friend for the longest time; even though there's a lot going on right now, he'll realize that someday."

Remy lets out a deep, shuddering sigh that she didn't realize she'd been holding in. "Thanks, Taka."

Naomi spins around. "Remy, you're up."

Now Remy wishes she did have that biscuit to stuff her mouth with. "What? Up for what?"

"You took that elixir, too, right?" Naomi says. "Sit here. Let's see what that potion did to you."

———◆———

Naomi has prodded Remy's face, examined her mouth, even taken her blood. But, no matter what sort of tests the older girl runs with her myriad of vials and potions, she keeps shaking her head. "Nothing. Nothing at all."

"What do you mean?" Remy asks. She glances over at the couch;

Jack, Ellie, Cam, and Taka are sitting on the couch, where Naomi banished them all after Cam kept hovering, trying to see every step.

"The traces of the potion are there"—Naomi flashes her paper invention, which shows the same "*January 1*" lettering as Cam's—"but I can't seem to find any side effects. Your labs are all normal, your vitals fine."

"So, this love potion had no effect on me?" Remy asks.

"It . . . Unbelievably, it doesn't seem like it. Have you lost any memories?" Naomi asks. "I know that's difficult to gauge, but you scrolled through your phone when you showed Cam the pics of you two, right? Was there anyone you didn't recognize?"

Remy shakes her head; she'd wondered that, too, and already looked alongside Cam. Her, Cam, Ellie, Jack, Lia, Minami . . . Remy recognizes them all.

Naomi pauses, glancing to look over at the couch, and then leans in close to whisper, "Okay, because of the potion that you took, I have to ask this: Are you in love?"

"I should be," Remy replies, softly.

Naomi's eyes track her gaze over to Cam, who's laughing with his brother about something.

"Do you know . . ." Remy hesitates. No one knows about her real fortune from Mr. Yoshino anymore, and she's not ready to share it, still. But the question burns in her gut. "I'm wondering . . . since that soulmate potion didn't work, will I never fall in love?"

Naomi bites her lip. "I'm not sure, honestly. I've never seen a potion as potent—or volatile—as what you drank. I mean, they've been banned for ages. No one even studies love potions anymore because of that, and their scarcity."

Remy's stomach lumps up, as if the potion has solidified into a rock.

"I'm sorry," Naomi says. "I'm trying to think of an antidote, I promise. The good thing is, it seems like you don't have any side effects so far. Maybe that countdown is just matching Cam's, because it impacts you if he forgets your shared memories, permanently. The thing that

I'll try to figure out is how, and why. But keep an eye on things, okay? Let me know if anything—anything at all—changes."

Remy nods numbly, adding Naomi's number into her phone.

What if my fortune is the reason why the potion didn't work? What if Remy is the reason why Cam is now cursed?

Remy

As Remy's world slowly but resolutely crumbles to an end, clearly the most logical solution is to sit at the table, laugh about nothing, and stuff fried chicken into her face. To pretend like she's not in love with Cam, like this isn't hurting more than anything before, she does a damn good job of convincing everyone she's ravenous and totally okay, and now she's going to keep pretending the crispy drumsticks are all she needs to make her heart happy.

Cam, who switched seats with Taka, seems to be watching her out of the corner of his eye, rather than eating. He's picking away at one of the biscuits—for reasons she doesn't understand, Japan's KFC punches holes into the middle of them, like donuts—as he studies her. Maybe he's wondering what made the two of them best friends.

"You should eat," Jack says, nudging one of the paper buckets toward his younger brother. Even Cam's older brother is worried; Cam's not acting like himself.

Cam reluctantly pulls out a crispy chicken thigh and sets it on his plate. He still looks as unhungry as ever.

Remy tosses over a small packet of maple syrup, without thinking, and Cam brightens. As if on autopilot, he tears it open and drenches his chicken, but just as he's about to bite in, he pauses. "You knew."

Cam's got an incredible sweet tooth. He loves sugar-doused cereal.

He'd willingly tickle-fight Remy for the last homemade matcha cookie they'd baked together. In the same way he had—at least, before the soulmate potion—always accepted Remy as she is, the only constant being that she changes from day to day, her favorite moments are when Cam can be himself, too: that insatiable curiosity for finding answers (*especially* if there are no answers; he's always attracted to unsolved puzzles) and that just-as-insatiable sweet tooth.

"I had a feeling you might like it," she says with a laugh, even as her heart aches. *I always knew.*

He cracks a smile—the first real smile since all of his memories of her went out the window, and Remy can't help but cling to it, trying to press it into her mind.

Because, even if he's forgotten her, there's no way that she'd ever be able to forget him.

Cam

C am liberally douses the chicken with more maple syrup, though it's supposed to be for the biscuits. Sugar has always made his brain feel clearer. He bites in, the coating satisfyingly crispy, then—

It's Father's Day; he and Remy are fourteen years old, and trying to make dinner for Mr. Yasuda and Mr. Kobata.

"Dad?" Cam pops his head into CharmWorks, his father's shop. It's internationally known for its exquisite bullet journals and stationery that imbue users due to a special secret: magical spells for confidence and mental fortitude. The store is bustling, with Mr. Yasuda at the register, ringing up customer after customer.

"What is it, son?" Mr. Yasuda asks. He's far more polite than usual when he's got a store full of people watching him. Cam wishes he were more like this at home, too.

"Do you want karaage or steak for dinner?"

Mr. Yasuda puffs up, glancing over to the line of customers watching this father-and-son interaction. Most customers know about Cam's mom passing away, which makes this even more precious in their eyes, probably.

"Some karaage sounds nice," Mr. Yasuda says, with a flash of a smile. Cam's dad, as cranky as he is, can never seem to turn down Japanese-style fried chicken.

Perfect. Plan decided. Cam heads across the alleyway to Remy's house, with a bag of potato starch in hand.

"He wants karaage," Cam declares, the moment he steps inside the Kobatas' kitchen. Remy looks up from where she's flipping through a dessert recipe book, probably searching up some new concoction to attempt. Cam's always loved her trial baking runs, even the ones that end up in a sweet, soggy mess. As long as it's sugar, and not baking soda, like what happened a few weeks ago.

Remy and Cam are ready to make the karaage. Except they forgot one crucial part: they don't know how to cook.

So that's how, a few hours later, the Kobatas' kitchen looks like a bomb has gone off in it. It's okay, they'll clean it up later. They need to fry the chicken first.

The oil is hot and ready, the chicken is prepped. Everything is going fine, until Remy drops in the first coated chicken to fry.

Remy lets out a shriek of pain; the moisture on the chicken has sent oil splattering all over her hand.

He jabs the stove knob off and holds her carefully. She's gritting her teeth, but the whimper she lets out tears Cam's heart into two. How could he be so damn useless and not study this up beforehand? How'd he let his best friend get hurt?

Cam turns the faucet on to drizzle out cool water—not cold, according to Google, because this time he's not going to fly by the seat of his pants, he's going to do this right. He holds her hand as she lets the water run over it. No matter how quickly Remy's skin can heal with a magical burn ointment, he can't forget that he should've taken better care of her; that he was the one who let her get hurt.

Later, when they're sitting on the rooftop of Cam's house and eating their karaage together, Remy pulls out a bottle of magical sweet-and-spicy sauce she ordered all the way from a home chef in Fukushima, Japan, and plays music from his favorite indie band, ChemiCold. She leans against him, laughing as his eyes well up from the heat, but he can't stop eating it. Because, with her, life tastes good.

Cam reaches out to brush his fingers against the side of Remy's hand. The star-shaped burn mark is faded, but it's there, like that memory that clicked into place, bone-deep and real.

"I remember," he says wonderingly.

"Your memory's back?" Remy lets out a gasp, lighting up like he's just told her he's saved the world. He wishes he had.

Cam quickly backtracks. "That time we made the fried chicken. Father's Day, back when we were fourteen."

"Oh." Remy's voice is small. "*Oh.* Just that."

Even if Cam doesn't remember much about her, he can tell she's trying not to show how much she hurts.

Then, Naomi, sitting on Cam's other side, and who's been apparently watching this whole exchange along with the rest of the group, says, "*I know!* It's a key switch. *Recreating* a memory."

When Remy's brow wrinkles in confusion, Naomi continues, "It seems like Cam's memories aren't totally gone. I think that it's because memories aren't static."

"That makes sense," Ellie says, nodding slowly. "You make them, but when you remember them again, they're different."

"Still don't understand," Jack mutters.

Ellie nudges him with a smile. "Take the day the four of us found Mochi at the park. I can recall the way she was shivering and looked so sad and lonely. But do you remember if it was cold?"

Jack frowns. "Hm . . . Wait, it was summer; people would've been using the barbecue grills, right?"

"I didn't remember that it was smoky," Ellie says. "Not until you brought up the barbecue."

"True." Then Remy frowns. "Now I can't un-remember the smoke."

"That's how memory recreation works," Naomi says. "Simple as that. It's based on the five basic senses . . . Which might be the perfect leaping point for finding more memories, actually."

Remy's eyes shine, illuminated with hope, and the other five start talking about ways to trigger the rest of Cam's memories as they polish off the late-night Christmas dinner. But a pit opens up in Cam's stomach, churning with the feeling that he's going to let all of them, but especially Remy, down. This makes no sense. Why did the soulmate elixir erase all of his memories of her? His chest does a funny twist. But what if it's not Remy? What if there's someone back home that he has the biggest crush on, and he's forgotten about them?

"Isn't there a way for Cam to keep his license?" Remy pipes up. "Especially if he's remembering things?"

"Even though I'm here unofficially, having an alchemy license and taking a banned potion changes things. I can't just let that slide. . . ." Naomi studies her thoughtfully. "*Unless* he's back to the same state as he was before he took the potion, before his flight. Then, when the Tokyo Magical Bureau offices open back up, I guess I won't have any reason to file my report."

"I'll find an antidote by then!" Cam says. "And keep my license!"

"Find?" Naomi shakes her head. "You do realize this is a two-hundred-year-old love potion? The Yoshinos aren't going to give up any hints. It's going to take a lot more than a smart brain to figure out how to even create an antidote to counteract it."

"How about two?" Remy says. "You and Cam could create an antidote together."

Maybe the photos *are* right. He grins at her in thanks, like she really is his best friend ever.

Naomi, on the other hand, shakes her head. "I don't know where to start. . . . Memory recreation is tricky. . . ."

Cam deflates. He doesn't even have until January 2. If he permanently loses his memories of Remy in a week—midnight, New Year's Day, to be exact—his future in magical alchemy will disappear just as quickly.

Memories . . .

He sits up straight. "Naomi, what if we use my memories? Isn't there some way to capture them to create an antidote? You said that the senses—taste and sight and all that—are a key switch. . . . Maybe that's what the antidote needs to trigger the rest of my memories."

Naomi tilts her head to the side. "You're right. . . . Adjusting this antidote to be a liquid key switch *would* work. In theory . . ."

"Wait, wait," Taka says, waving his hand. "I know where we're going, and it means no more chicken. No Christmas games."

"I just need to do a *little* thinking." She pulls a notepad out of her pocket, scribbles on it, and tears out a page. When she offers it to Cam, she murmurs, "What are you doing tomorrow?"

Remy casually glances at the paper. "What's that, Cam?"

"Oh." Cam looks down and coughs, his throat dry. "She was wondering—"

"I was inviting Cam to my house tomorrow night," Naomi says sweetly. Then she adds, "Do you want to come, too?"

Cam

When everyone is entranced by some story Taka is telling, Cam slips out to the balcony. There, finally, his introverted mind pieces itself back together as he stares out at the sparkling cityscape.

"Would you want to see the illuminations in Tokyo?" Remy asks.

"With you? Definitely," Cam says. "But with Jack and Ellie? No, thanks."

Remy laughs, and he can't help but feel like sunlight is blooming inside his heart.

Another memory. Like smoke, the rest of that moment disappears out of reach. Cam stays there, hand outstretched toward nothing, his back to the one girl who seems to have all the answers in her mind. The sliding glass door squeaks as it rolls open.

Jack and Ellie step out, Ellie keeping close to the glass door—she's never been good with heights. It's strange to be able to recall so many days he's spent with Jack and Ellie, but there's a white blur where someone else—Remy?—should be.

He can't even trust his own mind.

Jack leans against the railing. "How are you holding up?"

Cam looks over at his brother. "Tell me. Were Remy and I really like . . . Was she . . . What were we like together?"

"You looked at her like she was the center of the universe," Jack says, without hesitation.

"Did we . . . date?" Cam asks, curious.

This time, Ellie lets out a noise, like one of Cam's frustrated, match-making aunties back home, the ones who are always trying to match him up, though he always refuses. "You two should have."

"Then why not?" Cam asks.

"Question of the century," Jack mutters. "You'd never tell me."

"I've got a feeling that's why this curse happened," Ellie says. "You were too scared of being honest with your own thoughts. You've got to figure that out, Cam, or you're going to lose her forever."

"And your license," Jack adds pointedly, as if Cam isn't already *completely* freaking out about that.

"Thanks for the reminder," Cam growls.

How can he remember something—someone—he's forgotten? And in time for him to keep his alchemy license?

Then, the glass door opens again, and he can hear Remy's laugh close by—sharp and bright and beautiful—as she tells the others she'll be right back.

Jack and Ellie mutter something and disappear through the door. A smaller figure peeks up at him from under her messy bangs.

"Hi, Remy," he says softly, and he wonders at how familiar her name flows on his lips.

"Hey, Cam," she says back. He knows, without having to look—but he does anyway, to be sure this sliver of a memory is right—that she's smiling. She is. Remy's voice is like an experiment he's tested over and over again, with certain inputs triggering certain reactions. If he makes a joke, she laughs—nose wrinkling and all. If she cries over *Big Hero 6*, she'll want to watch it all over again, knowing she's going to cry again. If she—

He doesn't know the rest of her reactions and the formula that makes Remy truly herself, because he's forgotten it. And he *needs* to remember; he needs to get this cursed potion out of his system or he'll lose his license forever. That's what matters, right? He tries to keep his magical alchemy future in his mind—not that smile that melts him—when he says, "I have an idea."

Remy

The cold night air is sharp in her lungs as she avoids the urge to loop her arm into his, the way they used to, before the potion.

"Look," Cam says. "I honestly don't know you."

You do. *You know me better than I know myself, most of the time.*

"I have six days to get my memories back," Cam says slowly. "I was thinking about it, and you would know better than me—well, obviously—what might trigger more shared memories between us. I need your help to get my memories back so that I can keep my license."

Remy stares at him. Wishing he would remember their days together, wishing he loved her as she is now, messy and unsure about her future as she is. The one thing she'd always believed in was him, even if it was never him-and-her. Wishing she was worth more to him than his license.

"So, you want a list? I can give you a list of memories. Or we can go through those photos in our album." She tries to keep her voice light, yet the words cut too deep.

Cam seems to search for words as he looks out along the skyline, and finally down at her, studying her lips in a quiet line, her eyes turned up to his. "I think we need more than a list. Because you . . . I . . . I know you mean something, something incredible to me, even if I'm cursed to forget. If we weren't as close friends as those photos show,

I'd *never* be able to get my memories back. It's a lot to ask, but . . . for the friendship that we had, would you please help?"

Our cursed love. Remy smiles up at him, even though her heart is breaking. So. These are their last few days to spend with each other, before he forgets her forever. *I don't want to be alone with these memories, not without you to remember them, too.*

"I'm cursed with you," she whispers, but the breeze steals away her words. So she simply nods, and says, louder, "Of course I'll help you. But you better get me some damn good ice cream to make up for this."

He laughs quietly. "An ice cream in the middle of winter? Only you would want that—I think."

"I'll do this for the old Cam, then," she says. "In hopes that we'll find him again."

"The old Cam was a lucky guy to have you as a friend. And this new Cam thanks you, too."

Her heart breaks as she loops her arm around his. Yet, to her surprise, he leans into her.

Maybe he does remember, just a bit. She'll treasure every minute—and fight against that fate—until then.

Five Days Until New Year's Eve

TUESDAY, DECEMBER 26

Remy

Morning sun dances through the windows; a crystal catcher sends the rays beaming around the kitchen with hints of rainbow hues. Remy wraps her hands tighter around the mug of freshly brewed matcha from where she sits at the table, centered in the middle of the compact kitchen. If only she could solve her problems with one sip, just like this drink. Her matcha is imbued with another jet-lag charm, sharp with the scent of ginger, and every sip gives her life, but not answers. She glances over to Cam's still-closed bedroom door. She hasn't seen him since last night, since he, well, *forgot* her. Today is their free day, after yesterday's busy interview, but she doesn't even know what they're going to do.

"You two will be okay on your own today?" Aunt Kiyoko chirps, as if she can hear Remy's very thoughts, as she wipes the counter. "David and I will both be at work, but call us if you need anything."

"Absolutely, thank you." Remy tries to get up again to help clean the kitchen after their simple rice and egg breakfast, but Cam's auntie waves her back into her seat.

"Drink that all," the older woman says sternly, her eyebrows zipping down. "With jet lag and that mysterious whispering last night, I'm sure you're exhausted."

Remy chokes on her drink. "Did we wake you—"

"Not at all, I was finishing up some work. But are you sure every-thing is okay?" Aunt Kiyoko pauses in front of the table, leaning on the edge. "If it's something I can help with . . ." Then, she shifts, and chirps brightly, "Actually, I know that it might feel strange to confess your problems to me, so let me share what I do."

Remy will take anything that'll work. "Oh?"

"Matcha brownies!" the older woman exclaims, pulling a bag out of a drawer, beaming. "The answer to most of life's questions. This is infused with wish powder, too. With every bite, make a wish, and it just might come true." Then, she tilts her head to the side, a knowing look. "Must go, have fun, you two!"

"Wait, what?" Remy asks, bewildered. It's just her and Aunt Kiyoko—who's already halfway out the front door, so who is she talking about?

"Bye now!" the older woman calls, and the door swings shut.

Did Aunt Kiyoko just *ditch* her?

Then, a sleepy voice asks, from the other side of the kitchen, "Brownies?"

Cam rubs his eyes from where he leans against his bedroom door. His long-sleeve shirt lifts up to show a peek of a tanned midriff, and her throat goes dry.

"*Oh*. Um. Good morning, Cam." Remy basically shoves the brownie mix bag into her face, and tries to read the directions, but she *definitely* can't concentrate. "Wow. Incredible. This is so cool that it's matcha flavored. And it has a wish charm in it."

"I need sugar." He slumps onto the chair next to her.

I know, she wants to say. The Cam she knew never really woke up before liberal amounts of sugary coffee or tea.

"Want the rest of my drink?" she asks, nudging the mug over.

He takes a sniff, his nose wrinkling. "Is there extra sugar any-where?"

They both look around; the cabinet doors are all shut.

"I don't feel like rummaging through their stuff," Cam says.

"It's weird, right?" Remy echoes. "To be in someone's house, and they're not home."

Cam looks at her funny. "That's almost how I feel about forgetting you. I feel like I should be at home, but I'm not, quite. Something's missing."

Her heart flips. Cam . . . did Cam just say she was his *home*? No, no way. She's just misinterpreting the rambles of a sugar-deprived, jet-lagged, cursed somewhat-ex-best-friend.

Cam burrows his head into his arms, letting out a moan. "More sugar . . . I need brainpower to figure out how to make an antidote. . . . Matcha brownies sound amazing, but we'd have to bake them. . . . I need sugar *now*."

"I have your Christmas present," she says. Everything was so busy yesterday that she hadn't been able to give it to him.

Cam peeks out. "Does it have—"

"*Tons* of sugar." She nods, and Cam beams. When he looks at her like that, it's as if the crystal catcher is sending rays of sunlight straight into her heart.

Moments later, after digging through the bottom of her aqua-blue suitcase, she reappears in the kitchen, sliding a small green box in the shape of a Christmas tree across the table.

Cam looks embarrassed. He doesn't reach out for it like she expects.

"What is it?" she asks. "Sorry, this isn't anything much."

"I don't have a present for you. I shouldn't accept anything—"

Remy laughs. "That's because you *already* gave me a gift. You bought me the suitcase, remember?"

Cam brightens. "Seriously? Why'd I buy that ugly suitcase, though?"

"Hey!" she protests, laughing as she sits back down next to him. "I don't appreciate insults toward my present."

He pops open the box. "*Yum*."

But Remy groans. "Oh *no*."

She'd spent all night before their flight baking. The Christmas tree was simple enough: star-shaped sugar cookies stacked on top of each other, from biggest to smallest, and coated in enough icing to even satisfy Cam. But the corners are all crumbles and even the iced ornaments that took forever to make have cracked in half.

He turns his head to the side, looking at it thoughtfully. "I can get a sense of what it looked like. I love the ornaments—wait, is this one a pair of rose-colored spectacles? And that one's a glass beaker? Remy, this is genius."

Her heart skips. This is the Cam she remembers and misses.

"Go on, have some. Get your sugar fix."

Cam never has to be told twice when it comes to sweets. He gently breaks off a corner and pops it in his mouth—

And gags.

Remy pales. "Shoot. No." She grabs an edge and takes a bite, and just as quickly spits it out into a napkin. "*Ew!*"

"I think you mixed something up." Cam chews diplomatically. He also looks like he might be dying. "It's, uh, very unique, though—"

"Spit it out, spit it out!" she cries. "I grabbed the white pepper instead of baking powder!" The spices and baking supplies are on the same shelf back home, and she was likely daydreaming about this trip instead of focusing on the cookies like she should have.

Cam, though, swallows his bite, even with Remy protesting. He quickly gets up to fill a cup at the faucet, and thirstily drinks a full cup and a half. Then he turns, and they stare at each other.

"Were you trying to poison me?" he asks. "Is that what that soulmate elixir gone wrong was about? You're my best friend, but you're trying to get rid of me, too?"

Remy's face burns, until she sees the corner of his lip curve ever so slightly. "Cam!" she protests, and he bursts out into laughter.

"What *happened*? I know you're never good at baking, but that was a new low—"

He freezes, as does she.

"You remember?" she asks, in a small, hopeful voice.

But Cam rubs his forehead with his fingers. "Just a flash of memory. You made me snickerdoodles, I think. They ended up being so hard that Minami used them as hockey pucks. A few other memories of your baking, too, but it's a mess every time. A good mess, because you're really trying . . ."

"A mess." She glares at her lumpy, broken Christmas tree. Then, she picks up the brownie mix. "I'll redeem myself, I promise."

Cam

This morning has been a strange wake-up. First, the message on his phone—a note from himself last night: *Do you remember Remy yet?*

No. Yes and no.

Then, when Remy brought out the Christmas tree cookies, he knew he *had* to figure out a way to remember her. No one could look at that homely stack of cookies and icing and *not* want to be friends with the person who made it with all their heart (though lacking skills in the baking department).

Remy taps the bag of brownie mix. "Your auntie left it out for us. Apparently, these are magical, and can help grant wishes."

"Wait, you want to make the brownies?" Cam asks. His mouth still burns from the peppery fire of the so-called sugar cookies. "How about you hang out here? I'll make them."

Their hands reach out at the same time for the mix, but she's slightly faster, and his hand lands on top of hers.

Their eyes meet from across the kitchen table, in that split second.

They. Are. Holding. Hands.

Well, technically.

And—whoa. His body reacts instantaneously. In that sliver of a moment, his ears heat up, his words fall straight out of his brain, and his heart ricochets like he's pumped it full of so many elixirs that he can't even make sense of what's going on.

"I—uh—sorry," he stammers.

Remy's cheeks turn pink. "Oh. No worries. Um, let me go make something for you to drink."

She quickly hops off her seat, turning toward the counter with her back to him, too fast for him to see her reaction.

But—he needs time. He needs to figure out what the hell just happened.

That was not the physical reaction of someone accidentally brushing hands with their best friend. Last night, Ellie had patted his shoulder; Naomi—Professor Watanabe—had prodded him to test him; he had even brushed hands with Taka when he'd handed over syrup packets. None of them had stirred up a feeling like *this*. Even if his memories of her are gone, something about her is in his system.

Especially because of how he wanted more.

More. Worse than a sugar craving that he can't fulfill.

He'd wanted to pull her forward, closer to him. Greedily. He wanted her to soothe the confusion in his mind, like she'd be his sunshine after last night's mental rainstorm. He wanted to rest his head on her shoulder, and simply breathe her in. . . .

Cam lays his head back down on the table. What in the world is going on?

"Tired?" Remy asks.

"Totally jet-lagged," he lies.

In just a few moments, Remy is sliding over a freshly made mug of matcha with that gingery scent, but there's nothing that woke him up more than their brief touch.

He drinks it, anyway. "Thanks. This is great. I feel more, well, myself now."

She laughs. "At least I can't mess up a drink. How about we both make the brownies? If you help me, I can't mess up that badly. That's always worked out before."

I'd do anything as long as it's with you. The thought bursts into his mind, and Cam has to do all he can to reel it in before he says it out loud.

What. The. Hell.

He jerks the mug back in his face, and nearly chokes on another gulp of the sharply gingery drink. When he comes up for air, all he can stammer out is, "Um, yeah, definitely need those brownies."

———— ◆ ————

This is excruciating. His mind is popping up with all these thoughts about Remy; noticing the brightness of her smile, the way her hair falls over her cheek and he wants to brush it away, her witty remarks that make him laugh as they make the magical matcha brownies— imbued with a wish enchantment. He needs all the good luck and wishes in the world at this rate.

His head is reeling, trying to figure out what is going on. Because, if he were to draw a Venn diagram, the feelings for Remy as his supposed best friend and *these* feelings have no overlap. But, here he is, holding the bowl of brownie mix, as she spoons it into the tray, trying not to breathe her lotion scented with citrus and peonies; a perfect match for the way she's bright and sweet, because as good as it smells, it sets his brain in a weird Remy-obsessive loop all over again.

"Where's the oven?" Remy asks.

He looks around. The kitchen is still immaculate: the brownie mix bag had turned into a bowl the moment they'd opened it up, and all they needed to add in was water and two eggs. But, to her point, there's only the small dishwasher, the sink, and the refrigerator. A microwave sits on the counter, and he peers closer.

"Look, there's an oven button," he says. "I've heard about this before. Japanese microwaves—even the non-magical ones—have way more settings than our usual American types."

"Neat. Way more efficient," Remy says.

When they have the tray inside, Cam eyes the bowl that Remy's still holding. "I . . . I'm hungry."

She laughs. "I've seen that look before."

"I mean, there's a little left on the sides, I don't mind being the sacrifice to see if it tastes good."

"Oh, you're *so* noble." Still, she offers up the spoon. Except, well, she tilts it to his mouth, and he has no clue if she means for him to eat it straight off of it, or if she's giving it to him, and his heart pounds—

But then she moves it closer to his hands, and his stomach sinks, though he's still on a Remy sugar high, as he takes the spoon from her. Of course she wasn't going to feed him.

But he sure was ready to lick off that batter.

Cam sits back down—he needs something to rest on—and tastes the pale green mix. "Oh, it's good. I need to bring some back as souvenirs."

"That's a great idea." Remy perks up. "I bet my parents would love this, too. Can I try some?"

Cam gives her the spoon, and he can't seem to drag his gaze away from how her eyes crinkle in the corners as she licks it right near where his mouth was.

"Mm, it's delicious."

He can't stop staring at her mouth. *Get your mind straight, Cameron Yuji Yasuda.*

But, with Remy, he can't seem to. Then, she looks at him strangely.

"What?" Did he just say his thoughts out loud?

"You have some batter on your cheek."

He tries to wipe it off, but she only giggles. "More to the left. *Your* left."

Apparently, he can't tell right from left or anything apart, not with the way Remy's looking so closely at him.

"Want me to help?" she asks.

He can't speak, but nods.

Remy steps to his side; when he's sitting like this, she only has to lean a little to reach his cheek, since he's way taller than her. He can't help but notice that their legs are only centimeters apart.

This close, he can see the freckles dusting her nose and cheeks. She has a stray hair that he wants to tuck back into her bangs, and he also wants way, way more. He wants to read her mind, to dig into everything inside, to understand everything that makes Remy, *Remy*. And the way she looks at Cam makes him feel like she *sees* him, right into him, all of who he is.

"Right . . . there." Her touch is as gentle as morning light; the warmth of her fingers fills his soul with a soft heat, making his heartbeat pulse erratically. It's like an elixir he could drink for the rest of his days, but never have enough of.

"Got it," she says, her voice dipping.

He wants to lean into her touch, and she isn't shifting away. If he lifted one hand up right now, he could pull her chin down, and capture her lips in a kiss, and he'd finally get the sugar rush he didn't feel when he tasted the batter.

Rinnng!

Remy jumps away, glancing at the counter, where her phone is flashing with an incoming call. "Oh. Right. Ellie's probably wondering if we're awake."

She washes her hands quickly before going to pick up her phone, and Cam's mind is left reeling. He and Remy—they're like an experiment that he doesn't understand the hypothesis or the conclusion of. But what he knows is this: the way he reacts to Remy is nothing like a relationship with a best friend. He wants to label this as intellectual curiosity, but he can't lie to himself. It's . . . it's something more.

That soulmate elixir wiped out his memories, but he wants to get them back. If he only has until January 1, he needs to figure out what this is. Because there's something about her that's more addicting than sugar, and he needs answers . . . before he forgets her forever.

Remy

Remy hangs up the call. "Ellie said Jack's still catching up on his work, but she and Taka were wondering if we're free to grab lunch."

Cam casts a longing look at the tray of brownies that he's just set on the table. "I mean, lunch sounds good, but . . ."

"Let's eat the brownies first. I'm hungry." She's not. The ginger matcha is still sloshing around in her stomach after *that* way Cam had looked at her moments before.

Cam starts cutting the brownies into perfect, oh-so-Cam exact squares. Even with a ruler, he couldn't cut them more perfectly.

"Want to take the first bite?" he offers, gesturing at the tray.

"You think I managed to poison them again? You measured the water, I cracked the eggs. There's no way I can mess up two eggs—I think."

He laughs, his eyes shining in that way she loves so much. A frazzled knot inside her heart eases. After last night, she was wondering if he'd ever look at her like that again.

Her heart pounds. *Her* Cam is still in there, somewhere. She just has to find him.

Cam lifts one of the perfect squares onto a paper napkin and slides it over.

"A potion for your thoughts?" he asks.

For now, it still has to be a secret, a secret she'll do anything to make come true this last week they have together.

"Just thinking of my wish," she says, and then she takes a bite. Creamy matcha sparkles in her mouth, breathing life into her like Saturday-morning walks through the farmer's market with Cam, their sides almost touching. The sweetness reminds her of all the cupcakes from their favorite magical bakery that they devoured as kids, the hint of enchanted courage giving her hope to believe that they'll always be together, always be best friends to the very last of their days.

Then, she knows exactly what she wants to wish for.

Cam Yasuda, she breathes out, her words a silent declaration from every part of her heart, *in this next week, I want you to love me, as I am now. As you are now. Even if you don't remember our past, maybe by making you fall in love with me, you'll remember something. Remember us.*

She wants to open the window and yell this out into the Tokyo skyline. Tell the whole world. But Cam, who's sitting across from her, is quiet and oblivious in his own sugar-induced bubble, and she has to do this right. Get the old Cam's memories back one at a time, and also make the new Cam fall in love with her, as she is.

It's a ridiculous plan. His memories are wiped; she may never find the Cam she loves and remembers. But she can't sit around and watch him drift away from her.

After all, maybe love doesn't need labels, but she'd always wanted to believe that Cam had feelings for her, just a little bit. And if what she feels for Cam isn't love, then she has no idea what love is.

Remember us, Cam. She wants to tattoo those words onto her heart so that it pulsates with every beat. *Fall in love with me, Cam.*

"How do you like the brownies?" Cam asks, breaking their silence. "Did you make your wish?"

"They're perfect. As is my wish," Remy says, with a wink.

He smiles back, and in that moment, she believes that perfection can really happen. That, through this week, Cam will truly fall in love with her, and his heart will be hers.

Remy

"According to the directions," Remy says, checking the crumpled paper one more time, "Naomi lives . . . here?"

She and Cam stare between the messy ink lines and the bridge that they're standing on. It arcs over a small stream with thick trees lining each side. In the middle of winter, shadows swathe the branches, but in the spring, this place probably blooms with cherry blossoms. Remy can almost imagine the petals flowing through the air, light as tiny, little pink clouds.

Sure, there are houses on either side of the stream, but . . . there's *nothing* on the bridge. Yet the note clearly says, "*Walk onto the bridge, stop in the middle. My place is on the right.*"

Remy rubs her eyes; she's tired. After she and Cam had lunch with Taka and Ellie, they checked out a movie theater in Roppongi with Jack after he'd finished studying for an upcoming exam, and then tried out an okonomiyaki restaurant—traditional Japanese savory pancakes—for dinner. It's been a whirlwind of a day, but they still have to visit Naomi. The chance of a solution glimmers like a streetlight in the distance: somewhat close, but too far away to see the future clearly.

"What about that?" Cam leans over her shoulder, pointing to the bottom of the note. It's hard to read with his proximity; Remy can barely breathe. What she does manage to inhale is tinged with his slight jasmine tea scent—that shampoo he uses, with a sugariness that matches all the sweets he devours. It's so very *Cam*, and she wishes she could spray that scent all over her blankets to wrap herself up in.

Remy squints. "*Knock on the railing and say, 'Naomi is going to be the top magical alchemist in the world.'*"

They glance at each other skeptically. A cat wandering past also shoots them a curious glance, its tail flicking like a question mark.

Knock, knock. The wood is smooth under Remy's knuckles.

"*Naomi is going to be the top magical alchemist in the world*," they say.

"You made it!" The whisper comes out of nowhere.

Cam and Remy stumble toward each other with surprise, and for a second, she clings to him. Then, blushing, she just as quickly takes a step away. *Please don't notice, please don't notice.*

"Are you okay?" he asks gently. His hand hovers out like he wants to hold her up.

"Just . . . surprised." And embarrassed beyond mentioning, but nothing new there. Then she stares over his shoulder, eager for a distraction. "Look! A . . . a . . . *house*?"

Where there was absolutely nothing but thin air, a glass creation swirls into place on top of tall glass stilts. The railing—which had been totally solid a second ago, has vanished and been replaced with a set of mossy stairs leading to the front door, where Naomi grins out at them, like it's not an incredible load of magic to be standing in a house that *surely* hadn't been there a second ago.

"Sorry about that silly line. My house chooses it for me, and it has a mind of its own." Naomi waves them up the steps. "Come on in."

Cam

Cam should probably be looking at Naomi's place, like Remy is, but that sudden sensation of Remy bumping into him flickers a memory. Like a vial bubbling over, it's seeping all throughout Cam's consciousness.

Didn't Remy always get scared during movies? Did they ever go on movie dates?

"Earth to Cam," Remy is saying, tugging at his sleeve. In a daze, he stumbles after her, and into Naomi's house.

"What *is* this place?" Remy asks, as they take off their shoes. "I've never seen anything like this before."

"On our way up to my lab, I'll give you a tour," Naomi says. "No one gets it when I explain this place to them. You have to see it to believe it."

A few seconds later, Cam and Remy are following Naomi around the small, one-bedroom house, complete with a balcony and tiny roof-top garden, with enough space to hang laundry. The walls are made of glass—"Like you saw, no one can see it, so no one can see inside," Naomi explains—and the bigger houses lining the street don't even match up to how magical this place is.

They make their way upstairs, and Naomi opens the door to reveal a rooftop garden, with a wide grassy area perfect for lying out to watch the stars; she closes it again. "Uchi, onegai!"

"What's wrong?" Remy asks. "That looked *gorgeous*."

"I need . . ." Naomi turns the knob again. "My laboratory."

Cam blinks as the door swings out. Where there had just been an open area, all of that has vanished and been replaced with small bookshelves, and a few display cases tidily filled with glass jars and vials. Fluffy beanbags are scattered around the deck, and he can just imagine sinking into one of them as he thinks over formulas for an elixir. There's a huge glass box with refined magical dust sitting on a shelf, one of the biggest Cam has ever seen. Best of all, Naomi's laboratory opens up to the sparkling night sky.

"Whoa," he says.

Naomi grins as she strolls out onto the rooftop. "When I have guests, this is usually a garden; that's why the house-magic had that set up. But, normally, it's this. There's more here that I don't keep in my lab at school, especially my top-secret projects."

Remy shakes her head in awe as she and Cam settle into the beanbags.

"But . . . *how*?" Remy asks. "I've never seen magic like this."

"You've been to a magical cottage before, right?"

"No," Cam says. "Or, at least none that I can remember." He glances over at Remy, who's laughing to herself. "Have I?"

"We haven't been, but Ellie showed us pictures a few summers back," Remy says. "Well, you know how magical cottages are supposed to help stranded travelers, so Jack and Ellie stayed there for the night—"

"Never mind. Forget I asked. I don't want to know about my brother's love life." Cam turns to Naomi, who's been watching this exchange with amusement equaling the laughter leaking out of Remy. "Save me."

"Wait, I haven't heard about this from Ellie, either," Naomi protests.

Remy gives her a big smile. "Then we have a lot to catch up on."

Naomi raises an eyebrow. "Deal." Cam tries hard as hell to push down that flash of jealousy. Okay, he was jealous of Taka inching near Remy before. Now he's jealous of Naomi and Remy giggling their heads off at Cam's expense. Like, is there *anyone* he's not jealous of? He's not a best friend; he's a watchdog.

Remy takes pity on Cam's scowl, and waves at Naomi to continue with her explanation.

"Like Remy was saying, the way magical cottages work is that they show up for a magic-aware traveler in need. I was . . . I was having a tough day." Naomi glances away, out at the lights strung between the trees, her eyes distant like she's back in a moment years and years ago. "I stumbled on this house, and despite being in the middle of Tokyo—or maybe *because* of its location—no one had lived here in the longest time. Thanks to its proximity to so many people, raw magic had collected in every corner, loads of it. It's the most powerful magical cottage I've ever seen. It can create almost any room I want with a whispered wish. The only thing this house *doesn't* let me do is study it. It shoots me straight out the front door and onto the bridge if I try. Here, look at this." Naomi grabs a pair of rose-tinted glasses and slides them on, glancing between the two of them. "Hm. What I thought."

She hands them to Cam. "Try these."

"Wow, these are the Leon Rosé line," Cam says in awe, running his fingers along the thin, slightly pink-hued wire frames. The lenses are almost clear, with the barest hint of rose. "I've seen them in the *Magic Times*. Didn't the patent go for a million?"

"A pair's now a hundred thousand yen—so about a thousand dollars. I got one pair through my research grant," Naomi explains, grabbing another pair for Remy. "And I have an anonymous benefactor who always sends the latest, so I have an extra set. Super rare for academia, really. Go on, try them."

"No glasses can be worth a million." Remy slides them on, her eyes widening. "Never mind. I stand corrected."

Cam tries on his pair. "Damn. Naomi, can I keep these?"

Raw magical dust shimmers through the shadows, illuminating the world with light. With these glasses, it looks like the sky is gently snowing. Tokyo is full of wonder and joy, like Cam had always expected.

Remy laughs at something Naomi is saying, and Cam turns to

look. As he expected, her joy is creating the sparks of raw magical dust, shimmering out from her body and joining the snow at their feet. *Snow?* When he looks at Naomi's house, the walls, the bookshelves, everything is no longer glass. They're solid white from all of the magical dust. "Whoa."

"Yeah," Naomi says, following his gaze. "Compare that with standard rose-tinted glasses."

Remy digs out her pair from her bag and tosses them over to Cam. He slides them on easily, like he's done this a thousand times before. It's like he's putting on a sweater that used to be an old favorite, but he'd stuffed it in the corner of his closet and forgotten about it for a while. With Remy's old glasses, everything is fuzzy at the edges.

"Those new glasses are the value of MagiTech." He switches back to the new lenses, and as a reflex, he rubs at his eyes. But these glasses don't make his eyes ache the way Remy's hand-me-down glasses do. "I've read so much about it . . . but this is my first time experiencing this in person. This is the future of magic, isn't it?"

Naomi nods. "Absolutely. Technology is one of the best ways for us to get magic-enhanced tools into the hands of the general public, and it'll be huge when this is cleared through the magical government."

"MagiTech is neat and all, but . . ." Remy leans in. "Were you able to figure out an antidote?"

There it is. The question that's been on Cam's mind all day.

"Cam's the one who helped me figure this out. I'm not going to do anything." Naomi pulls a small tablet onto her lap. "*You* are." She types a few words onto the screen. A few seconds later, a printer spits out two tiny pages.

Cam blinks as she hands one each to him and Remy. It's not paper. It's a Polaroid.

Where the picture should be, there's a mirror, instead.

"This is a charm," Naomi says. "Using MagiTech that I've gotten— like those glasses, and a few other tools—I've been spending this whole day perfecting it."

"What do you want Cam to do?" Remy asks.

Naomi smirks. "It's not about what *I* want, honey. It's all about you. I have a theory based on memory collection, after seeing Cam spark a memory last night. There's a whole deep world of magical ideology based on this, but the brief of it is that memories are like little film reels in the dark of our minds. By focusing on those thoughts, it's giving them attention. Think of them as solar-powered, if you will. You'll need to recreate them, to a certain extent, and shine light on it so that it can recharge, and then that recollection will trigger the lost memory."

"But, how?"

"That's where my theory kicks in," she says. "Senses are, well, sensual. Meaningful in memory creation and idealization, when we live through the memories again. I still remember the sour taste of the plums that I ate in my auntie's orchard; whenever I have plums, it brings me back to that day, and my relatives talking over me." She shudders. "Thankfully, that's where the memory ends. But those are the kind of memories that can be triggered. Within these memories, I'm hoping there will be some sort of answer of where that soulmate potion—because it should've worked, from all the analysis I've done—went wrong."

Naomi nods past sets of computer screens to the far end of the rooftop garden, where there's a single burner on, with a vial bubbling on top.

"That's the antidote?" Remy pushes off the beanbag in an instant, Cam following in her wake.

Flames are spouting blue from the Bunsen burner, turning into an almost see-through rose gold at the bottom of a glass vial. It's bubbling with a clear liquid that almost looks like boiling water.

"From the small amount of that soulmate elixir that I extracted from your blood, I've been able to analyze it down to the molecular level; it's fascinating. So I took its essential building blocks: the trigger for love, synthesized dopamine, norepinephrine, and oxytocin. I added a *ton* of ultra-concentrated magical dust to amplify the effect, and added in five pinches of moon powder for the five days you have left."

"Wow," Cam says quietly. "It sounds ready."

She shakes her head. "It still needs that key switch. I've created a testing vial"—she waves her hand at the next burner over, where a wide glass filled with a soft blue liquid sits, unheated—"but it should be staying clear to show that it's negated when I mix samples of the two potions together. I just don't know what's missing."

Cam wracks his brain for an answer. "I wonder what it is . . ."

"Memories," Remy says.

"If you can collect enough memories, I can infuse them into that potion to reverse the loss," Naomi says.

A solution. An antidote. Cam breathes out. A way to figure out how he feels about Remy, and what all these instantaneous, kick-in-the-gut sensations are when he's near her.

The idea settles in the air, like an invisible string tying them together.

"There's a cost, though," Naomi says. "I tried my best, but just like that potion had side effects, there's no guarantee this one will work, either."

Remy and Cam glance at each other.

He pauses, an answer on the tip of his tongue. A potion is what got him into this, but hopefully it'll be what fixes things, too. Remy turns her head, watching in an owlish way, and he's got a feeling that she's done that countless times before: patiently waited for him to speak; totally unlike his dad, who expects an immediate response in one second flat, or he thinks it's nothing worth saying.

"I need to try," Cam says flatly. "MIT will revoke their early acceptance—well, if I got in. I won't be able to get in anywhere else without a magical alchemy learner's license, either." His fingers drift to his back pocket; it's unusually light without the comfort of that rose-gold card. Only five days until it's gone forever.

Remy's lashes lower and she frowns. *Shoot.* He's insulted his best friend of seventeen years—even if he doesn't remember her.

He stammers and quickly adds, "And our friendship, too. There are all these blurred-out spots in my memories. Combined with what everyone's saying, with the pictures of us in my phone, clearly, they're you. But it's one thing to know and one thing to *feel*."

Then, to his surprise, she meets his eyes, burning brighter than the stars above, burning brighter than the magic dust flowing from her. Faintly, he notices letters flash on the lens of the glasses: *Determination; a side effect of hope. Feeling that achieving one's goals is possible.*

Even his glasses believe in them.

"And I need my best friend back," Remy responds.

Cam turns to Naomi. "I'm fine with whatever risks this has. I'm ready."

Cam

"Load up the magical film and snap a pic." Naomi holds out a small, black, old-fashioned camera. She demonstrates how to flip open the back and place in the film. "Think of it like a charmed selfie."

"That's it?" Remy asks.

"You have to trigger memories," Naomi says. "So, remember, the fundamentals of memory recreation: trigger any of the five senses to evoke the strongest memories. Taste, sight, smell, hearing, touch. Just like that Christmas fried chicken sparked a recollection through taste. Remy, your goal is to find things in Tokyo that align to strong memories for you and Cam—you have to have been in these recollections together for this to work."

"And take a picture when—or *if*—he remembers something?" Remy asks, a tinge of doubt in her voice. "What if he doesn't?"

"Drink this," Naomi says, grabbing the glass bottle that's simmering on a Bunsen burner on one of the shelves and gesturing toward Cam. "It'll help unstick the memories in your mind. It's got nearly two hundred grams of refined magic dust."

He takes a sip; it's bubbly like sparkling water, with the hint of a strangely familiar smell . . . his mind flashes with recognition: the papery scent of a new puzzle, fresh out of the box.

"A puzzle?" Cam frowns.

"We do puzzles all the time, back home," Remy says. "Is it giving you a memory?"

"Nothing specific." Cam shakes his head. "Just helping me remember things we do together, I guess."

"I could use some memory help to pass tests," Remy mumbles.

Naomi laughs. "You don't want those things you learned in high school to be at the forefront of your memory for all time."

"Fair enough, I'd hate to repeat high school forever." Remy shudders.

"One more thing." Naomi takes a big breath, nodding at Cam. "Think of this moment. Think of everything you have in front of you. The next hundred-and-twentyish hours. No classes. No school. No parents. You have a city at your fingertips, and you are going to *live* like that."

Remy clears her throat. "We've made tons of plans. Places to eat, things to see—"

"Definitely keep those plans," Naomi says. "But think of what might remind Cam of the past while you're building a new present. That spirit, that feeling of ichigo, ichie."

"Ichigo . . . ? Like, strawberries?" Hopefully the potion he's sipping will help his Japanese.

Remy scrunches up her forehead, translating it quickly. "More like 'a once-in-a-lifetime chance.'"

"Every moment is one chance in a lifetime." Naomi sighs. "Honestly? We've all got the world at our fingertips, and no one seems to do anything about that. They just keep living like tomorrow's guaranteed." She stares at them, eyes blazing. "The day I found this house, I realized nothing can be taken for granted. With this week, you'll understand that, too. Maybe this week is about you two finally living like you're alive . . . because you're *really* going to lose out if you don't start living your life."

Cam downs the rest of the potion. It tickles all the way to his stomach; he's never ingested this much refined dust all at once. With the glasses, he can tell his body gives off a slight shimmery glow.

"Ah." Naomi gets her pair back from Remy, and nods. "It worked.

One part of the theory is complete. Now, take a picture of you two, together."

Remy and Cam shoot each other confused glances, but Cam awkwardly steps closer to her. The scent of peonies swirls up, and his throat goes oddly dry.

"A picture will get his memory back?" Remy asks.

Naomi groans. "Is that your 'picture-ready' pose? You think that's enough?" She shakes her head. "Follow me, both of you."

She guides them to the side of the house that overlooks the bridge. "Look at this."

Remy leans against the railing. "Ooh, this spot is beautiful."

Cam joins her. The stream trickles from underneath the house and down through the neighborhood. Overhead, the full moon sweeps its light over the world, taking away the darkest shadows of the night. Even with the houses behind the trees, it's like they've snuck into a secret part of Tokyo.

Without saying a word, they walk the perimeter of the rooftop, until they make it to the area above the bridge.

"Not too loud," Naomi warns, who is trailing behind them with the camera in hand. "If we pass the railing, the house's magic no longer dampens our sound."

"So someone would find this place?" Cam asks.

She laughs. "No, they'd think the bridge is haunted, probably."

"Oooh," Remy says, low and spooky. Then she turns to Cam. "Do I sound like a ghost?"

"You sound like you've just caught Mochi eating your shoes," Cam says, and Remy lets out a peal of laughter, leaning on the railing for support.

A salaryman walking below them jolts; he's heard Remy's voice. Cam claps a hand over Remy's mouth, but then she prods Cam's sides and, dammit, she knows *exactly* where he's ticklish. He lets out a snort; the man spins around in confusion, trying to locate the sound. Remy tries to muffle Cam, but they both start laughing harder, so much that they have to sit down, with stitches in their sides.

Naomi holds up the camera and there's a loud *click!* It flashes bright. A second later, the film develops, spitting out the side: Cam and Remy are grinning like they've never been happier, their cheeks red and eyes tearing up from laughter. Something snaps into place in his mind. This is how they used to be. A memory comes crashing over his senses; a key switch.

Cam is eleven years old. The most recent potion that Cam made was a success: a joy-filling potion. But he's stuck on his next experiment, a stained-glass potion that turns an ordinary pane into a whirl of beautiful colors, though just for a minute. He's stuck, that is, until Remy bakes him the most misshapen, partially burnt oatmeal raisin cookies ever.

They're perfect because they're from her, even as much as she apologizes.

They're perfect because she made them even though her older sister always teases her for not being able to set foot in the kitchen without causing a mess.

They're perfect because she knows how much he loves sugar, and how it helps him think.

He doesn't tell Remy, but it's the first time anyone has baked anything for him since his mother passed away. And, when he polishes off the batch, he even figures out his missing ingredient—thunderstruck glass shards—and the potion is a success.

Suddenly, they're in high school—*college apps suck. That's a universal truth anywhere, but especially at Palo Alto High, with everyone gunning for APs and extracurriculars to one-up one another in college apps. So, when Cam sends in his early decision packet to MIT and Remy turns in her submission to TMU, they go to Minami's house to celebrate. But they sneak up to an empty room, playing Candy Crush on the couch and chewing on (slightly burnt) cranberry scones that Remy has made for him.*

Memories spark, like lightning-bright camera flashes, and then they're on the flight over to Tokyo—*Cam's eyelids are drooping; the rumble of the plane's engine is making him tired even though he refuses to pause his annual* Fullmetal Alchemist *anime rewatching marathon. . . . Then Remy nods off, her head shifting and leaning onto his shoulder, and his heart pounds in his chest. He doesn't feel so sleepy anymore.*

Remy. His best friend. The memories are sharp and poignant, filled with contentment that Cam wants to chase. To hold. To have Remy as all his own, as more than a best friend.

"Keep taking photos, one for each of the senses when you trigger the memory," Naomi says. "Once you take the picture, drop it in here."

She gives Remy a vial no bigger than the length of her hand.

"It's solid ice," Remy says, giving it a swirl. "How can putting a picture into *ice* work out?"

"Try it," Naomi says.

"Okay, but if this doesn't work, I get to live here," Remy warns. "Your house is pretty amazing."

Naomi raises an eyebrow. "Thankfully, I tried this part earlier, so *deal.*"

Remy drops in the rolled-up photo. Instead of clinking against the ice, the second it touches the surface, it burns into a flame. And, when Cam and Remy look closer, the top layer is a little melted; an opal-hued liquid swirls at the top, sparking with a rainbow of colors.

"It melts!" Remy breathes out in awe.

Naomi grins at the vial proudly. "As soon as it turns into pure liquid, drink it, Cam. If this works well—at least like the simulations I ran—this will help trigger all of your memories again."

Cam eyeballs the vial. "That melted less than a millimeter, and there are about five centimeters in there."

"That's why it has to be a meaningful memory. Key-switch-level meaningful," Naomi says. "Remy, that's up to you, since you're the only one between the two of you that can recall the times you had together."

Remy nods, lost in thought, as Cam takes the camera, the set of magical film, and the vial. Thank goodness it's winter, and his thick jacket has plenty of pockets. Everything fits into his chest pocket, even the camera. Instinctively, he wants to keep it close. When he looks up, Remy's eyes linger on his.

He can almost hear what she'd say. *Five days. Are you ready, Cam?*

Then she grins, pulling out her phone. "Ooh, I've got an idea."

Naomi and Cam watch Remy in bemusement; she's on the warpath as she types away on her phone. It doesn't take a best friend to know this.

"A few adjustments to our schedule," Remy says.

Seconds later, his phone dings as an explosion of emojis fills his inbox.

WEDNESDAY, DECEMBER 27

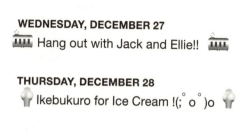 Hang out with Jack and Ellie!!

THURSDAY, DECEMBER 28

Ikebukuro for Ice Cream !(˚ o ˚)o

FRIDAY, DECEMBER 29

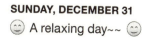 Arcade Game Day (˚ ⌣ ˚)

SATURDAY, DECEMBER 30

Souvenir & thrift shopping in Shimokitazawa

SUNDAY, DECEMBER 31

A relaxing day~~

MONDAY, JANUARY 1

 The flight back, ugh!

Remy's voice catches. "I sure hope this works. . . . If not . . ."

"It'll work," Cam says firmly. He holds out his arm to Remy. "Want to remake memories?"

It sounds like a cheesy pickup line, and he wishes he wasn't just the biggest alchemy dork in the universe, trying to talk to the prettiest girl he's ever met.

But her small hand—cold as ever, even under the toasty heat lamps—slides around his elbow. She says, softly, "We've got a city with our name on it. Ichigo, ichie."

A once-in-a-lifetime chance.

The camera is heavy in his chest pocket. He and Remy race down the stairs, out the front door, and onto the bridge. Naomi's house disappears into thin air, but a trace of her voice floats from the rooftop, "Have fun!"

Cam and Remy start walking along the sidewalk, and his arm is extra warm with her touch, like it's something he's been missing ever since that fateful night at Beni's Apothecary.

Maybe that's true: without her close by, there *is* something missing. When he sees her, he tries to deny the connection they have, but he senses it deep in his bones. Cam looks up at the night sky, searching for a shooting star. A vague recollection stirs in his memory. Isn't that something Remy does? Searching for good luck and magical chances?

Not that a shooting star could be visible in Tokyo, with all the lamps along this street—

A faint glow streaks across the sky, weak against the bright city lights, but there. It's a sign. Cam silently breathes out his wish into the world. *I don't know enough about what the old me was like. But maybe we're not supposed to be constantly stuck in our old selves, and this is a chance to embrace something new. I want to know who the new Cam should become, and understand this way I'm feeling about my best friend.*

He looks down at his arm again, snug with hers.

I want to follow wherever Remy takes me.

Four Days Until New Year's Eve

WEDNESDAY, DECEMBER 27

Cam

Cam hangs out on the couch, blankets piled on him like a warm version of the rumored snow that the weather forecasters keep saying will happen this week. The morning darkness wraps around him; he woke up at 4 A.M., unable to get back to sleep.

The mini Christmas tree lights flicker merrily. Even though Christmas was two days ago, most people in Japan seem to keep their lights up to celebrate the new year. It's kind of nice, and he likes the way Remy gets a dreamy-eyed look whenever she sees a bunch of them.

A noise makes him look up; a quick glance at the wall clock shows it's barely 5 A.M. He sits up; a figure is slipping out of the second bedroom to the front door.

"Remy?" he whispers. Uncle David and Aunt Kiyoko are still asleep.

She spins around. "Shoot. I didn't mean to wake you." She gestures at her peacoat. "I was just going out for a bit since the jet lag is still waking me early. . . ."

"Can I go with you?" he asks. "Maybe we can recover another memory."

Her eyes sparkle. "Get dressed in five? We can get an early breakfast with more sugar than the brownies."

"I'll be ready in two."

Yesterday, they were only able to recreate tiny memories: sipping on 3D latte art from a café called HATCOFFEE reminded Cam of the spring break they spent experimenting with latte art with Remy at her parents' tea shop; seeing a Shiba Inu dance around their owner reminded him of playing fetch with Mochi, Remy's dog. Little yet precious moments of their friendship, but nothing that's melted more than a millimeter. He could use whatever help he can get from Remy.

———◆———

Remy leads him through predawn Tokyo, faint streetlights glowing through the semi-dark. They follow directions on her phone through alleyways, over bridges, and up a small hill (a mountain, in Cam's sleepy daze), and then finally to a quaint coffee shop nestled among the trees at the top. A little wood sign lists that it has just opened at 4:30 A.M.

The waiter bows the moment they walk inside, where it's toasty warm, and Cam already begins shedding his sweatshirt.

"You were going to eat breakfast by yourself?" he asks. This early, all the other tables are empty except for the nice table by the window, overlooking the city. A guy sits there by himself, looking out at the view.

"Damn, if he didn't grab that, we'd have the best seats in the house," Cam says.

The waiter clears his throat. "My apologies, but all our tables, despite being empty at this early hour, have been reserved for this morning, and I'm afraid I don't recognize—"

"We're with him," Remy says, gesturing at the person already sitting.

The waiter coughs. "A guest of one of the Old Families. My apologies; please, follow me."

"Wait, Old Families?" Cam echoes, following Remy. "Who?"

"I heard something about certain families being more prominent in the area. I guess it works well for reservations." She grins, stepping forward. "I was going to bring back some of their pancakes for you and your family. But, actually, Taka said he was awake, and we were going to chat about TMU."

Taka turns around in his chair, waving at Remy. Then an eyebrow quirks up as he sees Cam over her shoulder.

Cam curses under his breath. He *invited* himself to be a third wheel.

The moment they sit down, the waiter bustles over with mugs of coffee and menus. Taka rubs his hand through his hair, yawning.

"Late night?" Remy asks. "Or, long morning, already, I guess?"

"A friend is moving overseas to model, so I wanted to spend some time with her."

"Oohh, a girlfriend?" Remy asks, pillowing her hands under her chin.

She's such a romantic, except when it comes to her own life, Cam thinks suddenly. Then, just as quickly, he's filled with a sense of melancholy. How does he know this?

"Nah, she's definitely not my girlfriend," Taka says. "I've sworn off dating. Anyway, hungry for some soufflé pancakes? Best in all of Tokyo."

To Cam's questioning look, he says, "Think of a regular, flat pancake, but five in one. Super popular in Japan. They're like ten centimeters of pure, fluffy joy in an edible form. Plus, this place serves them with a jolt of hidden energy, so you'll feel fueled throughout the day."

"Hmm," Remy says. "Maybe I'll get the chocolate hazelnut and strawberry soufflé ones . . . Or maybe the maple bacon set . . ."

"I can get one of those and we can split," Cam offers.

"You are the *best*." She grins at him, and Cam's certain: Remy is better than any sugar or caffeine he'll ever find. "But wait, there are a few more pages I want to look through . . ."

"Do you live with your family?" Cam asks Taka, to kill time. "They don't mind that you come back so late? Or, well, early?" His dad always got grouchy when Cam slipped into the house after the parties at Minami's, even though if Cam had been home, he'd have been holed up in his room and not seen his dad, anyway. Ah, the joys of an overprotective parent.

Taka laughs. "My parents and I haven't seen each other in about two years, ever since I graduated high school. They always thought I was out of my mind thinking I could get into TMU without them paying my way in."

"Oh," Remy murmurs, setting her menu down. "That's right, your fortune."

Taka explains for Cam's benefit, "Uncle Michi—that's Mr. Yoshino, from the Good Luck Café—read my tea leaves, right when I was going to drop out of school."

"He's your *uncle*?" Remy exclaims. Then she glances around at the other tables, which have been filling up, and adds, "Wait, then can't you get us in with Beni?"

He shakes his head. "I've been cut off from the rest of the family. Because of my uncle's fortune-telling, I went forward with applying to TMU. My parents didn't know that the only thing I promised myself was that if I got in, I'd cut ties cleanly with them. I donated their money to TMU, I gave away everything they gave me, and worked to get myself where I am today. The entire family hasn't heard from me since the last time my parents were threatening to kick me out for being a disgrace and being too much like a New Family."

The way Taka had slipped out to "make a call" right when Remy's fortune was supposed to get read . . . the hat he'd worn low over his eyes . . . It finally connects for Cam.

"Why'd you go back that day, then?" Cam asks.

"Honestly? I was never expecting to find it again," Taka replies. "The Old Families of Tokyo don't want anything to do with me, and I figured the Good Luck Café would be the same, too. I thought the magic that had helped me get kicked out would've kept me out."

"Damn," Cam says. "I'm . . . I'm sorry. Wait, is this that whole Old Family thing the waiter was talking about?"

"Yeah, do you not have that in California?" Taka says. "Here, especially in Tokyo, there's a split between the New Families and the Old Families. The old ones are those who have had magic and wealth traced back to ancestors beyond the Heian Period. Then, there's the

New Families, the ones who stumble onto magic by accident or marry into it; those families are outcasts from the Old Families."

Cam and Remy stare at each other in surprise.

"I mean, you mentioned your family after the interview, but I didn't know it was anything like *that*," Remy says.

"I wouldn't wish this on anyone else," Taka says. "It's a power struggle, with the head of the New Families continually trying to prove themselves, no matter what it takes. And the Old Families grasping at whatever power they can keep, all for themselves, trying to twist life like puppeteers. That's why Uncle Michi and the rest of my family do things like show off their power through the café, or Aunt Beni puts it on display through her apothecary, but they never share the secrets behind it with anyone else."

"That's not fair," Cam says.

"They know. What's fair for them is unfair for everyone else, but they want it that way. That's why I had to leave them. That's why I'm nothing in their eyes, but still rejected from the New Families, too. It's rare to have friends like Naomi—she's, I guess, an outcast on her own, being the prodigy that she is. And Ellie and Jack couldn't care less, probably because they always have each other." There's a strange note to Taka's voice, something that reminds Cam of last year, on his birthday, being home alone but his dad had forgotten their plans to eat dinner together and was wrapped up with work. Cam had pretended it wasn't a big deal. . . . Hadn't Remy showed up later with a lopsided birthday cake, though?

"You're doing really well," Remy says fiercely. "I saw your Instagram profile, and you've got *amazing* jobs on your résumé. Like, model for BEAMS? That's like, a dream come true to even *buy* a shirt from them."

Taka laughs. "I bet I have a shirt from them you can have; brands give me free stuff all the time. I usually donate most of what I get, anyway."

Cam can't even be mad at this guy for the way Remy squeals in delight. Out of anyone, Taka seriously needs some Remy-inspired light in his life. But he's almost ready to start working at BEAMS—as a cashier, anything, to get Remy a shirt, too.

Remy tilts her head to the side. "But . . . if you're comfortable, tell us more."

"More . . ." Taka crinkles his forehead. "There's not much to say. My parents always told me I was dumb. They'd say it only made sense that my grades sucked, because I couldn't be good at anything."

Remy splutters. "Didn't the other interviewer—that scary-looking guy with the glasses—say you're at the top of your class?"

"I am. But my parents have impossible standards." Taka grits his teeth. "They wanted to keep me small."

"That's the worst," Cam says. His dad is no better.

"I'm sorry," Remy adds softly.

Taka clears his throat, looking around. "I need to run to the restroom."

He heads toward the back, but he slips outside to stand there, hands shoved in his pockets in the freezing cold, head bowed. Cam wishes he could stand there, too, and say, *I understand.*

Remy's lips narrow with fury. "I can't believe Taka's parents are like that. Their own kid. He did the right thing, even if his parents still try to gaslight him."

Cam looks at the menu, but his thoughts are too tangled to concentrate on anything else. "Taka's strong. The last thing you want is to live your life with narcissist parents hovering over your shoulders, always blaming you and playing mind games."

Something thick and heavy is stuck in his brain, like a scab he doesn't want to peel off. Those words yank at its edges, exposing the still-raw wound underneath.

Blaming you.

His breath stutters as a memory sweeps over him.

Cam

SIXTEEN YEARS OLD

Cam's father is red-faced as he pounds his fist on the kitchen counter to emphasize each word, as if all of Palo Alto can't hear this argument already. Jack's yelling back at him from the doorway, standing with his suitcase, his voice nearly hoarse.

"I'm *leaving*," Jack shouts. "You can either accept my choice to move to Japan, or push me out of your life, but I'm still leaving."

"You're deserting your family *and* the shop after all I've done for you—"

"After how you've treated Ellie?" Jack thunders. "Do you think I'll stand for that? For the ways you bad-mouth her when you think she's out of hearing? I thought you had changed, but there's no end to this, is there?"

"She's not good enough for my son—"

"She's too good for me," Jack hisses. Then, he looks up and down at his dad, as if seeing him for the first time. "Especially for someone with a father like you. So maybe if she's not good enough for your son, then . . . then, I'm not your son anymore."

From where he stands in the middle, Cam can see how Jack's fingers are white as he grips the suitcase handle, shoving the door open as he leaves. Yet Cam also knows that after this, his father will curse and cry and whisper his wife's name, and stare up at the ceiling and ask where everything went wrong.

But it doesn't take long, after all.

Before the door even closes—quietly, because perfect, brilliant Jack doesn't slam doors—Mr. Yasuda turns to Cam, his eyes rimmed in red. "Son, you won't do that to me, right?"

Guilt seeps into Cam's bones, twisting his words and thoughts. Is he being played like a puppet? Or is this what it's like to be the star—and only—child?

His dad stares, waiting for his answer. Will Cam be the son he has always wanted to be in his father's eyes?

"I'm not looking to fall in love anytime soon, if that's what you're worried about," Cam says. "I've got college to focus on, right?"

Mr. Yasuda nods sharply. "That's my boy."

His smug satisfaction as he heads off to the shop weighs Cam down with guilt. How could he say that, when he cares so much for—

Cam

PRESENT DAY

The memory *pops!* like a bubble, disappearing without a trace. Cam grasps for the rest of that recollection, a million questions looping in his head with no definitive answers. Was that what he thought—that college is more important than love? Yet, if that was the case, why would he take a soulmate potion? How is that cursed potion pulling memories *without* Remy from him? Did this have to do with her? Is it because his dad never wanted Cam to be happy around her? The thought slithers into his brain, an insidious poison.

What if she was the one thing that made him happy? His true soulmate?

"What would you like to order?" The waiter steps up to the table.

But Cam can't speak. He searches for answers, only to find more questions. His heartbeat swells like crashes of thunder, taking over his ears. *Breathe. Breathe.*

Then he realizes it's Remy speaking. "Breathe, Cam. Breathe in for four, out for six. That's the pattern that you use to relax. Breathe."

In for four, out for six. He breathes in and out, following the sound of Remy's voice, soft and comforting, as she helps bring him back to earth, floating down from the storm clouds.

His sneakers press against tiles that are squeaky. Curls of a breeze from the front door opening brush against his neck, sharp and refreshing. He touches the outside of his mug, coffee scalding his finger into realness through the ceramic. The waiter has shuffled away, wiping tables by the front of the store. Finally, he looks at Remy, who is quietly watching him, and his world settles into place. She's the most grounding part of this all, having her next to him. "Thank you."

He digs in his pocket and pulls out the camera and clicks. A few minutes later, a picture of him sitting at the table, the beautiful view of the river to his right, and the edge of Remy's arm to the left, appears on the film. When he rolls it up and inserts it into the vial—with Remy holding it for him—nearly a full centimeter melts. So. It meant something, more than any of the other memories. . . .

"Wow," Remy whispers. "Just about three centimeters left. That was some memory."

"The only thing that made it better was you," he says. "Thanks for helping me."

Her eyes are soft. "I'm your best friend, Cam. Even if you don't remember me, I'm here for you."

There aren't enough thank-yous that could cover the way her words are like the first rays of the morning sun, wrapping around him and filling him with light.

"I remember enough to know that I need you as my best friend," he says, cracking a rueful smile. "But wow, that memory makes my head hurt."

"I know just the fix." She beams back. "I ordered soufflé pancakes for all of us. I hope that was okay. I got the maple bacon for you."

"The more sugar, the better," he says. "That's my new motto."

He's grateful for Remy, in more ways than words can explain. She gives him a smile sweeter than the pancakes sizzling in the kitchen, and he's pretty sure his real motto is, *Remy is sweeter than sugar.*

Remy

It's a little before seven o'clock when the sun begins inching over the skyline. The soufflé pancakes—the fluffy delights that felt like they were eating slices of the moon—are long gone. Remy, Cam, and Taka are sipping on coffee as they chat about Cam and Remy's plans to take a day trip with Jack and Ellie to Kichijoji, a city on the outskirts of Tokyo, later in the day.

Something about this is nostalgic. Remy searches her memory; she could've sworn that she would whip up a hojicha latte, and she and Cam would go up to his rooftop to spend a quiet Saturday morning . . . Or maybe that only happened once or twice? She rubs her forehead, trying to remember.

Then, the whole café—which has completely filled up—goes quiet. The sun rises along the Tokyo skyline like their soufflé pancakes, melting golden butter on the tips of towers, lines of glistening maple syrup pooling over train tracks, and coating shimmers of powdered sugar light on the rooftops of houses. It is all at once too bright to look at, yet a sight that Remy can't seem to pull her eyes away from.

Remy wishes she could bottle this up. She could pop the cork every once in a while and let the memory float out, and remember how it felt to have Cam and Taka right next to her, just like this.

But she knows the reality is that this will never happen again. Every sunrise and sunset is a once-in-forever thing, and when it's gone, it's gone forever. Ichigo, ichie.

As they head out of the café, the sun paints the morning a golden yellow. *Every day has a sunrise like this; it's up to me whether I see it or not.*

Even though the pressure from the potion-gone-wrong is still pressing down on her, somehow, it's easier to breathe.

Cam

Cam groans as they step outside and a blast of cold air nips at their faces. "I forgot my heavy jacket back at the apartment. And I'd totally promised to bring the hand warmers, too." They'd split up duties: Ellie had planned out the day, Remy had picked out their lunch spot, Jack had figured out the train schedule, and Cam was in charge of hand warmers.

"Brr. It *is* cold." Remy rubs her arms. Her pastel-blue peacoat isn't enough for the cold Tokyo winter; it's gotten significantly colder day by day. Cam has the vaguest stirrings of a memory of trying to buy her a thicker jacket, but she'd been too worried about him spending money on her, even though he'd wanted to. He should've just bought the damn jacket.

Cam moves to unloop his scarf around his neck, but he's too slow.

Taka holds out a soft, silken scarf in soft grays like the cloudy sky above; it's from some sort of famous brand that Cam's seen his richest classmates back in Palo Alto wear. "I got this from my gig yesterday, but the color isn't my thing. Want it?"

Her eyes widen. "No way, I'm totally going to spill something on it."

"It's okay," Taka says, gently stepping close to wind it around her neck. "I have so many of these."

She smiles up at Taka as her shoulders ease. "Thanks. I feel warmer already."

Cam's fists curl, but he can't say anything. Damn this guy and his classiness.

Remy's phone buzzes; it's Ellie, sounding as cheery as ever—she's likely already guzzled up her daily matcha latte and checked off half of her to-do list. "Morning! Ready to meet up?"

"Um, mind if we meet a little later?" Remy asks, glancing over at Cam. "We need to pick up some stuff."

Ellie laughs. "Sounds good. There are trains nearly every fifteen minutes, so no rush. Just text me when you're heading to Shinagawa."

Cam's stomach sinks. "Sorry, I forgot about our plans today. . . . I was just so surprised that you were heading out that I just grabbed the first sweatshirt I found. How about I head back to the apartment really quickly, and I'll meet you at the train station?"

"I can go with you—or, wait, want me to pick up the hand warmers?" Remy asks.

Taka pipes up, "There's a convenience store around the corner that'll have that. Want me to take you there?" He quickly checks his watch. "I've got some time before I have to head to my next gig."

Cam protests, "I don't want you to have to pick up my slack. . . ."

In reality, something in his gut twists about leaving her alone with Taka. Even her having his scarf around her neck makes him feel weird.

"You know I always have your back," she says softly.

Those words melt something in him.

"Thanks, Remy," he says, and she beams.

It's better than a dazzling sunrise to see her smile like that.

Remy

Remy and Taka make small talk as he guides them past another branch of Kinokuniya Books—Remy makes a mental note to go back later—to a convenience store at the corner. Remy's been shocked to find how *actually* convenient these tiny shops are in Japan. Everything is prettily organized, and there is everything from soft-serve machines to socks to bento lunches. Like, she could live off everything in these convenience stores.

Taka grabs a basket and methodically picks up a few packs of hand warmers, and Remy wanders behind him.

"Your focus is amazing," she muses out loud. "I'd have forgotten and gotten caught up in everything else here . . . like snacks." Remy inches toward her favorite aisle.

Taka grins. "You probably need some travel snacks. Good idea. I also should pick something up, too."

"You're too kind," Remy says, and he lets out a surprised laugh.

But then he pauses, glancing at her thoughtfully. "Speaking of forgetting . . . So, we all know that Cam lost his memories of you. I can tell it's a struggle—you two have a whole history he doesn't remember. But what does that mean for you? It didn't seem like you lost your memories of him, right? Or are you losing your memories of someone else?"

How can Remy remember someone she's already forgotten? She

can only think of Cam and the way that they were together. Sure, there were others, but . . . they weren't *him*.

Doubt slices at her until she pulls up her phone as they loiter in the drinks aisle. There, even though she's checked multiple times already, she flips through the massive load of pictures of her and Cam, hanging out almost every day. "I don't see anyone else."

She doesn't have to wonder about the *others*. Her flings, where every pair of lips was compared to Cam's, where she'd run her fingers along their jawline and wonder how they could ever compare to him. Those are in the trash. But even if she forgot their names, those people wouldn't matter.

"Let's talk about something else?" Remy asks.

"Yeah, sorry. The weather? Breezy, but not too freezing."

Remy snorts as they linger in the instant noodles section. "It doesn't have to be that bland."

"Okay, future travel plans. Top three places, go."

"Um . . . Somewhere with the northern lights, Greece, and my bed."

Taka does a double take.

"My bed as in, like, to *sleep*. I want to nap for the next hundred years, until this all blows over. Preferably with my life figured out and my best friend with his memories back. He can also be a hundred and seventeen years old with me, after that long nap."

Taka laughs. "Being a vampire might be the solution."

"Do you know one?"

"Only me. Can't go into the sunlight because my skin gets rashy, and garlic is oh-so-good, but gives me the worst heartburn after."

Remy stops in the middle of the aisle, a salaryman dodging around her in his rush to get out, and stares flatly at Taka. A vampire. *Vampires can't possibly exist, but then magic shouldn't, either. . . .*

He stares straight back, serious as hell.

Except for the twitch of his lips.

For the first time since taking the cursed elixir, Remy truly laughs. A full belly laugh, the kind that bursts with joy like an oasis. Taka joins her, so they're the two weirdos snorting and giggling inside the convenience store.

"You got me!" Remy wipes away the tears at the corners of her eyes. Oh, hell, she needed this laugh so bad.

Taka picks up a bowl of instant ramen with black garlic, something she's never seen in California, and pops it into the basket. "Remy, you need to try the local ramen shop below my apartment. It's the best, ever, even if my clothes that I hang outside smell like garlic sometimes."

"Guess you can't be a vampire after all."

"Want me to bite you to find out?" Then—"Hey! I'm not target practice with potato chips. The basket is *here*."

"I was aiming for *you*."

Taka only pretends to poke her in the cheek with the ice-cold side of a Häagen-Dazs matcha mochi mini cup—another snack for later. The other shoppers seem to notice, so Remy's voice dips into a whisper. "Top three favorite ice cream flavors?"

Somehow, Taka can even make "Top three worst moments of college" hilarious. Remy's stomach aches from laughter by the time they make it to the candy aisle.

The display behind Taka catches her attention. Remy was going to pick up something with chocolate . . . Goldsticks, maybe. Why does she like Goldsticks so much, anyway?

I'm forgetting Cam.

The sudden pain shoots through; a throbbing headache. *Goldsticks are my and Cam's favorite snack. Of course.*

"We . . . we should go," Remy says. Taka gives her a curious look, but doesn't push for answers. In mere moments, he pays—despite her protests—and they head out the door.

They walk toward Yūtenji Station. Cam should be there any minute now, and Taka is riding over to Jiyūgaoka Station for his modeling job. She's loaded down with just a few bags and heavy thoughts. Remy can't help but think of that nighttime walk with Cam, before the love potion, before everything went wrong. The way she'd laughed, thinking that their closeness was forever. But even by then, Naomi had already walked into Cam's life. Is *that* why the potion erased her, so that Cam could focus on the new girl? Is Naomi his soulmate? Above, the midday light sears bright, but it still doesn't chase away the winter cold.

She misses Cam, the best friend she knows. Every moment, even if it's simple flashes of the past like lying out on her bedroom floor and knowing he's popped her favorite so-buttery-it's-basically-oozing popcorn or that he always jolts upright at *all* the slightest scary parts. It's feeling like, as they lie there, breathing and laughing and being silly, their hearts are totally in sync, and she can truly tell him anything, even about her date that she kissed during junior prom—except that she loves him (and that she wished that her date had been him)—and he'll understand.

Remy barely notices as they turn into the train station. Her thoughts are caught in a web of *Cam, Cam, Cam*—and that's what she blames when she stumbles over an edge of the tile. Taka drops his bags—his food slams against the floor—and his arm shoots out to keep her (and her dignity and her baggage, mental and from-the-convenience-store) from falling face-first onto the cold tile.

"I'm sorry." Remy's cheeks blaze with embarrassment.

"You were lost in your thoughts." Taka helps her regain her balance. She tries to grab his bags, but her hands are tangled in her own, and Taka's already kneeling on the ground picking up his food.

Then, a voice calls, "Remy? Are you okay?"

Cam. Her heart pounds as he weaves through people to get to her side, scanning her face with worry.

"I'm fine," she says, giving him a smile. "Just . . . was distracted, you know, trying to think of ways to remember things—I mean, get you to remember things. We should go."

Cam nods, but before he and Remy head to their train, Taka holds something out.

"Wait," he says. "I got these for you. A snack for later."

He places a small box in her hand, and Remy looks down. It's a box of Goldsticks, in a matcha-strawberry flavor she's never tried before.

"I saw you looking at them," Taka says, "so I thought you might like it."

"Those look good," Cam says, glancing over her shoulder. "Oh, shoot, our train is leaving soon. Let's go, Remy."

Cam starts heading toward the ticket gate, and Remy's heart twists. He doesn't remember their favorite snack at all. But Taka noticed at the convenience store, and he seems to notice her hesitation now, as he glances with a soft perceptiveness between her and Cam.

"I'll take it with me?" he offers quietly.

"No way," she says. "These look great. I want to try this new flavor."

But the edges of the box dig into her skin as she follows Cam. Nothing is the same without her best friend that remembers her, not even a simple box of Goldsticks. She needs *her* Cam back, so they can try this box together.

Cam

Kichijoji is a lively neighborhood in Tokyo, known for its streets crammed with shops, a spacious park, and the Ghibli Museum, named after the world-famous animation studio. The briefest of memories settles into place. He'd become obsessed with the movie *Howl's Moving Castle* when they were ten, and they wanted to create their own four-legged moving home. For his birthday that year, Remy had baked him a gingerbread version, and used a motion spell to bring it to life. It'd been right after he'd been struggling over his mom's passing, and the little things she'd done had meant everything to him.

After their hands are cupped around toasty-warm crepes—the caramel Goldsticks crepe was calling his name—Ellie turns to them. "I want to show Remy a few shops; would you rather follow us or hang out here?"

"Go for it," Jack says quickly. He's clearly been on enough shopping trips. "We'll be fine."

Remy darts forward.

"Here," she says breathlessly, pushing a piece of paper into Cam's free hand. "I came up with a few ideas on our way over."

He unfolds it while juggling his crepe, and takes a look.

TOP THREE KICHIJOJI HIGHLIGHTS FOR CAM

1. **Crepes!** There's a super-popular crepe stand outside the Kichijoji train station! I made some a few years back, but mine . . . might have fallen apart.

2. **Daiya Street.** Check out the magical emporium and a thrift shop next door to each other. What better match, right? Totally reminds me of that San Francisco trip where you and I switched off between alchemy shops (you, of course) and thrift shops (me, of course)—with loads of boba in between.

3. **The Ghibli Museum.** Since you love *Howl's Moving Castle* so much—because of your favorite cranky, wonderful Calcifer—we *have* to check out the museum!

Now that he's seen this list, he takes a bite of the crepe. And—there it is—the briefest flash of Remy.

She's much younger, in a long, flowy summer dress and a KISS THE CHEF *apron that she'd gotten for a steal at her favorite thrift shop, Wicked Threads in Mountain View. Cam holds a wonky-looking, squiggly pancake rolled around strawberries and chunky whipped cream, nothing like the perfect cones that were in the recipe's pictures. Still, he takes a bite, and it tastes like home: sweetness and kindness.*

"I was stuck on my experiment," Cam says slowly, and she nods. "But with this offering fit for the best of alchemists, I just came up with a solution."

She laughs, like he's being silly, but her smile shines brighter than any elixir he's ever seen.

"You—" Remy pauses, her eyes trained on the crepe in her hands, and Cam's pulled back into the present. "You've already crossed off the first item, though I guess you didn't get any memories?"

"I did, actually." Cam slides out the enchanted camera. "I remembered when you made me those crepes a few summers ago. They were the best."

"Really?" she asks.

"Really. Take a photo with me?"

He loves the way she leans into him as he holds up the camera. He wants to wrap his arm around her and pull her in closer.

Together, they snap a picture and watch the photo melt into the vial; he wishes he could've kept a copy. Because, with that recollection and the way she grins up at him in the present, he feels like he's eaten a thousand sugar-laced crepes.

———————◆———————

The magical supplies emporium is *amazing*—Cam can tell, even from where he and Jack stand outside. This shop is one branch of an international chain called Good for Goods, but it's so quirky and full of a million different things that Cam would've never guessed that it could be duplicated. There's everything from crystallized moonlight to stewed burdock root in root-shaped glass jars. Wood shelves are filled with nostalgic cauldrons and high-tech glass burners. Along another wall, there's a New Year's display of red and gold omamori charms, which look like little cloth rectangles, hanging from shimmering ribbons. Each charm has a specific purpose, ranging from general good luck to acing tests. Maybe there's one for "*Not Messing Up Your Life.*"

Around them, the non-magical shoppers pass straight on by. Cam figures they probably see a storefront with a COMING SOON! sign or perhaps an old alleyway. But, for the life of him, Cam can't seem to move. He stares at the window, but his mind is occupied with worries about trying to get his memories back, losing his license, whether he and Jack are actually okay—

"We should go inside." His brother stuffs his hands into his pockets. "Isn't it cold out?"

Cam lets out a grunt, but he doesn't move. He can't find it in himself to walk inside. What if he never gets his license back? What if he can't test out what crystallized moonlight does when infused with bottled firework sparks? What if he—

The panic swells, buzzing louder than the other shoppers passing by, and his throat constricts. His vision narrows, his head spins.

Remy's voice echoes in his mind: *Breathe, Cam. Breathe in for four, out for six.*

Four and six. Aren't those unlucky numbers in Japan? The pronunciation for four can also mean death; six for nothing . . .

But these are the numbers that worked for him, time after time. These are the numbers that Remy reminded him of. Cam takes another deep breath in for four seconds, finally finding himself again. Maybe they aren't so unlucky after all.

Jack shifts, and Cam can feel his older brother trying to read him. "How about we head over to Inokashira Park? That's where the Ghibli Museum is. We can hang out there and wait for Ellie and Remy to finish their shopping."

"Sure," Cam says gratefully.

It's only a five-minute walk, back through the train station and threading through the smooth stone path, to get to the park. There's a brick café to the right of the leafy entrance, which reminds Cam of something. A coffee shop he saw in Tokyo? Or maybe back in California . . . He remembers a flash of some café on a corner, and wanting to take a friend there.

Jack and Cam quietly wind through the trees, bare in the cold winter. Even the paths and grounds have been swept immaculately—no surprise in Japan.

"You're worried about the antidote, right?" Jack asks, gently breaking the silence. "I've asked a few friends, but they've got nothing on Naomi's skills, so I think you're in the best hands with her."

"Thanks. I'm definitely lucky to have her help." The incomplete antidote thuds against his chest, from where it's zipped into his jacket. Hopefully, he'll get enough pictures for it. "Still, I can't believe my license is suspended. Hell, I can't imagine what Dad will say when he finds out."

Cam hasn't said a word to his dad, other than texting that he'd arrived safely in Tokyo. His dad had simply responded, *"Ok. Don't forget about your shift on Jan 3. I need coverage for the post–New Year's bullet journal rush."*

"Don't worry about Dad," Jack says. "Dad is going to be Dad, no matter what we do or say."

Their past fight is fresh in Cam's mind.

The closed door. Jack is gone, and he's not coming back.

"Son, you won't do that to me, right?"

"Are you—" Cam pauses, unsure how to explain his waterfall of worries. "Did you want me to take your side?"

Jack blinks. "My side? For what?"

"That argument you had . . . right before you left."

The furrows in Jack's forehead deepen, like Cam's not making any sense.

"I thought you wouldn't want to see me," Cam admitted. "I thought only Ellie would show up at Shibuya. . . . I mean, we don't message a lot, like, other than happy birthday and basic stuff. I know it's because we usually talk in person the most, and it's been weird because we're so far apart now . . ."

Jack stops, and Cam's stomach lurches. He's totally said the wrong thing.

Then, his older brother puts one hand on his shoulder, looks him in the eye, and says, "When I said we're okay, I meant it. What Dad does or says will never come between us. We can't count on him, but at least we have each other. Got it?"

Cam nods slowly.

"Seriously, I mean it. I never want our dad to wedge himself between us. No matter what he does or says to me, or even if he tries cutting me off. Dammit. I should've explained things better to you."

"It's okay—"

"It's not. I'll try to communicate better, Cam."

"*Dad* needs to communicate better. It sure as hell isn't fair that we got stuck with a dad like him." Cam sighs. "I couldn't look at him the same after he yelled at you that way."

"We could have endless discussions about what's fair," Jack says gently. "But I'd rather accept that he'll always be the way he is—because he'll never change—rather than change myself for Dad. I'm happy living for myself, and I want you to find that happiness, too. I want to be the kind of brother that supports you through what *you* want, not what Dad wants. I'm here for you, okay?"

The anxiety that's been like tangled yarn in Cam's chest slowly eases, unknotting and fading away into a blissful peace. *Jack's not mad at me after all.*

"I guess you've gotten better at explaining yourself these days," Cam says, finally, and gives his brother a grin.

Jack laughs. "I should capture that on video. Ellie would be ecstatic to hear that."

Cam finally looks around. They're standing in front of a huge lake, filled with groups of friends cheerily laughing as they paddle around on swan boats.

That's how it is, isn't it? Jack and Cam might be stuck with their dad, but they'll always have each other to paddle alongside with, together.

"Hey," Jack says. "For better or worse, life isn't filled with sunshine all the time. It's gotta rain every once in a while, and there are always going to be some struggles. But that's what makes it life."

Knowing this, knowing that Jack doesn't hate him for not speaking up when he and Dad were fighting—this is a tiny step toward normal. This is a ray of sunshine through all the Dad-related storm clouds.

"We should probably head toward the museum." Jack studies the swan boats. "Do you know that any couple that rides a swan boat on this lake supposedly gets cursed?"

"I've had enough of curses," Cam says, wiping all ideas of taking a boat onto the water with Remy out of his mind. "So, where's that museum?"

Three Days Until New Year's Eve

THURSDAY, DECEMBER 28

Cam

Time is *flying*. One moment, they're wandering through the exhibits of Ghibli Museum, and Cam swears he just blinks and it's a whole new day, and they're in a building called Sunshine City, in a completely different area of Tokyo. Sunshine City—though not an actual city—is big enough to be one, with loads of stores, arcades, a movie theater, a planetarium, and even an aquarium, where they're headed to next.

"Whoa, we're high up. We've got a whole city at our fingertips," Remy says, peering out of the elevator window at the Tokyo skyline. "Ready to get the rest of your memories?"

The elevator jolts to a stop, and she almost loses her balance, but Cam reaches out; instead of stumbling into the window, she bumps into him.

For a moment, the world slows.

"Sorry," she whispers.

Don't be.

The slight chill to the air melts away with just her touch. The area where she brushed him feels like it's tattooed onto his arm. Cam manages to say, "Are you okay?"

She nods, briskly stepping out of the elevator, but there's a pink tinge to her cheeks. "Thanks. I think the aquarium is this way."

He breathes in the faint, addicting scent of Remy's skin that lingers, and his heart skips a beat. In that moment, he'd noticed how Remy is the perfect size for him to pull into his arms and tuck right under his chin, just like he's always imagined—

Always imagined? Old Cam, dammit, if you're this obsessed with her, how come you never confessed? Because Cam can't deny the way his mind and heart react to Remy; something about her sparks pure joy without any magical dust needed.

As they wind through the ticket queue, he's still searching for that memory. He can't remember beyond this flash of recognition. The rest of his body remembers her, that's for sure, even if his brain doesn't.

But, to him, that isn't love. In alchemy terms, it's a research paper without a true conclusion, like friends with benefits. He *needs* to figure out what happened before he caves in to kissing her, like he has desperately wanted to, these past few days.

He's never been on a date—as far as he can remember—but he knows that for him, love isn't a crush. Love—whenever, if he ever, feels it—will be real after a thousand days and a thousand nights of being with a person who lets Cam mess around with his potions, and maybe joins in with him, too, and knowing that person lets Cam be Cam.

He has a feeling that person just might be Remy.

Though he can't believe he'll love a person more than magical alchemy. His best days are when he can keep experimenting on and on, without an end in sight. He likes diving into archaic magical tomes and testing out different things. His worries about Dad simply wash away, stuck outside his research bubble. With alchemy, Cam can change things. He can change the future for patients like his mother, for families before they become broken like his. *That's* why he needs to go to MIT more than anything else.

Well, all of his dreams will be useless without his license.

He'll be doing just what his father wants: following in his footsteps, and taking over a shop that he likes, but that he'd never truly love working at. Stuck forever.

"How many tickets?" the boy behind the counter asks.

"Two, please." Cam slides in front to pay.

Remy protests. "But—"

"You're doing a *lot* for me," he murmurs. "This is the least I can do."

When he opens his wallet, though, he's running a little empty on cash—2,400 yen per person isn't cheap—but it's worth it. It's worth it, if this will work.

It's worth it, if this can count as a date with Remy.

When the boy slides over their tickets and a pamphlet, Remy clutches them, beaming with delight. "I've always wanted to come here. Thanks, Cam."

His heart clenches. He'd catch her from falling, buy her tickets, anything, any day, if she'd smile at him like that every time.

As they start walking through the aquarium, he doesn't really register the glistening fish swishing past thick reefs, or the flying penguins exhibit. He can't stop glancing over at Remy. So, instead, he pushes himself to run through theories on why he took the soulmate potion.

He may not know what happened, but he *knows* there's something he's missing in his past, like he's trying to recreate a potion from his notes and half of the directions are wiped clean. Maybe this is the key to understanding what went wrong. He has to figure this out.

It was for his love of magical alchemy. Well, he can't deny that's what his life revolved around—at least, when he had a license. But it's *more* than that, somehow . . . Related, but *more . . .*

Was it to impress Professor Watanabe? Naomi's mind and lab are incredible. Still, as much as he admires her work, he doesn't feel in *love* with her. . . . Though, maybe the soulmate potion erased those memories?

Was it to impress Remy? Why did they never date if they have such chemistry?

They turn right toward the jellyfish tunnel. The air has a hint of marine to it, like someone lit a candle named Ocean Life. When he catches a glimpse of the calm blue waters, filled with dazzlingly bright jellyfish, Cam is plunged into a memory.

Cam

Cam and Remy are on the cusp of starting sophomore year, and the end of summer vacation is right around the corner yet a thousand years away. This camp has everyone from ages eight through seventeen, but the only person Cam has been interested in spending time with is Remy.

But all he has to do is spend a minute too long changing into his swimsuit for his best friend to get swarmed by admirers. That late afternoon, when he jogs out to the beach of Lake Tahoe to meet her, a few of the other campers are already gathered around her, talking about a bonfire later that night.

When he steps to her side, one of the guys shoots him a Look, but Cam uses his height—he's taller, though skinnier. He's been following Jack's workout routine at night. The other guy flicks his eyes up and down, but doesn't say anything. Cam doesn't grin, though he damn sure wants to—

Remy's hand tugs on his sleeve, so sweetly. "Hey, BFF."

The other guys shift forward, interest reignited. Cam has been friend-zoned to the moon and back.

"Want to go?" she asks softly, and his knees feel like they're going to buckle. He could lose himself in that gaze of hers that shifts the rest of the world aside and puts him in the center of her universe. When she looks at him, they're not the Beauty and the Geek; they're simply Remy and Cam, forever.

Still, that tall guy is asking his "BFF" out, grinning as he says, "Before you head off . . . Remy, what're you doing tonight—"

From the lake, one of the little kids from the youngest group of campers, probably around eight years old, runs out screaming. "Eric! Eric, one of the girls saw a monster in the water!" He runs straight to the tall boy trying to hit on Remy, and Cam thanks his lucky stars for this interruption.

One of the other boys looks like he's just crapped in his pants as he hops awkwardly out. "She saw the Loch Ness Monster!"

With the water lapping at their heels, a counselor is scolding a tiny girl, probably around the same age as the boys. "We don't spread lies here!"

The girl seems dead serious on continuing her prank. "I swear I saw it! It had teeth as big as my arms!"

"No! Don't let it get me!" another of the younger boys screams, running amok. Except one of the waves pushes him over, and he flails as the water tugs him back. "I'm getting eaten!"

Cam mutters under his breath, "It's a wave . . ."

Remy giggles. "I heard about a place you might like. Follow me."

The counselors are trying to shepherd the rest of the campers out of the water, but Cam can't say no, not with her eyes glittering with mischief.

Remy grabs a bunch of rope lying out by the pile of tubes, and wraps two together. Cam helps her drag them behind the dock, away from the hysterical campers and overwhelmed counselors, shouting like the world is about to end.

"You scraped your leg? Shoot, let's go get the first aid kit."

"Don't worry! There aren't any monsters."

"What do you mean, you're going to livestream this? That's against camp policy!"

The waves take Remy and Cam out into the middle of the lake, like the currents are assisting with their getaway. When they float apart, the ropes tug the tubes back together. With their bucket hats, loads of sunscreen, and the sun beaming, it's the perfect summer day.

"There's no such thing as a Loch Ness Monster." Remy laughs, stretching out. "Out of anyone, we would know."

"Yeah, but that little girl is telling that to a bunch of kids already running around wild without their parents. That's adding fuel to a fire."

The blue, blue waters surround them. Blue as the bikini strap peeking out of Remy's tank top, blue as the sky above that he wants to soak up.

Like magic, they float out to an island, no bigger than the size of his dad's stationery shop; compact enough to see the other end through a thicket of trees. Cam wonders if it's enchanted, because it seemed to come up out of nowhere. His guess is confirmed when Remy points at a sign that also seems to appear out of thin air, staked into the white sand. "Look. This is what Minami told me about. Pretty amazing, right?"

WELCOME TO SHOOTING STAR ISLAND. ENJOY THE S'MORES, AND STAY TO WATCH THE STARS.

"It's even better than she described," she whispers, in awe.

Cam has been wondering if he should suggest heading back—they were only floating for five or ten minutes, but the coast is already out of sight—but he just as quickly squashes those thoughts.

Next to a small fire pit already dug into the sand, there's a picnic box filled with Tony's Chocolonely chocolate bars—Remy's favorite brand—and fluffy marshmallows and graham crackers. There are even little metal roasting sticks and a matchbox-sized charm for enchanted fire, too.

Remy tosses the charm into the fire pit and it blazes instantly. Cam and Remy sink to the ground and wiggle their toes in the sand. It feels damn good.

"Can we stay here forever?" Remy asks.

Cam thinks of going back to his lonely home, with his dad who is too immersed in his work and getting money to care about what his youngest son is doing. Then he thinks of Jack, and how hard it is to live in the shadow of someone who is absolutely perfect all the time. Is that why Cam is so into magical alchemy? Because if it gets him into MIT with a full ride, then it's something his dad will finally be proud of?

Remy quietly lays her head on his shoulder. Somehow, he has a feeling she knows what he's thinking without him having to say a word. After his dad and Jack had gotten into yet another fight over the summer, he'd told her how he felt like he didn't fit in at his home, and she'd listened and listened. She'd passed him tissues as his shoulders shook. Then she leaned her head on him, just like this.

He wants to stay here forever.

Remy shifts to get up when he starts moving. He shakes his head at her, wordlessly asking her, *Stay?* He hides the words he wants to blurt out: *Stay. Be with me forever.*

But he can't ask that, when he knows someday she'll leave him, too. She'll go on her own way, to college, to new friends, a different life from his. They only have now, these few moments. So, as late afternoon shifts into an early, blue-gold sunset, he'll ask her to stay, for a little longer, as he roasts a marshmallow just right, folds it between a graham cracker and a mountain of her favorite chocolate—because there is never such a thing as too much chocolate.

Finally, his hands sticky with chocolate and marshmallow, he holds his creation out to her. Instead of taking it from him, she bites into it right away, her lips brushing against his fingers.

He can't breathe.

Then she's pulling him down to sit, and guiding the s'mores to his mouth for a bite. Even though he protests—he'd made this for her—he can't refuse.

They share it in turn, bite by bite, and Cam figures he's turning into a s'more himself, toasted marshmallow cheeks from the way she laughs and a melted chocolate heart as she feeds him another mouthful. He's got a crumbling graham cracker mind from the way she licks her fingers; this moment feels unreal.

This is better than making out. This is more intimate, closer. The people that Remy dates might make out with her, yet they don't have this. They don't have Remy at their fingertips. Every bite is sweeter and more dangerous than the next.

Cam swears he doesn't believe in love. He doesn't believe in love, unless he's with Remy Kobata.

Cam

The memory ends way too quickly, and Cam is left staring at the jellyfish tunnel, his heart feeling like it's swishing away as fast as the floaty creatures. The water looks just the way it did in that memory, but it glimmers with a new realization.

Damn.

The scent of s'mores and sunscreen is so heavy in the air it's like he's still there. . . .

But *why* did he take the potion? If he already had his soulmate, what reason would there be for a soulmate elixir?

Or, maybe he got this flash of a memory because the old Cam *didn't* love Remy anymore, and that's what he needs to figure out. A lot of time has passed since that summer camp to now—almost three years—so things could've definitely been different by the time he'd taken the soulmate elixir.

Either way, he needs to capture this memory.

Cam scrambles for his camera and awkwardly takes a photo. The picture develops: he looks wide-eyed and confused, and jellyfish float aimlessly behind him. With a twist of his wrist, he drops it in the vial.

The potion melts, and this time it's a few millimeters, more than any of the ten-odd photos he added today.

Four centimeters left.

At least . . . at least Cam's remembering something.

The sweet taste of marshmallows haunts him as he glances over at Remy, standing in the middle of the tunnel. She's completely beaming, staring up at the jellyfish like they're her best friends. Cam's gut clenches. He wants her to look at *him* like that. . . . Before he took that cursed elixir, was he still in love with her then, too?

His heartbeat picks up—did she . . . *might* she love him?

Two Days Until New Year's Eve

FRIDAY, DECEMBER 29

Remy

The arcade buzzes brightly as Cam and Remy stroll through the machines, looking for their next game. They've got a handful of hundred-yen coins in their pockets—each worth about one US dollar—that will pay for a try or two. The bright lights from the machines, the prizes . . . it's like they've walked into a real-life version of Candy Crush. Except there's no timer that counts down to give them more lives . . . and their coin stash is running seriously low.

Yesterday had been the absolute best, and Remy still has high hopes that today will be just as amazing. With that memory Cam had collected at Ikebukuro's aquarium, they'd melted another centimeter. For some reason, he'd turned a funny shade of red when she'd asked him about it, and finally admitted, "It was that day at the lake." That was more than enough description; her mind unfurled the rest, though she wishes she could relive that sunny afternoon that melted into a velvety darkness . . . just the thought of those sweet marshmallows makes Remy crave pure sugar running through her veins.

So today, they should be able to make just as much progress. It's been so clear in her mind: a day in the game arcades in Shibuya, something they've talked about *forever*. Surely it will be attached to a memory the way that aquarium visit was, if not stronger. They'd spent afternoons tucked into the corner of the Palo Alto Bowl, before it closed, blowing their allowance on fifty-cent crane games. Cam used to love the curly fries there . . . or was it those thick slices of gooey cheese pizza? She rubs her forehead. Probably, knowing Cam, it was both.

Though, despite her best efforts, all her plans aren't working today. They haven't been able to win a single prize, but worst of all, Cam has been getting absolutely *zero* memories.

At the drumming game, just like the taiko demonstrations at the summer Japanese festival back home—Cam just shakes his head at Remy's inquiring gaze.

When they try crane game after crane game, trying to win a Shiba plush that looks exactly like Mochi, her family's dog—the red-gold Shiba only ends up *farther* away from the drop slot.

She doesn't remember them being this bad at games, but maybe she's not remembering things right. . . .

No. Remy takes a deep breath, scanning the aisle of machines for their next target. It's just the stress, the lack of luck . . . that's all.

"Look at that!" Remy points at a tall, thin machine where Goldsticks are stacked up three boxes high, forming a tower of sugary goodness.

"We have to win that." Cam looks like he's drooling.

"I'll win it for you, no big deal." Remy grins. "Or you'll win it for me. Share the spoils?"

"If it means getting to try any of these special-edition flavors, count me in."

Five minutes later, their hands are still empty of Goldsticks, and their pockets are definitely missing their previous stash of coins.

"Darn it," Cam groans, rubbing his forehead.

Remy fishes in the pocket of her jeans. *All gone . . .* Then, her fingers hit against the curve of cool metal. One last coin.

"I owe you for getting us roped into this," she says. "How about I buy you a regular-sized box at the Lawson on the corner?"

He laughs. "How about I do that? If you lose again, I'll get you a box at the conbini. It can't hurt to try just one last time."

Remy gulps. The coin is heavy in her hand, but she takes a look at the setup the way she does before a level of Candy Crush. *Maybe this is a sign. If I can get the Goldsticks here, I can get Cam's memories back.*

She used to do that all the time: make one-sided bets with the universe.

If I ace this chem midterm, I'll confess to Cam.

Or, *If the light turns green in five seconds, I'll ask him out to prom.*

It always seemed to be a sign when she never won. Like the universe was telling her, *Cam isn't the one for you.*

She studies the boxes. If she hooks the crane around the bottom edges, surely it will come toppling down. Or maybe if she just knocks the crane straight into the middle? But they'd tried that, coin after coin, and the crane arm had bounced off uselessly.

"I think those girls are waiting for their turn," Cam says quietly. Remy peers into the reflection of the glass. He's right. Two elementary school kids and their mom hover a very polite distance behind them, but the girls are eyeing the tower of Goldsticks with a longing that Remy recognizes well. It reminds her a bit of Cam when he's craving a sugar rush.

This is for Cam. She needs to win this not to confess, not to get his memories back, but just for him, as he is, in this moment.

Something makes her move the joystick to the bottom right, but just a little higher than their previous attempts, so that it knocks against two sets of boxes at once, and then—

The entire tower of Goldsticks boxes tumbles straight into the chute. Lights flash as the machine recognizes their victory. Moments later, Remy and Cam are cheering, hugging their boxes.

"We did it!" Remy says gleefully.

"*You* did." Cam laughs. "I just watched. And failed, earlier."

"It's all us," she responds, loyally. It's true: she would have been at the convenience store getting only one box without his faith in her.

They start to head to the door; they've used up all of their arcade game money, anyway. But as Remy juggles the boxes, she overhears the girls and their mom talking.

"We'll wait for the staff to reset the machine," the mom is saying.

"But I only have three hundred yen," the girl responds.

The older girl adds, "May-chan's right. They tried and tried. What if we don't get any?"

Remy's heart sinks. She knows what it's like to always have to be conscious of her money, and to feel like she'll never win. She asks Cam in an undertone, "Would you mind—"

The old Cam would already be nodding, but the Cam of now only looks questioningly at her. Then he looks over at the girls before glancing down at the stacks of Goldsticks boxes in their hands. "If we gave some to them? I think that'd make their day."

She grins.

Moments later, they're empty-handed. And they didn't get any memories. But as Remy glances back over her shoulder at the laughing girls, clutching their towers of boxes with surprise and joy, maybe they're not so empty-handed after all.

———◆———

The train car rattles her and Cam together; not that there's much room to move. They've hit rush-hour traffic, and salarymen with their dark black suits, wiping their foreheads and necks with handkerchiefs, fill the car. Most are reading novels or browsing on their phone.

Now, in this quiet, Remy's thoughts are churning. How can they get more memories? Maybe they'd been trying too hard. Is "trying too hard" a thing when it comes to Cam's beloved magical alchemy license, though? She'd been so certain that the clanging noises, the flashing lights, the pile of Goldsticks, *something* should've triggered a memory for Cam. If not of the bowling alley's games, at least of the puzzles they'd spent afternoons fitting together or that day at Santa Cruz Beach Boardwalk where they'd snuck off from their then-arguing siblings to run through the haunted house (Cam had been helping her through; then he'd screamed when he'd bumped into a wall; after that, Remy had simply patted all the "ghosts" on the head as she cry-laughed her way out). Today should have triggered *something*.

Or perhaps things just didn't mean the same to him.

Remy mentally shakes herself out of this funk. Of *course* their shared memories are different for him versus her. The way he processes things—analytical, like each day is a new elixir that he's creating, and he's testing things out to avoid any experiments going wrong—is way different than the way she processes things—one day at a time, and avoiding thinking about the future.

The train is packed. She can't even inch her fingers into her pocket to get her phone to check on her email. She's waiting on the results from the TMU interview, but her inbox is disappointingly empty. The salaryman to her right is holding on to the bar above her head; it's a total invasion of privacy, but there's really no space for anyone. After they'd gotten on, a wave of salarymen rushing in had squished them within the sea of people.

Then, she pauses, a suggestion from Naomi popping into mind.

"Mind if we make one more stop before we get home?" she whispers to Cam, not wanting to be a loud foreigner.

"Sure," Cam says, "but where?"

"It's called Mitsukoshi. . . . I heard something about it is pretty cool. We can hang out there until the commuter rush is over."

The doors slide open, the announcer's monotone ringing over the intercom. "Next stop, Ginza. Next stop, Ginza."

"Can we get off here?" Cam asks hopefully. "It's . . . a little crowded."

"That's an understatement." Remy laughs. "Just a few more stations until Mitsukoshi-mae."

It's humanly impossible but *more* people shove their way into the train, and the rest of the riders quietly and automatically shift, packing themselves closer and closer. The windows are fogging up; at least what little of the glass she can see.

"Stay behind the yellow line, and please wait for the next train," the announcer says sharply. "The doors are closing. The doors are closing."

It's when she's craning her neck, her arms protectively clutching her bag to her chest, to see if anyone else is seriously trying to sneak on board, that two things happen:

1. A group of laughing, slightly red-faced salarymen, probably heading home from an early business dinner, tipsily shove their way onto the car, causing another wave of quiet but insistent shoving.

2. The salaryman holding the pole over her head shifts, and the briefcase in his hand starts to slide loose, heading straight toward her.

Hell.

That's the only thing Remy can think before her life flashes before her eyes. Cause of death: briefcase on the Tokyo subway.

The reason she'll likely come back as a ghost, to haunt the living: she never got to kiss Cam Yasuda.

The briefcase starts to come down, but it doesn't hit her, and she doesn't get to live out her dream book life as Jane Su in *One Last Stop.* Instead, Cam snatches the briefcase and shoves it back at the man, who mumbles an apology.

In the next second, the announcer is snapping at that group of salarymen still shoving their way in, insisting they get off.

As the crowd shifts, like easing out with a breath, when the group finally leaves, Cam says, "Come with me."

He tugs Remy by the hand, threading through gaps between people, until they're at the wall, by the far door.

"That asshole." Cam swears under his breath, glaring back at the guy who'd almost knocked Remy out.

"I'm fine, I'm—"

Another push; the drunk salarymen are trying to sneak back on. Elbows and briefcases shove Cam and Remy. He slides around, cocooning her. Her back is pressed against the train wall and Cam's body is her shield. His arms, above her shoulders, prevent anyone else from sticking their briefcases anywhere close.

She stares up at him; he doesn't have anywhere else to look except down. The train lets out a buzz and it's finally moving, yet Remy's mind is already spinning. She can't tell if she's been here for only a few seconds or the best ten minutes of her life. Remy wants to stay here forever, protected and safe with Cam. What would it feel like to kiss those lips? Would that touch spark a memory?

Her heart thumps as the train swings on a turn, throwing her forward and into his chest.

"Hold on to my jacket. Hold on to me, if you need to," Cam says. He glances away for a split second—is he *blushing*?

I'm seeing things, Remy tells herself, yet the next turn doesn't leave her much time to think, because it throws her against him again.

This time, she grabs onto the lapels of his coat. She can feel the pressure of the other train riders pushing against Cam, through his body, and he loses some of his space, sliding even closer, so that her head presses against his chest. If it were quiet on the train, maybe she'd be able to hear his heartbeat. She can hear her own thudding in her ears, and she curls her fingers tighter around his jacket.

Remy can't remember the last time they were this close, but it feels so damn good.

Cam

Cam glares at the rest of the riders over Remy's head, and they inch away. If another briefcase comes flying toward her, he's going to chuck it out of the window. Maybe with its owner, too. At this point, anything is possible so long as it keeps her safe. . . .

And Remy . . . he looks down.

She's safe in his arms. Her forehead presses into his chest with a weight that is so comfortable and right.

Cam's heart pounds; surely Remy can hear this, but she doesn't move. If anything, her hands curl tighter to the lapels of his jacket like he's the only thing anchoring her.

A flash of a memory—*a school dance in middle school; Cam protecting Remy from an unwanted advance. The only brilliant idea he'd had was to ask her to dance, but he'd never expected his heart to thump like this. . . . Nerves. Pure nerves. After all, this is his first slow dance. . . .*

The announcer hums, "We have arrived at our next stop, Mitsukoshi-mae."

The doors burst open, letting in the cool winter air, and the salarymen and other riders push them out, shoving them unceremoniously onto the concrete train platform.

"That literally was like being a sardine in a can," Remy says, with a laugh. "Thankfully, we're all in one piece, right?"

"Seriously," Cam says, distracted. This isn't making sense. The old Cam would've done anything for Remy. . . . Was that why he took the potion—*for her*? But why would he do something like that, when he knew his license would be at stake, and that things could go so wrong? He has more questions than answers. Usually, he loves that about the experiments he does, but something feels off about this one.

The glass vial is heavy in his pocket: it's half-full of the solid part, half-full of the melted antidote. There's still so far to go. When he finds out why he took the potion, what if the answers change their friend-ship?

Because, honestly, he catches a glimpse of pure happiness in these moments with her. When she was in his arms, seconds ago. When she's laughing here, on the platform, with passersby shooting them confused looks . . . Where she is, where they are together . . . it's *home*. He's falling for her, as he is, even without all his memories. He—he doesn't *need* the past back if they can always be like this, in the way they are now.

That bone-deep want seeps out into his every breath as she slides her arm into his, tugging him toward the station exit.

Remy

The automated doors of the Mitsukoshi Department Store slide open softly, like little Mochi curling around Remy's ankles, vying for her attention. Just like her dog back home, everything in Mitsukoshi is calling out, "Look at me."

"Ellie said department stores in Japan were special, but this is really something," Remy says, stopping to take everything in.

"Wow," agrees Cam, pausing alongside her. "This is just the food floor?"

White tinsel and fairy lights are draped all over shiny glass counters without a single fingerprint in sight, making Mitsukoshi sparkle from wall to wall. Workers in crisp uniforms bow to shoppers, inviting them forward. To the left, there's a display of fluffy red, white, and gold New Year's cakes that Remy would gladly inhale in a bite. To the right, handmade jelly candies gleam like jewels in treasure chests. All this food is going to make Remy's hard-earned cash fly out of her pocket with every counter she sees.

"Naomi mentioned there's a magical section, too." Remy checks her messages. "It's . . . *between* floors?"

"Um . . ."

"I'm serious!" She shows him her phone screen. "'Ride the escalator up from the basement; step onto the next set of escalators within seven seconds. On the next escalator, exit at the enchanted doorway in the midpoint by walking through the right-hand barrier.'"

They stare at each other. Remy wishes she'd brought at least *one* of the five Tokyo magical guides she'd bought from Kepler's Books, when she was counting down the days until the trip back in Palo Alto. But those tomes are sitting in her suitcase. They surely would've had something on this. The idea of jumping off an escalator mid-ride sounds like an absolute prank.

Cam

I want to go, but I'm not sure I can walk into thin air." Remy glances down, dejected. "Maybe we should just stay with the non-magical sections."

Seeing her look like this makes his stomach drop, like he's fallen straight off the escalator. His head is still buzzing from the way she'd fit so well under him in the train. Right now, he should probably take some time away from her. He needs to reprogram his brain to *not* say something stupid, like how her closeness almost brought him to his knees.

"How about you wear the rose-tinted glasses?" Cam suggests. "Won't you be able to see the doorway, if it's magical?"

She blinks. "You're right. I think I read about that in one of the guidebooks." Then, Remy pauses. "But you'll come with me, right?"

Dammit. He's got a weakness for the way she looks up at him, like he can really do something. If she has all her memories of him, doesn't she know that he's not that kind of guy? He's not Jack, strong and handsome and reliable, that kind of moody-quiet that everyone falls for. He's just Cam, the spare instead of the heir; the guy that his classmates pat on the head because he's *cute* and sweet, but nothing that great.

He checks himself, his damn circular thoughts.

What if she sees *him*? And thinks that he's good enough for her?

"How about you wear the glasses . . ." Cam says, outlining the plan before his brain can shut down this fly-by-the-seat-of-his-pants Cam and think logically. "And lead me?"

"That's perfect." The way Remy smiles at him should be illegal.

She slides the glasses on, looking a little hipster with the rose-wire frames, and threads her arm through Cam's, tugging him forward. "Let's go."

Cam can't speak. His memories might be lost, yet he knows he wants to keep that image of her against the train wall, staring up at him, forever. He wants to hold on to this moment of the two of them, intensely close, him relying on her for his next steps.

He lets go of trying to keep control of things, as she leads.

Toward the escalator they go, arm in arm. Surely they're getting odd looks, but Cam doesn't see anyone else.

All he can see, the only person he can think of, is Remy.

They come to a sudden stop at the bottom of the escalator.

"I can't," Remy blurts out. She glances between the escalator and the side door. She's not bad with heights like her older sister, though he doesn't know how he remembers this about her.

"What's going on?"

"Honestly?" she says. "I'm not sure I trust magic anymore. Not after it did me dirty with that potion."

Not trust magic? That's been the center of his existence: the potions that are full of potential, the magical alchemy books thick with dust and questions waiting to be solved, even his dad's shop that has supported their family.

Remy holds out the glasses. "I don't . . . I don't think I can wear them. On second thought, I'd rather not look."

"Let me?" he asks softly, and to his surprise, she nods.

Cam can't stop the way his heart swoops as he takes the glasses from her hands. Her fingers are cold. She's more scared than she's letting on. He slides them on quickly, and wraps his fingers around hers.

Remy

Oh. *This* is what holding hands is supposed to feel like.

"Your hands are freezing," Cam says, as he rubs warmth back into her hands.

He's technically not even holding her hands—he's rubbing on them to chase away the cold—but Remy's body is on fire. It feels like her heart is being cupped in his soul, like he'll always be supporting her, caring for her.

"We, uh, should go," Remy says. "Escalator. Glasses. Floor."

Cam gives her a weird look.

Was she always this awkward on dates? No, she used to be smooth. But before, her heart wasn't on the line. And after this week, all of that is over, gone, ended—like the way that she and Cam used to sit at lunch, their knees casually knocking against each other like it was no big deal. It was a big deal to her, even if she wouldn't let on to it.

Then there were the days that they'd sneak a hojicha latte out from under her parents' noses, passing it back and forth as they—

Her mind is blank. Where did they go? Was it the library? They had studied, hadn't they? Or was it another movie night—

Why the hell can't she remember?

That damn love potion. Is it erasing her memories, too?

"Are you okay?" Cam asks. "Remy?"

She focuses on him: his scrunched forehead, worrying over her. Just the sight of him centers her. No, she hasn't forgotten Cam. She remembers everything, even that time he slipped and fell on his butt while Rollerblading. He had been so sure he'd be a natural at it, especially after being able to skateboard, so it'd been too cute when he'd squeaked in surprise.

It's likely the jet lag and early mornings that are tiring her out. That, and running around Tokyo, trying to get Cam's memories back. That's why she's more forgetful these days.

"Just a little nervous . . ." Remy says, her heartbeat pounding. Okay, maybe they can stand here until closing time, and he can rub her hands into eternity.

"Can you trust me for the next minute?"

She drinks in the honesty burning in his eyes. She wishes she could read him the way she can read almost anyone else at their school: Kaon was 85 percent a tease, 15 percent interested in her. Sanghoon was definitely only hitting her up for free green tea through her parents, and she didn't begrudge him for that. See Hee was experimenting, but weren't they all?

Weren't they all . . . except for Cam.

She had never let herself fool around with her best friend. She never wanted to be the one that he dated just before he found The One in college. With Cam, she can't survive being the Second-to-Last Girl, the way she is back at their high school. Basically everyone she's dated has found a long-term relationship after being with her. With Cam, maybe he would mean it when he says, *Let's stay as friends, okay?* But that wouldn't be the same. It would've hurt her more than anything.

"The next minute is all yours," she whispers. *And every moment after.*

"Close your eyes," Cam says, and Remy willingly obliges. He laces his fingers into hers. "I promise, I won't let go."

Her shoulders relax. A few steps forward, guided by his hand, and then the escalator hums under her feet.

"The halfway point is in a few seconds," Cam whispers under his breath. "Oh, damn. The glasses *do* show this exit, but I can't see what's beyond . . . Let's get off to the right, in three . . . two . . . one . . ."

With a tug of his hand, he pulls her to the right. Remy digs her heels in. *No, no, wait, she's not ready . . .*

"It's here," he's whispering. "Remy, it's—come on, we're going to miss it—"

The far more logical part of Remy should open her eyes and stay on the escalator.

"Come with me, Remy," he whispers.

Damn his smooth voice. If this week is all she has, maybe it's time to enjoy this moment. With that, Remy follows Cam into thin air.

Cam

"C am!" Remy squeaks out. "Do you . . . do you see this?"

They, unbelievably, have not fallen headfirst off the side of the escalator.

A sign floats overhead, suspended in thin air:

WELCOME TO MITSUKOSHI'S BETWEEN-FLOORS
Find your way through the Past, Present, and Future

There are three paths that split out from where they stand, each looking like portals into entirely different worlds. Other magic-aware shoppers step off the escalator, in a whoosh of cotton-candy-scented air, and walk around them. Clearly, Remy and Cam are the only ones new. Yet, for once, he doesn't let everyone's glances get to him.

"Oh!" Remy says, her eyes lighting up with recognition. "I remember now—Ellie did a whole case study on this place for a school paper. This one's special because it's split into three sections: Past, Present, and Future."

An announcement blares overhead: "We are closing in one hour."

"We're running out of time!" Remy exclaims. "Ooh, look at Memory Lane! Is that like the past? My cousin Jin would love that, he's super into history."

He loves how her eyes sparkle with delight; he could stay like this forever. But she'll notice if he keeps staring at her, so he takes a look around.

The entrance separates into three long, winding corridors with no end in sight, filled with enticing storefronts and restaurants that shimmer with possibilities; Cam feels like they might be doorways to enter another world.

The hallway on the left leads to historical Japan. The shop fronts are filled with dark fabrics and oak countertops, contrasting with bright red signs ranging from THOUSAND-YEN ARCADE—which, at ten dollars a try, sounds pricey, but the magical prizes are supposedly more than worth it—to HANDMADE PICKLES AND PORTRAITS. There's a vendor that Cam wants to beeline over to; the man turns rounds of rice crackers over a grill and calls out, "One hundred yen for a chance to see a glimpse of history with every bite!"

The path in the center is labeled THE PRESENT. A magical manga store and a cosmetics shop at the front of the corridor draw in customers with cheery, plasticky displays, and there are plenty of hovering banners that say, BUY NOW, PAY LATER or NO TIME LIKE THE PRESENT. A few kids—would this have been what Remy and Cam were like years ago?—giggle, pulling each other to an enchanted candy store with a reminder in the window: ENJOY THE MOMENT AND TASTE THE JOY OF LIFE.

Clearly, the lane to the right is Future Street, aptly filled with robots and medical equipment. Things are more blocky-looking over there, with steel doorways and counters, and ads made of blinking laser lights. A woman in high heels trots forward, snapping her fingers at a disheveled assistant scrambling to follow in her wake. "Come on, we don't have all the time in the world. Good things are awaiting."

"Which way should we go?" Remy asks.

Cam wavers, glancing at Memory Lane. The technology of the future pulls at him, but the past and now immediately feel more comfortable.

There's no future if there's no past.

A little ways down Future Street, a crowd gathers in front of a strange store. It looks like it's full of boxes, and Cam would have likely passed right by it if he hadn't read Ellie's case study.

"Pinch me," Cam says.

Remy turns from where she's drooling over a magical candy shop from the present, and leans over.

"Ow!"

"You asked."

"I mean, not on my cheek." Cam laughs, rubbing his face.

"Where, then?" Remy replies tartly. "Your butt? Because, I mean, it's cute and all, but I'm pretty sure that's off-limits."

Cam's face burns. "No, I, uh . . . look!" He points wildly at the shop he'd been gaping at.

Remy spins around, and her jaw drops. "No way."

They're staring at BOXED; the crowd in front is buzzing with excitement. Unlike everything else from the sleek, stainless-steel future, this store is brown. Like, cardboard-box brown, and it's literally in the shape of a box. The window display, which looks like it was made by a Tetris master, is full of boxes around the size of Cam's hands put together, with minimalistic labels, like "*Robotic Dog Vacuum*" or "*Self-Writing Book*." But surely a box can't possibly fit . . .

"A car?" Remy says, voicing his thoughts. "Wow, ten million yen. So like a hundred thousand dollars for a car that looks like a golf cart?"

The woman in high heels steps in front of the crowd and points at the car. A clerk hurries to her side; with a swipe of a card, the boxed car is hers. The clerk leads her and her assistant to a white platform in the center of the street, and everyone gapes as the assistant sets down the box, the cardboard sides unfolding and expanding. It's not any ordinary car; it turns into a levitating drone. The woman slides in behind the futuristic wheel, and her assistant takes the passenger seat. Moments later, after a few pushes of a button, the drone lifts up, taking them toward the ceiling; a chute opens, and they disappear.

The crowd gasps, and starts talking among themselves.

"Test runs allowed for interested buyers!" the clerk calls, over the clamor.

Remy sighs wistfully. "Who *has* that kind of money?"

"We do." Cam winks. "Let's test it out."

He holds out his hand, and she stares at him with questions in her eyes. "Really?"

Cam's world shifts when she slides her hand into his, and their fingers lace together. This feels like home; this is what he's been trying to recapture. That memory of his father, the house in stark white . . . he never truly belonged there.

This is why he has to recover his memories, so that he can understand what held back the old Cam from telling Remy that he was in love with her. *If* the Cam before the potion still cared for her in that way.

But, for now, he tugs her forward, so they can head to the future together.

Remy

The future sparkles. They slide inside the car, and the door snaps shut; the moment they sit, holographic belts shimmer over their laps, and the car begins moving.

The test drive narration begins. "Welcome to BOXED's exclusive car-in-a-box. A portable getaway solution, an easy party trick for the magic-aware. These cars, researched and developed at the local world-famous Tokyo Magical University, are renowned for their cloaking and anti-collision charms, creating a safe way to travel for the wealthiest of the magic-aware in a set of exclusive, private roads for BOXED users in the Tokyo Metropolitan area. The Tokyo Magical Bureau is testing a potential release to the general, non-magical public with a roadmap planned for . . ."

The voice drones on, but Remy's too busy looking at the path ahead. "Wait, seriously? We're going out— *Wow!*"

With smooth acceleration, they zip *up*. Up, as in outside. The thick winter clouds obscure Tokyo from view, then—

They dip down, and the city glows. Over in Roppongi, blue and white lights sparkle from an ongoing illuminations display.

"This is the future," Cam says in awe, looking around the pod. "Shiny and full of miracles. Seeing the past with a bird's-eye view."

"It's like knowing how to solve the next level of Candy Crush already, even though you haven't even tried it yet." Remy laughs. "Though, as excited as I was for this, maybe I'm not a future-person much. I mean, I can barely figure out my own life."

"Really?" Cam says. "To me, at least in all the memories I've got of you, and what I see now, it seems like you always know where you're going. Your path is basically set with TMU, and it's your dream school. As soon as you figured that out, you never wavered. You started working a ton to get the plane ticket, and to figure out every next step after that."

Remy blinks. She's never thought of herself as having her life in order. It always feels like she's trying to catch up. "I mean, look at you, though. MIT early admission, the potential full-ride scholarship . . . all that work you do in magical alchemy? *That* is a real career path. Like, I think TMU is perfect for me because it'll let me explore different options, but you already *know* what you want to do."

"I guess everything is relative, huh?" Cam says. "You and I both think everyone else has their lives figured out, but we're all just . . . figuring it out as we go, aren't we?"

He's right. Maybe it's not a bad thing to be figuring things out, and to not have the answers.

A chime dings overhead. "Thank you for joining us on today's trial ride. If you would like to make a purchase, please make your way to any BOXED attendant. We hope you will look forward to the future."

The car zips back into Mitsukoshi Department Store and threads down a long chute to land straight in front of BOXED. The moment they step out of the car, it folds itself back into a tidy square, and a robotic attendant swoops in to pick it up.

Back in the crossroads between the past, present, and the future, Remy takes a long look at each of them. Cam follows her gaze. "Where do you want to go next: the past or the present?"

Before she has to think too deeply on her preferences, Remy blurts out, "Let's try the present. I want to stay in the now."

———————•◆•———————

The present feels good. Remy isn't questioning herself for things that she did before or struggling to decide what to do for the future. It just feels right.

So many fascinating shops beckon her closer, as well as countless delicious-looking restaurants, with displays of food that look so real that she can barely believe Cam when he says they're made of plastic. The sign to her right feels like it's speaking to her soul: DON'T DELAY, LIVE YOUR BEST LIFE TODAY!

"I want to go everywhere," she says, but there's definitely not enough time to check out the cake shop, the enchanted wallets atelier (which are charmed to keep spending down, despite the initial cost, by refusing to open up for unnecessary purchases), and the dog toy store, where she'd be able to find the perfect gift for Mochi. Then, she squints. "Wait . . . I know where we have to go."

She points out the pastel-colored shop beyond the atelier: CANDY HEART—SWEETS THAT ARE DELIGHTS TO EAT, AND MANY A MAGICAL FEAT!

"A candy shop?" Cam says, brightening. "I'm in."

The sliding pastel doors open with a burst of sweet smells, and a song appropriately named "Suga Sweet," by FAKY—one of Remy's favorite J-pop groups—pipes out of the speakers. A guy in a pastel purple uniform bows. "Welcome. Test out any of our candies, and if you enjoy your selection, please use one of the baskets for your convenience."

The shop is pretty crowded with people oohing and ahhing over the displays, but there's so much to look at that Remy doesn't even know where to start. Cam points. "Aren't those Hi-Chews available in California, too? I swear I saw them at Nijiya Market."

Remy picks up the long, shiny pack, filled with little chews. "Ooh! I read about them in a book last month, I've been craving some ever since. The main character associates each flavor with a different mood."

"You read books about candy?" He sounds intrigued.

"*Made in Korea*. It's a romance about two people who never think they'll ever be meant for each other"—she can totally feel herself turning pink—"but they're *way* more compatible than they first realize."

Somehow, Cam's ears look a little red. He grabs a green apple Hi-Chew. "What's this one for, then?"

Remy scrunches up her nose. Her memory seems to be failing her these days, but that moment of sneaking in a few more pages before her chemistry lecture started trickles back in. "To brainstorm things."

Cam scoops up a handful. "I need that."

"Grape is for focus."

He sweeps another set into the basket. "All mine, now."

Remy laughs. "Share some with me. Ooh, look at these!"

They're rolls of washi tape, but instead of being meant for sticking on bullet journals, it's edible strips of gummies that melt on your tongue—and then turn into the actual dessert.

"Try this one," Cam says, spotting some free samples. He offers her a pale golden roll, with tiny cheesecake slices decorated all over it.

She gives it a nibble. "Whoa. That tastes *exactly* like biting into one of those fluffy, jiggly Japanese cheesecakes. I want to buy out their entire stock."

When they get back outside, weighed down with pastel shopping bags—including special-edition Goldsticks flavors, of course—Remy checks her phone. "Oh, shoot. Don't we have dinner plans with Ellie tonight?"

Cam leans over. "It's 4:30 p.m. You mean, our dinner plans at five o'clock?"

She laughs. "See, this is why the future doesn't work for me. I'm way too stuck in the present."

"The future has good things, too," Cam counters.

"The future is like a spring trap full of worries, like, where's my email from TMU about whether I got in? It's supposed to arrive any minute now. What am I going to do if I don't get into my dream college? Ugh. The future is too much to think about. If I stay in the present, I don't have to worry about what I'm going to do for an Adult Job. I just want to hang out here forever, like this."

"So what about the past?" Cam chews on a strip of the cheesecake washi tape.

"The past is filled with all the wrong turns I took and how I never did enough to set myself up for the future and all that grown-up stuff. Here, in this moment, I can just *enjoy* the present."

"Looks like the future is sending us a message," Cam says, waving his phone. "Ellie's train is late. We can make a quick trip into the past."

Remy laughs. "As long as we have our bags of candy, I'm ready to go."

Cam grins. "Everything's better with sugar, whether the past, present, or future."

Cam

Maybe it's because the future and the present were so flashy and vivid, but something about Memory Lane's solid wood walls, and the way things are made of ceramic and wood and thick, heavy materials is comforting.

"I think I see an old-fashioned alchemy set." He peers through the dusty window of an antique shop.

"Let's go," Remy says instantly, and he loves her all the more—then he checks his thoughts. *Love? Where did that come from?*

But it's true. There's an allure to Remy he wants more and more of, every time he drinks in another of her smiles or hears her laugh. A thought flickers in his chest, warm and strange—she's an unsolvable elixir that he longs to analyze every part of, to understand, to touch.

He tries to concentrate on what's in front of him. The alchemy set is gorgeous. Thick, handblown glass tubes rest on a brass plate, with a small brass box with three rows of drawers. The top two rows contain glass jars, filled with herbs and extracts. The bottom drawer contains stainless-steel tongs and other tools.

"This would be perfect in my future lab," Cam says. Then he looks at the 100,000-yen price tag, quickly knocking off two zeros to roughly translate the price. It's almost a thousand dollars—a little less with current exchange rates. He'd only be able to afford this if it were a hundred dollars, max. "Well, maybe after I make some sort of amazing alchemy discovery, I can come back and buy this."

Not that it'll still be around by the time Cam gets his license back—if he ever does. He can't even imagine thinking of that future. Though, really, that's how he usually thinks: Why ever try to count on something that might not work out?

Then, a thought freezes him. Has he been too caught up to fully live in the present or believe in the future? Has he only been focused on MIT—a goal he's not even keen on, judging by the fact that he hasn't looked at his acceptance results? What if that's why the love potion turned into a curse?

He glances over at Remy to ask her, but she's preoccupied with her phone again, peeking at the notifications. The screen flashes with a pic of him and Remy; it looks like maybe three or four years ago, at the Santa Cruz Beach Boardwalk. They're both squinting as they laugh about some joke that Cam doesn't remember, of course.

"Is everything okay?" Cam asks.

"I got an email, but it was for something else. . . ." Remy says. "I'm waiting for the interview results . . . Taka said I should be getting either an email or a call by the end of today, max. See? This is why I hate worrying about the future."

"I'm sure they'll respond soon with good news." He feels the weight of his phone, too. If he *has* gotten into MIT, then he has to notify the alchemy department that he doesn't have his license anymore—which was the first question on his application. And if he didn't get in . . . He can already imagine the look on his dad's face. . . .

Then, Remy's phone buzzes loudly; she drops it in surprise. "Eep!"

Cam grabs it in midair and holds it out to her. She stares like he's holding a bottle of poison.

Remy

It's very likely *The* Call.

Her fingers tremble as she picks up, pressing her phone to her ear.

"Hello?" Remy says, her heart in her throat.

"Kobata Remy?" asks a deep voice in Japanese. "This is Hagiwara from the Tokyo Magical University Admissions Department."

It's the interviewer with the thick glasses. Her eyes meet Cam's as her heartbeat pounds rapid-fire.

"Yes, this is Kobata," Remy confirms in her best, most-proper Japanese.

He pauses—did she say something wrong? Does he hear an accent?—but then the man continues. "We had a very difficult round of admissions this year, as you may know; this was our largest and most high-achieving group of applicants yet."

Remy makes a polite noise, but she's too nervous to speak. TMU is *the* college for her. She can't imagine going anywhere else. She's dreamed of it for so long.

"To make our decision, we'd like to invite you to a final interview on January fourth at 10 A.M.," Mr. Hagiwara says crisply. "Please be prepared to show how you will contribute to the TMU community through your academic endeavors."

A sick feeling twists Remy's throat. "I—I . . . My flight back to

America is on January first, Mr. Hagiwara." It was the cheapest flight, yet also the only one she and Cam could afford. "My school starts on the third. Is there any way possible to meet earlier?"

"Our department is closed until the fourth. We hope to see you, Ms. Kobata, but we understand if you cannot make this meeting."

Remy slowly sinks to the ground as she hangs up. Her forehead grinds against her bent knees. She can't float a flight change, not with what little cash she has left.

"We have to get you to the interview," Cam says. "I'm sure you can skip a few days of school."

"But the cost?" Remy holds out her phone. "I just looked it up. It's a seven-hundred-dollar switch. I can't beg Ellie for a load of money. She and Jack are barely making it month-to-month; there's a reason we're staying with your aunt and uncle instead of their tiny place. My parents told me up front that they didn't have the money to send me to Japan for the interview. . . . I promised I'd be doing this on my own."

"You're not on your own." His eyes are resolute, and Remy's heart patters fast.

"I . . . I . . ." She peeks up from behind her hair that's a stringy mess all over her face. "But what else is there? I mean, I've applied elsewhere, but tuition is too high. I'll have to go the community college route. I can't even transfer in—TMU only lets someone in if a student has left, so there's only like one spot every year. I'll *never* get in."

Cam frowns, his forehead furrowing. "We'll figure something out. I know we will."

One Day Until New Year's Eve

SATURDAY, DECEMBER 30

Remy

If Tokyo is known for its bright skylines and neon lights, then Shimokitazawa, a small neighborhood only a twenty-minute train ride from Shibuya, is its fraternal twin. There are still big-city vibes, but Shimokita, as Naomi calls it, is cool and laid-back with winding streets full of thrift stores and quaint cafés. It's also where Remy stumbled across the Good Luck Café, but that isn't in sight today.

Still, all six of them—Cam, Remy, Ellie, Jack, Taka, and Naomi—meet where they had hung out just about a week ago, and start looking for a restaurant to have lunch together. For once, Jack and Ellie have the day off from school and their part-time jobs, Taka's taking a rest from his modeling gigs, and Naomi had needed a break from her research. It's coming full circle to be here, only thirty-five or so hours until midnight on New Year's Eve, though they have less answers than before. The antidote still has two frozen centimeters; when Remy had messaged Naomi about it, she'd confirmed: there are no shortcuts. If Cam can't trigger enough memories, the antidote won't work if it's not the full dose.

After their carb-induced haze from the best ramen of Remy's life, Ellie leads the way to a quirky little thrift shop. It's non-magical, crammed to the ceiling with vintage clothes, gadgets, and everything under the sun.

"This would be a great place to pick up an outfit for dinner," Taka says, looking around.

"Do we have plans?" Remy asks.

"My friend works at this incredible magical restaurant when she's not modeling. It's usually tough to get a reservation, but I know she can squeeze in a table for us. Except, there's a catch."

Cam clears his throat. "What is it?"

"There's a dress code," Taka says. "I suggest we check out this shop for something nice. Vintage is a must, but we've got to look sharp, too."

"Ooh, that sounds fun!" Ellie exclaims. "Remy, let's find something."

Ellie pulls her over to look at a set of dresses, but she glances over to where Naomi and Cam have drifted to a display at the front, to chat about the vintage computer sets. It ranges from an old-school tablet to black-and-white photos of old models of computers that literally took up an entire room. Apparently, Cam can make computers sexy and funny, because Naomi's laughing like he is *hilarious*. The sad thing is, Remy *knows* he is, especially when he gets into his nerdy little jokes that she loves, even if he always has to explain them. ("Why did the molecule walk into the bar?" "I don't know, Cam, why?" "Because they wanted an intermolecular special on the rocks." "Hah hah, wait, what?") And Professor Watanabe *does* understand his jokes.

"Hey, Ellie?" Remy asks, when her sister's studying a sunshine-yellow dress with a huge bow in front.

"Mm?"

"What made you fall in love with Jack?" she asks, quietly.

At least, she thinks she's quiet.

But a husky voice intones, with the seriousness of a movie-quality narration, "One day, Ellie Kobata slammed right into the love of her life, Jack Yasuda. She'd always admired Jack for being strong, for being handsome— Wait, didn't you say you noticed my arms—"

"Jack!" A very red-faced Ellie shoves her grinning boyfriend toward Naomi and Cam. "I'm sure Naomi's got plenty of nice clothes, but go tell Cam to look for something."

Jack leans down to place a kiss on his girlfriend's temple and whispers something to her softly, making Ellie smile so bright that it hurts Remy's eyes. This is a side of Jack that no one ever sees, unless he's with Ellie.

Once Jack's with the others, her older sister stares resolutely at a stack of hair bows, her cheeks burning red. "Sorry about that. It's a fascinating question, something that I've been thinking a lot about myself, ever since"—she waves her hand at Remy, to wordlessly explain *that soulmate elixir gone wrong*—"and I'm not sure that even I have an answer."

"Oh." Remy's always thought her older sister had all of the solutions. Pre-Calculus? All of Ellie's old homework was saved on Google Drive. AP Environmental Science? All the homework *and* past tests. Love issues just seemed like the next box that Ellie would check off. "But you have an idea?"

"I bet Naomi would have a better answer with the research she does." Her sister absentmindedly rubs her red cheeks and glances toward Jack. "But for me, love is about more than just falling in love once. Real love is about falling in love every day. Love is about staying in love, and loving who your partner is and loving yourself in those moments. It's about being with someone who sees you as you are, yet also is someone you trust to be by your side as you become who you want to be, as you take chances, without holding you back. That's why I kind of hate that idea of a white-picket-fence future, two kids and a dog, all of that. Because that's a safety net and someone else's dream. I feel like real love is about the continual process of growing into who you want to be, and having someone who encourages and supports you through that—though maybe sometimes they play the devil's advocate"—she raises an eyebrow at her boyfriend, who's laughing with his younger brother—"but they don't hold you back from being *you* or the future you."

Then Ellie smiles. "At least, that's what it is to me. But, really, I think each person has their own definition of love."

Real love is about falling in love every day. . . . The words take root in Remy's mind, unfurling and blooming. *I've been trying to make Cam fall in love with me as I am now, even though I wasn't sure it'd do anything. I thought it might even be hopeless. But maybe that was a good idea, after all.*

So when her sister loops her arm into hers as they continue walking down the aisle of decadent vintage dresses, Remy lays her head on her sister's shoulder, wordlessly searching for comfort. Ellie's right; both her version of love, and that it might be different for each person. What's *her* version of love? How can she convince Cam that she's worth remembering?

She'd felt just what Ellie was saying before, hadn't she? Back home, she'd felt like that each time she knocked on Cam's bedroom door with a tray of cookies and he opened the door with a beaming smile. When they walked side by side at school, just chatting about Remy's latest baking experiment or Cam's next potion. The way that being around him had always filled her world with warmth; it had felt like *love*.

But . . . maybe Ellie's right about the other stuff, too. Maybe Remy has been putting herself in a stagnant place, staying comfortable with what things are with her and Cam, instead of what the future could be with them as a couple. That's why she had to depend on a fortune and then a soulmate elixir to help her, even though it ended up only screwing her over.

"I'm going to try a few of these on, okay?" Ellie says, drifting off toward the changing room in the back. Remy waves her off, sorting through endless velvety dresses that look like they've been plucked out of the night sky. If she'd worn a dress like this to winter formal, everyone would probably have thought it was some exclusive designer label. What she wouldn't give to be back in school, before this all happened.

"Everything okay?"

Her heart races, but she looks up to meet Taka's eyes, standing in front of her. Naomi's gentle laugh, pretty as chimes, echoes from behind them, a perfect contrast to Cam and Jack's huskier voices. She glances at her feet; sets of matching velvety pumps line the aisle.

"Oh, you know," Remy says, trying to laugh it off. "Just nervous about losing my best friend, memory by memory."

He frowns. "Is the antidote not working out?"

"I'm not good at magical alchemy like Cam, but I'm not sure that we'll be able to finish creating it. Not by New Year's Eve."

Truth is, Remy is terrible at magical alchemy—she'd had to rely on his tutoring to scrape through non-magical Chemistry—but she'd done everything to support Cam's favorite hobby. If that meant Cam could think better with sugar, then she'd learn how to bake. The first time she tried baking snickerdoodles for Cam, they were so hard that they almost broke his jaw.

But for him, she learned. Remy studied video tutorials and read recipes (even those boring, pages-long intros) to figure out how to make snickerdoodles (spoon, not scoop, the flour), caramel fudge, and even white chocolate ganache macarons in the shape of Baymax, for their movie-watching marathons.

"There's something more than that, isn't there?" Taka asks. "You keep double-checking to see if Cam's around. Like he's about to disappear."

"I . . . It's nothing." She's just too stressed out about Cam, that's all.

"I wish there was someone who looked at me the way you look at him," Taka says gently. "He's lucky."

Her heart sinks further. Does *Cam* notice the way she looks at him? If he's never noticed, through all the years they've been together—when someone they've just met can—what does that mean for their relationship?

That the next thirty or so hours won't be enough.

The cold, hard truth sears into her bones. She'd known this, from the moment that Cam had stared at her blankly outside the apothecary. She'd known from the way Naomi had offered only a hypothesis; there were no guarantees that Cam's memories would ever return, or that she'd be able to keep hers. Already, there are too many memories that are like Ellie's blotted-out watercolors, faint at the edges, the sharp emotions long gone.

Cam and Naomi break away from Jack to have a low, fast-paced conversation. Remy doesn't have to know what they're saying to notice how they're totally in sync.

Then, Cam's laughter joins Naomi's; Remy presses her forehead against the shelf, willing herself not to burst into tears.

"You deserve the person you want to love," Taka says softly. "If you love him, fight for him."

"I am." Her whisper feels like knives in her throat. "But no matter what I seem to do, it never is enough. If this elixir doesn't work out and he doesn't remember how much he means to me, he isn't meant to be by my side forever. I think he's falling in love with Naomi."

"Fate can't be that cruel," Taka says. "I don't think he's in love with her. She's his professional idol, and they've become friends, but he doesn't see her in a romantic way. He doesn't look at her the way he looks at you. *Fight* for him, Remy."

His earnest support makes her eyes prickle even more.

"I'm trying." Remy says. "I'm trying."

"I know." He hands her a handkerchief, and she's surprised to realize her cheeks are wet with tears. Taka leans against the shelf, quietly keeping her company. And that makes Remy's heart hurt even more.

Remy

The Shinjuku High-Rise towers over the rest of the city. The forty-seven-story building is like a little world in itself. The purring sliding doors let them in with a whirl of warm air, melting away the chill of the December night, to reveal sleek velvet couches nearly hidden by gigantic floral arrangements, and sparkling crystal light fixtures above.

"Are we in the right place?" Remy asks. This looks beyond what they can pay for—though no one can tell that from their outfits. She's wearing a fairytale-like pastel yellow dress that they'd pulled out from the racks; with its matching cape, it flows around her like she's a star glimmering in the night sky. Cam is in a tuxedo, a vintage piece, and the rest of them are also dressed to the nines. It's like a scene out of a Taylor Swift music video, glamorous and decadent.

Moments later, they're zipping up in an elevator like bubbles in a potion; as soon as they step out, a white-gloved host leads them to their seats. This whole restaurant is floating among the clouds. Even the table is carved in the shape of a crescent moon. They're next to a window showing the rest of Tokyo, shimmering like the jewelry sparkling on the other magic-aware diners. Taka was right to tell them to dress up; the others here look like they bathe in money. But the food is so damn worth it. Waitresses dressed in pretty kimonos flit in and out like shooting stars as they deliver meals fit for queens and kings, straight from the sushi bar in the center, where a duo of sushi chefs wield sharp knives and work like lightning.

"It's the freshest fish that Tokyo has to offer," Taka says. "And—before you worry about the cost, eat your fill. My friend is comping our meals. She owes me a favor or two."

Remy gapes. "You must've done something good to get a favor like this. You're my stomach's hero."

Taka laughs. "Anytime."

Waitstaff set golden bowls in front of them, filled with fragrant os-uimono to start them off. It's a clear broth with thin slices of mushroom and greens. With one whiff, Remy wants to drink it all in a single gulp.

"It's filled with a hint of heat, to combat the cold," Remy's waitress says. "Please, enjoy."

Cam swallows a spoonful. "This reminds me of something . . . Wait, didn't you try making me chicken noodle soup last year, Remy?"

She doesn't remember this. "Did I? I usually only make sweets . . ."

Then, the memory trickles back. It was after Thanksgiving, when Jack and Ellie had left on their flight, when Cam was feeling down about his older brother heading off on such a bad note. He'd gotten a nasty cold, and so she'd brought over a thermos of soup that she'd made from scratch. For once, she'd done everything possible to make sure she didn't swap in sugar for the salt, and she'd concentrated and concentrated through every step of the recipe, hoping more than anything that the broth might make Cam feel better.

"Oh, right." Remy laughs. "I almost forgot."

From her left, Naomi gives her a funny look.

Remy could use some of that chicken noodle soup right now. She tries what's in front of her; with one sip, warmth fills her body, but she can't bring herself to drink any more.

I am not *forgetting things.* Not now, when they're trying to fix things for Cam.

The more she tries to piece together her memories of her best friend, the more her hand shakes when she holds the spoon, so she puts it down. There's too much going on. She doesn't know how she'll be able to make the interview . . . and, even if she does somehow manage to change her flight, if she'll get in. The edge of heat from the soup has disappeared, and her fingers are forming into ice.

Before the next course, Remy slips out under the pretense of looking for the bathroom. A fluttering waitress offers to show her the way, but she shakes her off, heading out the entrance.

By the elevators, there's an area with a bench in front of ceiling-to-floor windows, mostly covered by a few plants. Remy presses her hand to the glass. It's freezing cold, but it soothes her.

That is, until someone says, "Remy?"

Through the reflection, she can see Naomi. "Hi."

"Sorry to disrupt you," she says. "I told the others I needed to go to the bathroom, too. Girls' run sort of thing. That'll give you some more time . . ."

To pretend to collect myself back together, even though I'm falling apart.

"I don't think there's enough time for this," Remy says, with a short laugh.

Naomi frowns. "I thought I was seeing things, so I wanted to check. But . . . you look like you're trying to . . . *remember* something? Wait. Where did you and Cam first meet?"

Remy freezes. "Um, Bing Preschool?" Then, she backpedals. "No, we were born in rooms next to each other at Stanford Hospital."

Naomi stares at her, furious. "You *promised* me you'd let me know if you were starting to lose your memories, too."

"I . . . Unless someone asks me like that, I can't tell if I *am*." Remy leans against the glass, wishing she could freeze time, so she could finally figure out answers to all her questions. It's beyond frightening that her past is slipping away. "There are things that don't quite seem to add up. And . . . it's like how Cam described it, that there's a blur when I know someone else should be there . . . I guess . . . I am losing memories, as much as I want to deny it. But why did he lose his memories all at once, and I'm losing them over time?"

The soft carpet is getting crushed under Naomi's pacing. "I keep wondering about that . . . and this *would* prove the Soulmate Study to be right . . . What if, before the potion, you both were already in love? So the potion backfired—which proves that love potions *should* stay banned—since you two were already in love with each other?"

Love? Remy jolts. "Um, I'm pretty sure it's one-sided." *Anyway, I'm not anywhere as fascinating to the new Cam as you are.*

"From what I've heard Ellie say, you two were basically together, but never made it official," Naomi replies. "My guess is that you were close to coming to terms with your feelings for him—were you?"

Guilty. Remy ducks her head. "I was going to confess during this trip. I even tried the day we got here, but I swear fate was trying to pull us apart. Like, I was full of excitement about our trip starting, and we were standing at that famous Shibuya Crossing. I thought, *Why not now? What if we could spend the rest of this trip as a couple?* Just as I opened my mouth, a bunch of tourists plowed through us."

"So you *were* close to confessing." Naomi rubs her chin. "Perhaps Cam wasn't. Maybe that's why he lost his memories all at once. There was—is—something blocking him from being truthful with himself, which is how the potion went wrong."

Remy's eyes burn. "If the old Cam didn't love me—"

"I'm not saying that," Naomi says. "Being in love and being ready to confess are two completely separate things. I was wondering why you hadn't lost memories while Cam had . . . but now I guess we have a hypothesis."

"Well, if I'm forgetting things . . ." Remy gulps. "Can you make an antidote for me, too?"

The older girl bites her lip. "The issue isn't the magic dust or the base of the antidote. It's what you and Cam have been doing to *make* it into a true antidote. The elixir I made for Cam is turning into the antidote because *you* are helping to spark the memories. He doesn't remember enough about you to guide you. Nor—since the time limit for the two of you is the same—are you going to have enough time to recreate the memories by midnight tomorrow?"

The ache in Remy's heart feels like a knife has slid in, twisting with every inch. She's been trying to change her future, but maybe there is nothing to salvage.

"We need to talk with Cam," Naomi says.

Remy's hand snakes out, wrapping around Naomi's wrist. "Please don't. If there's no way to make an antidote for me, too, then I don't want him to know about my memory loss."

Naomi breathes in sharply. "You think he'd give it to you."

"I don't know. But even if there's a chance, I can't let it come to that," Remy says. "So please, keep this between us. And if I forget him, can you take care of him for me?"

They stare at each other, face-to-face. Their eyes are both shades of brown, but Naomi's are edged with thick dark lashes that make her look soft despite all her sharp edges. Then she swears under her breath, glaring at the gorgeous, sparkling skyline out the window. "You need to make sure as hell that Cam gets his memories back. I need to go back to my lab."

She spins on her heels, and calls over her shoulder, "Tell me if anything—*anything*—changes."

———◆———

Remy stumbles back toward the dining room in a daze. But, at the entrance, she pauses, trying to adjust her cape. It's a thin, gauzy cloth, studded with bits of crystals, so thin that it slips through her trembling fingertips. She tries to retie it, but the strings tumble down.

A hand catches them.

Taka stands in front of her. "Need help?"

Numbly, she nods, and he adjusts the cape around her shoulders, his nimble fingers tying the strings into a knot.

"What's the matter?" he asks.

"Everything." The truth slips out, and she laughs self-consciously. "Well, the obvious . . ."

"You've been meaning to tell me something, haven't you?" Taka asks.

She looks away, guilt biting her insides. "I was a little too headstrong before, yeah. I think I need your help with TMU. Mr. Hagiwara wants me to come in for an interview when I won't even be in Tokyo anymore. And he wants me to show my academic excellence, and explain how I'd be an asset to TMU."

Taka swears under his breath. "Can't you stay longer?"

"I can't pay for a flight change," Remy says. "Tomorrow's my last full day. I'm not going to get in, after all."

"I'll pay for it," Taka offers immediately.

How much money does this guy have just lying around? "No, there's no way I can accept that."

Taka grits his teeth. "You have to. Hagiwara doesn't actually care about you."

She blinks. "Excuse you? This is *my* interview."

"No, no." Taka shakes his head. "That came out wrong, I'm sorry. But Hagiwara is trying to screw with me. He's from one of the New Families that keeps playing power games, even though he knows I'm not part of *that* family anymore."

"Wait, *what*?" Remy says sharply. "This is all because of *you*? Does he do this to everyone you know?"

"I'm sorry," Taka says, his eyes sad; still, he doesn't quite answer her question. "I'll do what I can to fix things. I'll get him to agree to an interview tomorrow."

"I can't tomorrow. I have to help Cam," Remy whispers. "It's our last day to do something to save his memories of me."

"You'd choose him instead of a future for yourself?"

"I'm not the type of person to abandon my best friend at the first sign of trouble," Remy replies. "Especially the trouble that I got him into in the first place."

"I respect that," Taka responds. "But I'm offering you a way to get in, without having to change your flight. Think about it. You can still take care of yourself, while making good on your promises to him."

He's right, even though the words churn in her stomach.

"I can't. I need to stick with Cam and see this through. It's my fault that he's in this mess. Maybe I'll figure out a way to earn some money to change my flight or something. Or maybe it's better if I just stay in California, anyway. Go to community college, use that time to figure out my path. This could be a sign." She clears her throat. "I'm heading back in."

Through the rest of the meal, she sits next to Cam, and she tells him stories about their experiments gone wrong: the day they had tried to make a potion that would create the perfect broth for ramen, based on the eater's preferences, but it ended up being so spicy that their mouths (and stomachs) burned for a full day; the time she'd suggested a book-reading potion to help her read faster, but it'd made her read slower, so she'd only been able to finish a single book that entire summer.

Cam laughs, even though with the slight tilt of his head, she can tell these don't trigger memories, even when she brings up the photos and videos on her phone.

There have been so many potions and experiments that have gone wrong, but they've made their way through it, haven't they? This trip is just one more example.

She hopes, more than anything, that tomorrow will be the day that they change their futures, together.

Still, when the meal ends, Taka gives her one last lingering look, before they all head their separate ways. The guilt hurts: Shouldn't she be taking care of herself? But her guilt for what happened to Cam is worse. She needs to help her best friend first. She needs to change what she's broken for him, and help him get his memories—and license—back.

New Year's Eve

SUNDAY, DECEMBER 31

Remy

As Remy and Cam wander through the entrance of Amagi Park, she still can't stop thinking about this past week. If it hadn't been for Cam losing his memories, this would have been the most amazing trip ever. The deep blue waters in the aquarium at Sunshine City. The day full of arcade games. The magical sweets shop in between the floors of the enchanted department store. Cam's laughter and smiles, each one so perfect. Yesterday's thrifting, searching through racks and racks of clothes with her sister, dressed to the nines for dinner at the Shinjuku High-Rise . . .

Her heart pounds nervously every time she glances at the date on her phone: Sunday, December 31. Tonight's the deadline.

For lunch, they'd gone to Kura Sushi, a chain conveyor-belt sushi restaurant that they'd tried once in California, but it hadn't struck up a single memory like she'd hoped.

They're *so* close to finishing the antidote. If only Cam can remember something. All they need is one more solid, beautiful memory. She wants her Cam back, her best friend that knows her down to the molecular level, nerdy alchemy jokes and all.

Their boots crunch along the gravel, and they turn toward a smaller path going toward a set of trees. Cam rubs his forehead; he's been distracted all day.

"Is everything okay?" she asks.

He nods, shooting her a smile that doesn't smooth out his wrinkles. "It's . . ."

She's quiet, waiting. The Cam she remembers talks things out.

This Cam is different.

"Never mind." He shakes his head and sends another smile that, despite everything, still melts her heart.

Remy gestures toward the center of the park. "I want to show you—"

At the same time, Cam nods at a bench. "Want to sit—"

There's an awkward silence. Maybe he's going to sit her down and bring a voice to the whispers that she's been trying to avoid: they're not going to fully create the antidote in time. Then she'll have to reveal that she's losing her memories of him, too.

"Sure—"

"We can stay—"

"Let's go," Cam says. "I want to see what we're here for. Is this like that time when I surprised you with the BTS concert tickets, right outside the venue?"

Remy freezes. *When was that?*

Then, the *brrring* of a guitar echoes through the air. Cam raises an eyebrow. "Now I'm extra curious. Did Jack start a band?"

"Close," Remy says, laughing. She takes a deep breath and loops her arm into his. He stills, yet doesn't move away.

"I'm sorry." She untangles her arm. "I should have asked."

"No, no," he says quickly. "I was just lost in my thoughts."

They never had to ask before. Cam would jokingly put his head on top of hers, like a little pyramid, when he got bored waiting in line. He'd always hold out his hand to pull her up if she was sitting in the grassy center of Palo Alto High School. Remy always loved walking arm in arm with him, just like this. It made it impossible not to fall in love.

"Let's go?" she asks, trying not to think about how her confidence has been shattering all throughout this week. No one from Palo Alto High School would recognize her, not like this. Remy, the flirt of the school, is now the failure of Tokyo.

She starts walking, pulling her jacket closer. Taka's scarf is wrapped around her neck, keeping her warm. She should've returned it when she had the chance.

Something floats onto her shoulders, feather-soft. Is it snowing? The weather forecast blaring from the TV this morning had foretold of a storm coming soon, but that was supposed to be late in the day.

"Hey," Cam says softly, from behind her. "You should take this."

He slides his mittens onto her fingers. Remy squeezes her eyes shut as his faint scent of jasmine green tea with a hint of boba sweetness washes over her. She can't imagine a world without him. Why, *why* does Cam have to do these things that keep making her fall in love with him?

"And my arm, too." He crooks his elbow. "If . . . if you want."

"Fine. No take-backs." Remy giggles, tugging him forward; she doesn't want them to be late. She relishes the way he feels against her, their arms tucked close to each other's bodies.

His phone buzzes loudly from his pocket, and she looks at Cam curiously. "Do you need to take that?"

He shakes his head again. "No, it's okay. Later."

Later . . . when he remembers her? Or . . . maybe when he doesn't . . .

Remy doesn't know what to think. What will they try to do tomorrow, after they've both forgotten each other? It's something they've never talked about; something she's never even wanted to think about.

She'd considered writing a letter to future Remy, but she knows herself well enough to know that she wouldn't fall in love with someone based on one letter. Even if she asked Ellie to give her the details on a boy named Cam who she used to adore, that's all it'd feel like: someone else's love. That's why it hurts to see Cam fading away right in front of her: because she understands how easy it would be for him to step away.

Remy, through watching Cam fade away from her, has realized: it's one thing to know, yet it's another to truly *feel*.

Cam *knew* they were best friends when the photos showed their shared past. But he didn't feel it, not until he started recapturing those memories, before relearning who Remy is now, with all her hopes for TMU, her love for her sister, even her chaotic baking skills.

If not for that, if not for Naomi's antidote, it would've felt impossible. If not for this antidote being the reason he could get his license restored, he wouldn't be doing this.

But the way he'd looked at her in the train, with her back against the wall . . . or that wildly red blush up his neck after admitting he'd remembered that decadent s'mores feast on the deserted, enchanted island . . .

That surely couldn't have been just all for his license . . . right?

They walk into the grassy clearing. The midafternoon gray sky is gloomy, but once Cam sees what's in the center, his face lights up brighter than the hidden sun. "Is that— No, it can't be."

A three-piece band is setting up. From the other paths winding through Amagi Park, other people are racing for front-row spots.

Cam grins. "Did you seriously manage to find my favorite indie band in all of Japan? Scratch that, my favorite band, ever?"

"All in a day's work," she says, with a wink.

Cam shakes his head. "You're truly unstoppable, Remy Kobata."

"I called in a few favors with Minami," Remy says, with a laugh. "That's all."

Cam loves ChemiCold, this indie band, in the same way that Remy is obsessed with BTS. When she heard that ChemiCold does a pop-up show every New Year's Eve, she knew she had to find out where they'd be in advance, though the band wouldn't announce the location until fifteen minutes before they started.

Minami, having connections through her social media influencer work, was able to get all the details, even for a supposedly secret concert like this. And to see Cam grin from ear to ear, Remy would give all the favors in the world to Minami.

Cam gazes in awe at the three band members who are literally ten feet away. "Remy, *this* is amazing."

Kei, the lead singer, waves, and the crowd of a hundred-plus people that has gathered around them screams instantly. He leans into his mic to shout, "Are you ready?"

With another roar from their fans, ChemiCold bursts into a smooth, fast beat, thrumming with the vibrant energy of Namina's keyboard, Koji's electric guitar, and Kei's sharp, rising vocals, like a bird shooting off into the sky.

It's beautiful, the way the music pounds through her bones and blood, stitching itself into Remy's soul. With the cold air biting her cheeks, Cam's mittens soft on her fingers, and the music thrumming on her eardrums, oh, Remy feels *alive.*

Cam slings his arm around her as they jump to the music. "Let's take a photo! Damn. Remember when V gave his hat to the girl next to you during the BTS concert? You were *so close* to getting it!"

A memory. He discovered another memory. Her heart jumps, and she lets out a joyful shout that melts into the music.

"That was the best and worst night ever!" she laughs. "I remember that now. You gave me your hat to compensate."

They laugh as Cam fumbles with the camera, pulling it out. When it develops, they laugh until they're almost crying: Cam is jumping so high that the camera only captured his chest; Remy's so short that the photo clips out everything but the top of her forehead. He puts it into the vial. Only a millimeter melts.

That night at the concert, she loved him so much that she thought her heart would burst when he slid his hat onto her head. But those feelings have only compounded and compounded since. Through this week, she's never been so in love with who he is, hoping and longing for him to fall in love with her, too.

Time is fleeting; the night is only eight hours away, but Remy knows with all her heart that she can—she *has* to—unlock Cam's memories in time. The vial is almost all melted. Getting her Cam back is almost, almost within reach.

Cam

Remy could not have chosen a better way to ring out the old year and bring in the new. Cam had never thought he'd be able to listen to ChemiCold, *the* ChemiCold, front and center.

The last notes fade out, mingling with the crowd's reverent cheers. The band begins taking pictures with fans, but Cam stands still in pure, euphoric shock.

"C'mon, let's get a picture!" Remy pulls him toward the line. Before he can gather his thoughts—not that he's sure he ever will be able to— Cam is face-to-face with his music idols.

"Hi," he stammers, a loopy grin on his face. The members of Chemi-Cold grin back, but now Cam's not sure what else to say. *Your music got me out of a tough time. I listen to your* Premonition *album on repeat—*

"Want a photo?" Kei asks, ever so politely, nudging Cam out of his silent shock.

"Right, yes, you guys are the best, thank you," Cam blabbers, his face flushing with heat. How does he take a picture? The magical camera? No, he hasn't had a memory yet. He has to take a real one. *Hello, brain, are you on?*

Cam scrambles to pull his phone out of his pocket. "Remy, you should join this shot—"

She waves him forward. "Let me take a pic of you and the band first."

He nods eagerly, passing the phone over. "Damn. Jack is going to be so jealous."

"Why is that?" she asks.

Cam frowns. "He's obsessed with ChemiCold, too—"

Jealous. That spine-tingling feeling flashes over him. A memory.

The memory.

Cam

Since Jack has left, any time Cam spends at home stretches out into a long, lonely void. It simply hasn't been the same.

The white walls echo with just Cam's footsteps when he does find it in himself to go home. When he enters through the back, he can see through the doorway leading into CharmWorks. Mr. Yasuda is there, always, cheerily talking to customers as he rings up another sale. That smiling store owner persona is nothing like the silent, cold man that Cam knows. When Cam works shifts at the store, he always stays out of his father's way, because seeing the artificial look to his dad is too much like seeing a wax statue: almost real, but just not enough.

Cam can feel the ghosts from the past, too. In the shadows, he almost sees Jack lounging out on the couch, plucking at his electric guitar in what Cam thinks of as *The Days Before*. Mr. Yasuda hasn't uttered Jack's name a single time in the past year. Even when Cam tries to bridge the gap in their infrequent family dinners, telling his dad that he just got honors for his latest semester, just like his older brother did throughout his last year at Palo Alto High School . . . silence. At least, Cam tries to tell himself, his dad doesn't try to cut him off.

But it's as if Jack simply doesn't exist.

That is, until the day of his flight to Tokyo. Until Cam stands at the doorstep, his backpack weighing down his shoulders—he couldn't spring for the cost of bringing a suitcase over, so he split the baggage fee for Remy's incredibly ugly suitcase—and he's wrapping his scarf around his shoulders. He's just about to head to Remy's, next door, so that her parents can drive them to the airport.

"Cam."

He jolts, not expecting his dad to have remembered his flight, even though Cam had marked it on the fridge calendar.

Mr. Yasuda stands behind him, back hunched forward, with the look of a bulldog. Stubborn, even to the last moment.

"You're still going on that trip with the Kobata girl," his dad says flatly, but there's a question to it. Cam knows what it is, after years of hearing Jack and his dad bicker: Why would Cam hang out with *her*, when the Kobatas barely make any money compared to the rest of Palo Alto? Why doesn't Cam spend his time with any of the richer students?

"Yeah, it's the last time I'll have a trip with her—with anyone, really—before I start college."

But, to Cam's surprise, his dad's voice softens. "MIT. Did you open the early decision results yet? I know it's a yes, but just to be sure—"

"Oh, yeah," Cam says vaguely, even though he hasn't even gotten close to checking the admissions portal yet.

Mr. Yasuda claps him on the shoulder. "That's my boy. After a stellar degree at MIT, you'll be able to garner business meetings with the best of the national suppliers, and CharmWorks will be catapulted to a new level of success."

"Uh-huh." That pit in Cam's stomach is beginning to open. His skills with magical alchemy were just a way for Mr. Yasuda to get his son into one of the top Ivy Leagues. It was never about Cam's passion for alchemy; it's only ever been about prestige. It's only ever been about his dad's shop. Cam has to get back to Remy's side, where he can breathe, where there's room for him to be himself. "Well, I have to catch my flight—"

"If you see Jack with that girlfriend of his, remember this," Mr. Yasuda says suddenly.

Cam snaps his head up, his heartbeat pounding in overdrive. *No. Don't tell me anything. Whatever it is, I don't want to hear—*

Mr. Yasuda steps closer, placing his hands on Cam's shoulders. "Remember, always. This is what no one tells you about love: it's cursed. It claws the insides out of you, it changes and twists everything you want until you're living, breathing for someone else. When they've gone and left, there's nothing left of you."

"Dad—"

Cam cuts himself off. His father is crying, those hunched shoulders shaking with emotion.

Mr. Yasuda continues. "Do you remember how your mom lay there, on the hospital bed, like she had all the time in the world? She told me not to worry. Not to worry! Like she was going to get better. She didn't. She didn't, and she just left us behind."

Cam can't speak. Words stick in his throat, painful as knives.

Then, Mr. Yasuda looks up to stare at Cam with reddened eyes. "Don't fall in love. You'll only be left behind. Before you know it, they'll be gone forever."

That's the truth, isn't it, Cam thinks to himself. Those words resonate more than his father will ever know, seeping into his pores like powdered arsenic, and clawing under his skin. This is what he's felt, time and time again as he remembers his mother passing away in his father's arms.

Cam nods, his throat dry. "I know, Dad. You're right. I don't believe in love. It never works out."

Don't fall in love. You'll only be left behind.

Cam

A flash of gray sky; he's back at Amagi Park, and ChemiCold has their arms draped around him for a photo.

This was a key switch memory. If not *the* key switch, the one where everything started going wrong.

The weight of the past is enough to make him stumble away from the band, despite their confused stares. The crowd quickly surges around him for their chance for pictures. Cam feels like the other fans have their hands wrapped around his neck, even as they just push on past. There's no room to breathe.

"Cam!" Remy's calling to him, but he can't speak.

This newfound recollection has punched Cam straight in the gut. He'd lost those memories of him and his dad—even though she wasn't in it—*because* all he could think about in that moment was her. That he loved her. That he wanted to be with her, but that he couldn't, not as anything more than best friends.

As much as he tried to deny it before, she was so strongly a part of his thoughts, his days, that it was as if she was really there with him, present in his mind—and in his heart—even if she wasn't in the memory itself.

This was why he'd never confessed to Remy.

This was why he had to let her go. He wanted her to make her choices for her best possible life, free of him and his narrow future.

He stumbles around someone, mumbling a hasty apology, but he can barely see where he's going.

He was too damn afraid, the way he's afraid now. His past changed his future; he'll be losing his precious best friend and alchemy license in the same night.

Outside of that clammy, hot crowd, as soon as he gets out and the winter breeze stings at his skin, he slumps onto the grass. His head reels as the darkening sky spins around him.

The truth isn't cold and strange.

His fear doesn't feel foreign, like something his body can reject. He knows that this is the truth; it's a part of him as much as his breath spitting in and out of his lungs. This second-guessing, this inability to chase things, the way his worries claw at him from the inside out, it's more him than his hands that tremble at his sides. He slides them back into his jacket, so that Remy can't see as she touches his shoulder.

"What is it?" Remy asks, but it sounds like she's speaking from far, far away. "Breathe, Cam, breathe."

what what what

All he can hear are echoes of his dad's broken words.

This is what no one tells you about love: it's cursed.

cursed cursed

cursed

Piece by piece, he feels the pain of this truth pull him apart, all over again.

He wants to be greedy, to keep Remy close, because she's everything to him.

Let her go.

But he'll only be able to dream about what could've been, instead of the ways he'll miss the softness of her lips and the roughness of her kisses. Because, he knows, if he were to taste her sweetness, he'd be done for.

Remy doesn't deserve someone like him. All the ways he's broken: his broken family, the way he's hesitant and has to calculate every risk like he's trying to test out a new hypothesis, and *is it worth it . . .* he hates all these parts of himself.

But, as it is, he's falling in love with the Remy that he knows now. Yet he can't love Remy like this. He can't let all the ways he's broken break her, too.

His love is cursed; he knows that now.

And he can't let Remy be cursed alongside him. He loves her enough to not curse her, too.

Let. Her. Go.

Hell, this is going to hurt. Even if he doesn't remember everything about her, that empty part of him that's been throbbing in his mind, like a migraine he can't shake, will be with him until the end of time.

She truly needs someone who loves her, completely.

If this is the last thing he can ever give her, it's his friendship cemented into a *forever*, but it's also a goodbye.

Remy is frantic. "Cam? What's going on?"

He stands up, dusting his hands off. He has to think fast. Remy can smell his lies from a mile away. It has to be the truth, but twisted. "I told Naomi I'd hang out with her tonight, to talk about alchemy."

"Oh!" Remy blinks with surprise, and Cam hates himself for the way she tries to say, brightly, "I think we have time before the dinner I set up at the illuminations in Yebisu, and—"

"I can't go." Cam tries to veil all the emotion from his voice, his eyes, his frown, the way his hands are shaking. It's impossible, yet he has to do this for her.

"I don't think this is going to work out," he says. "Let's just call it quits."

Remy opens her mouth, but no words come out. Then, finally, a whisper. "*What?*"

"I don't need the antidote anymore." He hands it to her.

"Wh—"

"I'm fine." His voice is colder than the winter air, and it cuts him to his core. It cuts every memory he's rediscovered with her; each sparkling memory that he's cherished like a jewel, and shattered them all into dust. "I've lost my memories of our friendship. I've been fine. I still remember everything I need: everything about alchemy, my parents, Jack. I'll be okay. But you're losing memories of me, right?"

Her eyes drop; he's hit the truth right on the mark.

"I can tell," he says boldly, even though it was just a guess. *Dammit.* He'd wondered—earlier, she hadn't remembered the concert that they'd gone to, even though as the fireworks sparkled at the end, they'd both sworn it was one of the best nights of their lives.

Remy looks *pissed*. "Why do you get to choose who remembers or who forgets?"

"I'm fine with what I'm missing."

The meaning of those words hits Remy straight in the chest. She stumbles back, the vial slipping from her shaking fingers and onto the grass. Cam rummages through his jacket, takes a photo of himself, unsmiling and all. Then he picks up the vial, uncorks it, and drops in the last photo.

"There." When the picture meets the surface of the antidote, it sparkles with light as it dissolves the last drops. It's fully liquid, and this heavy memory has melted the antidote completely. That joy he expected feels flat and dead inside his chest. "Drink."

She shakes her head.

"Remy—"

"Don't you care?" Remy sounds like her heart is bleeding with every word, and Cam tries not to breathe, because surely he's going to crack. "I know now that things weren't perfect—not if we're here, our friendship falling apart like this—but weren't we always *us*? Didn't we always live in a world all our own, being the annoying best friends that laughed at jokes no one else understood?"

"I don't remember how you and I worked," he says blandly.

If the Cam before the potion were to ask one thing from this current Cam, it'd be to save Remy. He knows this, a thousand times over. The old Cam wouldn't be able to accept the antidote, knowing that his best friend would be left in pain.

The vial trembles in her hands.

He repeats, "Look, this potion isn't going to do anything for me. So you should take it." Cam won't let himself look away when her eyes well up with tears.

"No. Why?"

"Please, Remy," he says. "Honestly, the memories you sparked for me . . . thank you. You and I, our friendship was good, but maybe it's just meant to be that: just a high school friendship. And I have people who have my back, that's all I need."

"You are what I need."

"I think it's time we both moved on."

A tear spills over, tracing the curve of her cheek. "I've spent years wishing for good luck, dreaming as I blew out birthday candles, and believing in a happily ever after, and it's all come crashing down like this. But if that's what you want . . . if you truly want to move on—"

Remy tips the vial up, and drinks it in a flash. One moment, her lips are to the rim; the next, she tosses it furiously to the ground, and it rolls under one of the bushes.

"For you." Her fingers curl into fists; her round eyes are sad. She wipes off her mouth with the back of her hand, like the antidote disgusts her.

Cam's heart aches. His fingers tense, wanting to cup her cheek, to wrap her in his arms and never feel the cold of winter ever again. This is the last time he'll see her and remember who they are to each other. This is the last time he'll be the Cam who is best friends with Remy. Even though it's only in this tortured, awful way.

As he turns toward the exit, his head tucked, each step is beyond agony; it's a cry for help with words he can't speak. But he walks away, quietly, until he reaches the cover of the trees, and then he runs.

He runs and runs until his lungs burn and scream. The clouds overhead crackle ominously.

"I thought alchemy would always save me," he says, and he's not even sure if he's saying it to himself, the stormy sky, or no one at all. "But it broke the one good thing I ever had."

Cam falls to his knees as rain pours down, icy and unforgiving, pulling him into one final memory.

Cam

Cam could stay in Beni's Apothecary for the rest of his life. There are a ton of potions behind the bar that he'd love to study. But they're not here for that. Cam knows that Remy hasn't been telling the truth about the fortune that she got yesterday. It wasn't about her TMU interviews. There's something about the way her eyes drop just a moment too fast, the way her teeth skim her lip and then bite down.

"I want to be sure that the fortune from Mr. Yoshino is right," Remy blurts out, and Beni Yoshino, the namesake and proprietor of this apothecary, raises her eyebrow.

Nervousness swells through Cam, like an elixir flowing over. What's her fortune actually about?

Remy's mumbling—something she never does. All Cam can tell is what she says at the end: "I asked if . . . if I had a soulmate."

"Wait . . . what exactly did Mr. Yoshino say?" Cam is too scared of the answer, yet can't stop himself from asking. *Me? Who is it?*

"He said that I don't have a soulmate," Remy says.

Cam's brain short-circuits. *Not me. How? Rather than no one at all—it* should *be me.*

I want it to be me.

The thought washes over him like the glasses throughout the apothecary have broken, and the elixirs have become a wave, twisting and pulling him underwater, until he can't breathe.

Somehow, Cam *knew*. He always knew that their futures weren't going to be together, but to hear it straight from a fortune-teller, someone who's *known* for his accurate readings, well, it hurts. It hurts like a fairy tale where he expected to have a happily ever after, but he finds out that doesn't exist: exactly like what happened to his parents. His mom passed away when he was ten, from cancer, and he doesn't even need a wicked stepmother to make his life miserable, not with his dad the way he is.

Yet—

I had always hoped it would be me.

————◆————

The rose-gold love potion sparkles through the veil of dust on the glass. Cam wants to understand it, down to the molecular level.

But the moment his fingers twitch toward the bottle, Beni's eyes cut to him. This woman knows exactly the power of what she holds, and he has a pretty strong feeling that she's not going to let him just waltz out with a restricted potion.

And he's not here to study it, not anymore.

The lies he spouts out come easily: *Can I take a sample of it? I can study its impact. . . . If you apply magic, you* can *solve things that normally might not work. . . .*

Anything. Anything to be with Remy, forever. His best friend has always been his world, even if he's pretended to be just her best friend. He's always wanted more. He's always wanted forever.

He has always loved her.

He and Remy stare at each other, half the elixir in her glass; the other half in his.

No matter what his father says, no matter how his father has been cursed by love, he doesn't want that to be him, too.

He wants Remy. He wants to always see the way she's wide-eyed in wonder. The way she smiles at him when she thinks he's not looking, and he knows his dorkisms and quietness are safe with her.

Even when she goes on dates with someone else, and he waits for her to notice him, even though, deep down, he knows he *should* make her notice him. Tell her the truth.

He has always, *always* been in love with Remy Kobata, and he's been too damn scared to say a thing.

The light from above meets the meniscus of the potion and sparkles like little rose-gold firecrackers, dancing on the surface.

He needs this, but it isn't for study.

She meets his gaze. "Cheers."

"Cheers," he says, hoping this potion will help him say what he's always wanted to tell her.

I love you, Remy Kobata.

I love—

The world tears those words from his mouth, and all of a sudden, he's standing in the street outside the apothecary, with a girl he doesn't remember—

He tilts his head to the side. "Who are you?"

Remy

By the time Remy can find it in herself to move, the sky has seeped from a murky gray to pooling into a dark, moonless gray black. The band is gone; the fans are all home with their friends, probably replaying videos of the flash concert as they eat traditional New Year's Eve toshikoshi soba, or prepare for their first shrine visit of the new year.

All Remy can replay is the way that Cam looked at her like she was dead to him. Like all the past seventeen years never meant anything. Even though he'd recovered a handful of memories, he never *felt* the same way she had, like each moment was more precious than a snowflake from the first snow of the year, unmatchable and one of a kind.

I've lost my memories of our friendship. I've been fine.

He drilled that into her, pushing her to take the antidote. Her tears are not dried, but it feels like they'll never dry.

Her phone rings. She picks it up instantly. "Cam—"

"Remy," the voice responds, and it's definitely not Cam. She stares at the number, some Japanese number. "It's Taka."

"I'm busy—"

"I was able to set up the final interview for you. But it has to be *now*. I need you to come to the TMU campus right away."

She doesn't have time for that. She has to try to find Cam, try to explain things to him, try to get him—

"Cam asked me to make sure you'd go, as a favor. He said that this was the last thing he wanted for you, as your former best friend."

Angry tears burst at the corners of her eyes. Damn him. "I'll be there."

Remy

Remy smooths down the dress suit Taka had shoved at her moments ago, waving her toward a restroom to change. She checks her face for tears, one last time. Her heart is lead; this is the last thing she wants to be doing. Still, she knocks.

A voice says, "Come in."

Her fingers want to drop her bag, spin on her heels, and race out into the sheets of rain that are pouring outside. She wants to find Cam, curl her fingers around his jacket lapels, and shake sense into him.

But he asked for this.

This was the last request from her best friend.

She pushes open the door of Office #13 of Tokyo Magical University, and stops short.

The guy with the black-rimmed glasses stares back at her from the other side of the desk. Mr. Hagiwara looks absolutely pissed, with his nose wrinkled and his lip slightly curled. Taka sits next to him, his fingers laced.

"Welcome, Remy," Taka says. "Please sit."

"This better be worth it, to miss part of my New Year's Eve with my new girlfriend," Mr. Hagiwara snarls. "Let's get this over fast."

She slides into the chair on the other side of the desk from them, wishing she didn't feel the itch of this suit that feels too new and starchy.

"Tell us why you want to attend TMU," Mr. Hagiwara says.

"I don't know."

Truly, she doesn't know anymore.

He looks like he's going to kick his chair back and walk out, but Taka raises his hand.

"At first, I didn't know why," Remy says slowly, correcting herself. Her heart is dry and empty, but she's recited her reasons a thousand times—some of the few memories of Cam that haven't disappeared yet. "When I applied, I hadn't even walked through the halls . . ."

Why? Why did she want to attend? Especially if she doesn't know what she wants to do, or what she wants to become?

No. That's not true. She's been forgetting her dreams. Remy had always wanted to become something. *More* than the Second-to-Last Girl. Going to her dream school has been her choice, from the very beginning to now, something she's always wanted to do for herself.

The way she's been able to interview for TMU, through the countless hours of working to earn enough for the plane ticket, the way she'd practiced just as many hours more . . . This truly is something that's all hers. But it's even more special, because her friends helped her, too. Thanks to Cam, thanks to Taka, thanks to Ellie . . . She wouldn't be here without those she loves—loved—wants to love . . .

So she has to fight through this—for them, and most of all for what *she* wants—and then fight to get back to Cam's side.

Remy stares straight back at Mr. Hagiwara. "Once I attend, I'll have a million reasons to stay. But what I've loved the most about TMU is that it allows students to *figure out* what they want to do—it's the highest-rated university in the world. I can have a safe place to explore who exactly I've always wanted to be. The way it's set up to allow exploration between career paths, whether the Magic Reversal Team or International Magical Relations . . . it's truly one of a kind. I've even reached out to a few alumni to ask them about their experiences, and it's all been glowing responses."

Mr. Hagiwara purses his lips, looking like a sour fish at the aquarium, all bubbles and no words. Finally, he says, "Tell me any inclinations of what you might want to do."

"As you can tell," Remy says, "I'm not sure. But I do like books; that's something that's called out to me ever since I was little. My best friend—his thing is always puzzles, but mine is definitely books. If we saw anything that mixed the two, we'd buy it right away, like a book about puzzles, or a puzzle about books."

She'd even found the neatest thing ever, for their first year at college: a book about the best puzzles and riddles in history, 365 days of them. Remy had even bought a copy for herself, so that even if they were apart, she'd be able to go through the riddles with him, too. But he won't remember her, even with that book, anymore.

Remy draws in a deep breath, the way Cam breathes when his thoughts are overwhelming him. *In four, out six.*

She begins again, feeling like part of Cam is with her, still. "That's kind of what I want to do, but with magic and books. It'd be neat to learn about Magical Publishing—which I know is a degree option here at TMU—but also have the opportunity to explore other courses."

"Hmph."

"Even being at this campus has given me new ideas. For the longest time, I wasn't aware that magical colleges even existed, even though I've been a member of the magical society since birth. What if I helped outreach for magical colleges like TMU? What if I helped future students find a place like me?"

Hagiwara blinks. "An admissions counselor. Are you trying to take my job?"

Remy flashes him a bright smile. "I think that TMU is amazing, and you're working at a wonderful institution."

He harrumphs, but he doesn't cut her down this time. In fact, he looks slightly *honored.* Then, he glances at Taka, lets out another sniff, and crosses his arms.

Taka slides in, asking Remy a few more questions, giving her reasons to talk about her past experience working in bookstores and her parents' tea shop, as well as the book club at school.

After her last answer, about how she fundraised to pay for one of her favorite authors to visit her school, Mr. Hagiwara sniffles again. Remy wonders if she should offer him a tissue, or the vial of *Cold Be Gone* that she has tucked in her suitcase. She also wonders if she should just walk straight out and go find Cam, to cut her losses.

But Cam had asked her to do this.

"I'm done here." Mr. Hagiwara stands up, jerking his head into a shadow of a nod toward Remy and Taka. He starts typing on his phone and strides out.

The silence stretches as Remy stares at the door. She'd tried so hard just for him to be *that* rude?

Finally, she asks, "Did he just— Why the *hell* does he think I'd want to go to this school with the way he's acting?"

Taka clears his throat. "Hagiwara's the only one like this at TMU, though he does hold some power. But that's why my role is to keep him in check, thanks to my bloodline and, well, my donation. I found out today that he just didn't want to accept you after he saw us together."

"Seriously?" Remy asks. She's had enough of being the one to blame.

"It's not your fault." Taka looks away, his shoulders stiff. "I never explained the rest of my fortune from Mr. Yoshino."

I don't see what this has to do with me, Remy wants to say, but that look on Taka's face changes her thoughts. "What do you mean?"

"Mr. Yoshino—Uncle Michi, I used to call him—told me that I needed to go to college at TMU to find the one person who would see me for who I am. The one person who would love me, when all else failed and crumbled around me." Taka's eyes met hers. "He said I'd meet this person the next time that I would visit the Good Luck Café."

"That could be anyone," Remy says, even though her voice is rising.

"Ever since that fortune—ask Naomi, she knows—I've been searching for the Good Luck Café a lot, just to get in and prove the fortune is wrong." His laugh is cold and cynical. "I wasn't ready to believe it. There's this phrase that you can't translate to English, not exactly. *Koi no Yokan*. The feeling when you look at someone, that you know that you'll fall in love."

I'd been thinking of Koi no Yokan, *too, when I walked into the Good Luck Café*, Remy realizes. But at that time, her thoughts were wrapped around Cam.

"I thought Mr. Yoshino . . . He's part of your family, right? How do you know he's telling the truth?"

"I'd never heard of Uncle Michi telling a wrong fortune. They definitely wouldn't dare do it directly to me."

"Well, that must be so nice to be so powerful—"

"But he messed up yours. On purpose."

"*What*?"

"Mr. Yoshino told you that you didn't have a soulmate," Taka replies. "That's a lie."

Remy's heart pounds.

Taka slides his phone over the desk, so she can see the screen. "Look."

It's a photo of her tea cup. She recognizes the white ceramic laced with gold, and the two blotches inside of it.

"I've learned some fortune-telling from my uncle," Taka says. "You're the spot in the middle; see how it wavers at the edges? You're still figuring out who you want to be. You try things even though you're not sure what the end result will be like, and that's something I really admire about you."

She's not here for compliments. "What's that blob to the right? There's that line connecting it to the center splotch of tea—not saying that I believe this—that's supposed to be me."

He swallows. "That's me. If you look at it carefully, it's in the shape of a bird, with its wings outstretched. The character used for my name, Taka, means hawk."

Remy can't breathe. *Taka is supposed to be my soulmate?*

"When I was younger, my family called me 'little warrior' as a nickname, because hawks represent warriors. That's the kind of person I am. I'd fight for you, if you'd let me. I'd take your side a million times over. Maybe you and I won't agree all the time, but you know I'd only want the best for you."

"Then why didn't you tell me this until now?" Remy hisses. She stares at the picture of her supposed future with Taka. "You're saying that I should've been soulmates with you—but you waited and waited? Until a week after your family told me I can't ever fall in love? Hours before I forget Cam forever?"

Taka looks down. "I didn't go back to my family to ask for the photograph until today. I'm sorry it took so long. I had a lot to get into place to start talking to them again."

Oh.

For the first time, she takes in Taka's weariness—the faint undereye circles, the way his shoulders are stooped. Remy connects the pieces of how he'd had to leave their hangouts early to rush off to a so-called gig.

"You shouldn't have."

He shakes his head. "Cam forgetting his memories . . . that happened in part because of me. If you had found out the real fortune, you might not have taken the potion with Cam. Maybe . . . maybe you would've given me a chance. Regardless, my family knows that you're not to be touched by them, anymore."

His promises are pretty, like light catching glass vials. She doesn't need to look closer to wonder if there might be poison inside.

"I won't let this fortune tell me who to love," she whispers.

His dark eyes are soft and sad. "I know. I've only known you for a handful of days, and once I found out the real fortune, I had a feeling you wouldn't follow what someone else says is your fate, not if you don't truly want it . . ."

He trails off, and she can almost hear the unsaid words, *But I wish you wanted to be with me.*

Remy's voice cracks. "I'm sorry. I can't be all things to all people, and I learned that a little too late. I have to get my best friend back from the mess I got him into, whether he remembers me or not. I didn't ask you to rejoin your family. I came here for the TMU interview, not, well, *this.*"

He looks at her, quietly, as if she's the one not seeing clearly. "Did you check your email?"

Again, that request. Remy fishes her phone out of her pocket, and stares at the pop-up: *Your Admission Results for Tokyo Magical University.*

With a quick flick of her fingers, she opens the email. *Congratulations, you have been accepted to Tokyo Magical University . . .*

Damn.

"You won over Hagiwara, on your own terms. But for you and me . . . I mean it. Maybe you don't believe in us, but I do. Maybe not now, but in the future," Taka says, as he stands up to open the door for her. "But for now, you have to go."

Remy hurries to the door, but in front of him, she pauses. With a twist of her wrist, she unwraps the scarf from around her neck, and hands it back to him. "Thank you, Taka."

"Good luck," he says softly, as she races out the door.

She has to find Beni's Apothecary. If Remy found it once, surely she can find it again.

Her feet fly over the ground. If she runs, she can cover the most area in the few hours she has left. She has to find it, before Cam's lost to her forever.

———— ◦ ————

One hour later, her soles feel like they're bleeding. She has hopped on and off the Yamanote train line more times than she can count, pushing past the groups of friends red-faced from drinking parties and families heading to their first shrine visit of the year. Surely the apothecary will be somewhere central. Somewhere that anyone can stumble across it.

Her phone keeps ringing. She shoots her older sister a message: *Looking for Beni's Apothecary. Let me know if you find it.*

It's not the new year, it's not, not yet. But seconds of searching turn into minutes and before she knows it, the clock in the station—she's in Meguro—rings solemn: eleven o'clock.

Remy stumbles out of the station and stares at the buses circling the roundabout, and the taxis traveling close behind. Headlights flash into her eyes; a moment of overwhelming brightness—then complete darkness.

She kneels on the cold concrete. Even scouring through that magical social media app, Mahine, hasn't given a single clue. Everyone else is busy posting about magical new year's festivities. Beni's Apothecary is probably hidden in some obscure corner of Tokyo that she'll never stumble upon, definitely not tonight, and maybe never. It might even be already closed right now.

Remy buries her head in her hands, ignoring the strange looks from the passersby. She lets out a shout, wordless and ringing with all the frustrations and all the things she never said to Cam when she could have.

"Remy." A familiar voice beams through the darkness, filling her heart with hope. A tall figure, swathed in shadows, steps forward.

Her voice cracks. "Cam."

Remy

Her heart beats out of her chest like her body is flying up into the clouds, spinning into the mist, bursting into snowflakes.

Cam, Cam, Cam.

But—the timbre of his voice is different, huskier.

"There you are," says Jack, headlights flashing over his face, and Remy despairs.

"I thought you were Cam," she whispers.

Jack kneels next to her. "Remy. *Rems.*"

He uses the nickname he'd used only when they were younger. Jack's trying his hardest to coerce her out of this endlessly cloudy, dark night.

"You're like a little sister to me," Jack says softly. "Seeing you in pain hurts. I want you to smile."

Remy tries to tilt her lips up, but they only tip back down as the tears threaten to spill over.

"I can't," she whispers, her voice hoarse.

"Ellie's been running around Tokyo looking for Beni's Apothecary for you. Me and Taka, too. Cam said . . . Cam said you're starting to forget him. That's hurting him, Rems."

"Cam said he's fine without me." Her head droops. "He gave me the antidote to drink. He didn't want it anymore."

"He didn't?" Jack frowns, like he's trying to work out something in his brain.

"That doesn't sound like the Cam I know." Ellie is illuminated by the light pouring from the exit of Meguro Station; instantly, her older sister swoops forward and engulfs her in a hug, even with Remy awkwardly squatting. "Why didn't you answer my calls?"

Remy leans into her sister's embrace, but looks questioningly at Jack.

"I messaged her that I'd found you," he says sheepishly. "She was worried."

"*Worried* is an understatement," Ellie says, pulling Remy up, and nearly dragging her to a nearby bench. She plops Remy in the middle, gathering her younger sister's hands in hers, and cuts straight to the chase: "Did you tell Cam how you feel?"

Jack coughs, eyeing a vending machine. "I should get a drink."

"I didn't—tonight was supposed to be the time, the night, after he remembered who I was," Remy says. "I had the plans, remember? Yebisu, with all the illuminations, telling him after this week of fun, and it turned out like this."

Jack quickly backs away. "I'm getting a drink."

Ellie shakes her head. "Didn't the soulmate elixir teach you anything?"

Her older sister is pouring salt *and* fire into Remy's wounds.

"But—"

"Look, for things like your college major, it's okay to be undecided and not have everything figured out," Ellie says. "But if it truly matters to you? If *he* is who you think about? I saw you two: you were both falling in love with each other, all over again, through this week. You don't have to have yourself figured out to be perfect for someone, so long as that person is ready to figure things out with you. It helps to have the same goals for long-term compatibility, but you don't need to have every single answer to be in love."

Those words fall into place as smooth as sliding mittens onto her hands and finding, impossibly, that they fit perfectly.

"Don't you love him?" Ellie asks, softer.

Remy wants to scream. Of course Cam is the one that she loves.

"When are you going to finally confess?" Ellie asks. "When you two are married to different people? When it's too late?"

Remy's throat is dry. "That's why I took the potion in the first place. I had been searching for the right timing."

"Life doesn't ring an alarm and say, *Hello, I'm here*," Ellie says. "You have to grab it for yourself. Magic only goes so far."

"I know. I *know* that I messed up because I wanted some sort of easy, magical way to make him fall in love with me, because I never did anything about my feelings. I was trusting fate in the form of a magical potion, but fate's really about the actions we take ourselves, right? I'm trying, though, I promise. Like, I worked so hard to apply for TMU. It's something I'm doing for *me*, and I've been giving it my all."

"And that's good. Because the future you want is right around the corner, if only you look for it," Ellie responds softly. "Take those big moments, and those quiet moments, too. The ones that no one realizes are perfect, but are so damn special. Even if it's just the sunlight dancing on the rim of a cup. Or a sip of tea before it gets too cold. Happiness is so fleeting, and contentment even more so. Life is about chasing happiness, Remy. Chase those moments that shine brighter than starlight, and spend time with those people who make your life glow."

That's Cam. Irrevocably, Cam.

After all these years, all the paths seemed to point to him. He is the one that makes her soul feel alive, even if it's been a secret she's kept to herself. She's kissed a hell of a lot of frogs, trying to wash him out of her mind, but nothing has ever washed away the memories of him. Cam is her home, the place where she belongs.

There's no damn way she's going to let some fortune or potion tell *her* who to love.

Jack shuffles over with warm cans from the vending machine.

"Do you want black coffee?" he asks. "I also got a café au lait and a hojicha latte. Any takers?"

Remy shakes her head, squinting at the line of stores across the street, where the buses keep driving past. A light keeps flickering on and off, like a beacon. "I need to find Beni's Apothecary . . ."

A figure walks out of the darkness.

Taka, with his scarf wrapped around his neck. His eyes are soft and sad. "Hi, Remy."

The bulb finally flashes on behind him, staying lit and illuminating a sleek silver sign, with black letters carved in deep: BENI'S APOTHECARY.

Ellie glances worriedly at the clock on her phone: it flashes 11:11. "The time—"

Remy pushes off the park bench. "It's not midnight yet."

Jack helps Ellie up as he gives Remy a worried look.

"Let us know if you need anything," Jack says, in that older brother tone, careful and protective. "Anything at all. Call us, okay?"

"Seriously, we're here," Ellie echoes.

Remy nods, but there's no time to waste. She spins on her heel, heading toward Taka. His shoulders soak up the amber-yellow lights, but his face is shadowed.

"I'll open the door for you," he says. "It's locked, except for family."

She looks up gratefully at Taka. "I couldn't have done this without you. So, thank you."

He flinches, like her words are a dagger, cutting into him. "Remy . . ."

They're standing in the doorway, his fingers gripping the handle, but something makes her pause. His eyes lock onto hers.

"Can I"—his voice is slightly jagged—"can I have a minute? Just one minute of your time."

She owes him a lot. A minute is the least she can give back. "What is it?"

His hand falls away from the door, and he shoves his hands back in his pockets.

"I was trying to decide whether or not to be honest with you about this . . ." He trails off, biting his lip.

"Say it." What's on his mind?

"I know. I know you have a lot going on," he says softly. "Now, more than ever."

Her stomach twists. There's a vulnerability in the way his eyelashes brush against his skin when he shuts his eyes for a moment, like what he's saying is paining him.

"But what I realized from separating from my family is that some-times we need to choose the people we want around us. We have to fight for them."

Fight for him, Remy.

Taka had encouraged her, from the very start. But . . . had he been thinking something else the whole time?

She reels back. "You're telling me . . . *this*"—if it is what she thinks it is—"now?"

This close, she can see the slight indents on Taka's eyebrow from a piercing. This close, she can see his barely visible sharp intake.

"I'm scared to lose you," Taka says. "I want to believe that fortune is wrong, but every moment I've been with you has been like a moment of joy from someone else's life. It's been brief, I know, but I've . . . I've never felt anything similar with anyone else. I told you, I don't date. I never found anyone who makes me feel the way you do, that lurch in my stomach, the ease of our conversations, the way I want to do some-thing, become something for you . . . Remy . . . I—I—"

From inches away, she can see the rapid rise and fall of his chest; well-built despite how he looks slim from afar.

"Stay with me, please," he whispers.

The pressure of their closeness is too much. She's forgetting something—something so damn important, it should be right at this spot with her. But she's got her phone, she's got her wallet . . . What is she forgetting?

I'm forgetting Cam.

"I want to be with you," he whispers. "I want to be the person that you'll never forget."

Taka has done so much for her, with the interview, with finding the apothecary, even down to his scarf when she was cold, or his handkerchief when she was crying . . . He's given so much of himself, without asking.

Her eyes blur with tears, her hand on the door.

"I can't be that person for you," Remy whispers as Taka bows his head. "Cam is the one I dream of. Cam is the one who I know, if he's by my side, I can get through anything. I want to be your friend, I truly do. But I can't be anything more, not when my heart belongs to someone else."

Taka lets out a soft, sad breath. He reaches his hand out, and at first, Remy thinks he's going to hold her, but his fingers rest on the handle instead. A lock clicks; the door is now open.

"I think I knew all along," he says. "You should go. My minute is up, and you have the rest of your life to get started on. Good . . . good luck, Remy."

His eyes catch hers, one last time, as she pushes inside the apothecary.

Remy

Beni's Apothecary is dark and subdued. It feels like Remy is walking through the Milky Way. Though it's past closing time, faint lights illuminate the bar; a man sits on a stool with the bartender before him, stirring up one last drink. Taka had let her in, but hadn't followed her inside, simply saying, *This is as far as I can go. I can't watch you chase after someone else like this, Remy.*

"Ah," is all Beni says when she sees Remy, gesturing her to the seat next to Mr. Yoshino.

It doesn't feel right to sit, not when she should be searching for Cam, but she needs answers. Beni pushes over a steaming, rolled-up towel. Remy ignores the shibori. She's not here for a casual drink.

"I need to change things," she says hoarsely. "That love potion—"

"I know," Beni cuts in. "I hadn't heard from my estranged nephew in years. Finally he showed up to try to get an antidote for you. Even I didn't see that one coming."

Her eyes sting. *Taka. Thank you.* She owes him more than she can ever repay.

Remy spins around to stare down Mr. Yoshino. "Why did you lie about my fortune?"

"We will do anything to protect one of our blood." Mr. Yoshino's lips are set. "We wanted you to believe it, to lean into it . . ." He sighs, and then admits, "But we never expected you to fight it in the way you did. To be able to find this apothecary so soon after . . . we realized it was a sign that we needed to do something. After all, you wanted to fall in love with someone other than Taka. Our interests are aligned. That was why Beni allowed you to take that love potion."

"Then—then, can you fix things?" The clock shows 11:28 P.M. There's really no time.

"The Old Families can't interfere anymore; these last minutes are yours alone. Between the potion and letting Taka feel like he's done his part in supporting you, the Old Families have been behind your back, Remy Kobata, whether you noticed it or not. We played chaperone to your little date in Future Street—not everyone gets to test out those BOXED cars, you know. How did you get exclusive, fully paid seats to the nicest magical dinner in all of Tokyo? Who do you think parted the crowds so that you'd get front-row access to that band Cam likes so much?"

Her heart thuds. She'd noticed how well things had come together, but she'd chalked it up to her planning and some almost-magical luck.

"It didn't work." Remy's heart tears with every word. "I drank a *soulmate elixir* with my best friend. I—I wanted him to fall in love with me. Why *isn't* Cam in love with me?"

"Because of fate," Beni says simply. "We learned firsthand why love potions are banned. There are too many variables, too many potential conflicts. . . . But most of all, because fate had other plans in mind."

Remy knows this.

She *knows*.

These years of stolen glimpses, heart-tugging moments. Nights of staring up at her ceiling, wishing Cam was wrapped around her. That damn longing of wanting to be by his side, to soak up the world with him, always. Always, that gut-aching longing.

But magic—one of the things that brought them together, a spark of shared connections and moments—that alone isn't enough to keep them together. Remy should have known that she and Cam weren't meant to be.

That she couldn't trust magic . . . if she couldn't trust herself to take action.

Magic, despite all that it is, isn't enough on its own. She needs to do something, too.

"It seems the potion won't be enough to make you two fall in love—and remember each other," Beni says. "Not if you may have been truly meant for T—"

"There's got to be something!" Remy cries out. She's wanted to be with *Cam* forever, for forever. "Naomi created an antidote. Cam wanted me to take it." Then, she adds, quieter, "There wasn't enough for two."

She sets the vial on the bar. With the faint overhead lights shining through the glass, the liquid of the full bottle swishes with rainbow hues, shimmering with magic.

Remy had only pretended to drink the antidote. When it'd rolled under the bushes, Cam hadn't even bothered to notice that it was still full. While Cam had easily dismissed their lifelong friendship, she couldn't stand the idea of being without him. She couldn't fathom a world without Cam to make (sometimes peppery) cookies for, to talk over his new experiments with, to solve the latest level of Candy Crush together . . . For her, no matter if he was at MIT and she was in Japan, she'd always wanted to stay best friends, even if not more.

So, of course she couldn't actually take the antidote. Not if it meant only she could be okay, and he'd forget her. What if he lost not only memories that she'd been in, but Jack and Ellie, too? What if he continually stopped remembering everyone in his life?

"With this antidote, surely there's something that you can do," Remy says desperately. "Taka said the Old Families have access to magic and potion books that no one else does."

"Well, then, this is interesting." Beni's lips quirk. "I heard from Taka about this, but he'd said you drank it all. When I looked into Professor Watanabe's paperwork, the molecular makeup is similar to the soulmate elixir you took, with a few subtle differences. The recipe is quite unique."

"Then there's a chance that this antidote might work," Remy whispers. "Can't you use that Old Family magic to double it for two? I want him to be happy." Her voice cracks. "Even if it isn't with me. I *need* to help him. I want him to have his license back, his memories back. I want *Cam* back."

Beni's eyes go up to one of the top shelves, where the empty bottle of the soulmate elixir sits, mocking her. Next to that is a thick, dusty potion book that Remy hadn't noticed before.

"Taka asked you to help me, didn't he?" Remy asks. "I'll never fall in love with him, so long as you help me with this."

Beni and Mr. Yoshino exchange glances, and Beni says, "Then you know. Taka is whom we must protect, and his match must be worthy of him. You are from a common family. It is better if you are not in love with him, for then there's nothing for him to reciprocate."

But Remy can tell: they're worried about the possibility that she could fall in love with Taka, even as much as they try to deny it could ever happen. That's why they went so far to try to get her to fall in love with someone else.

"I'll never fall in love with Taka so long as I have Cam. So long as you help me with this antidote, with fixing this mess. But—if you don't—"

Beni snaps, "You don't want to play games with the Old Families, little girl."

"I'm not. This is a plea."

Again, Mr. Yoshino and Beni exchange glances that Remy can't read.

"Fine. Make one specific potion with me, and I'll help you with the antidote," Beni says. "It requires strong emotions for this, but I can supply the magical dust—"

"I'm in."

"This may erase all of your memories of him," Beni warns. "It might undo everything you're trying to fix. Honestly, same as the initial soulmate elixir, I have no guarantees what I do will work."

This is the cost of playing with magic. This is the cost of Remy not speaking up when she could have. If she had done something before they'd walked into Mr. Yoshino's café, before this trip, at homecoming when they went as "just friends," or a million instances before. She and Cam could have been walking down the path of illuminations together, their hands entwined.

After they forget each other, they won't even walk side by side.

After this, her past with Cam might truly disappear after midnight.

With her heart in her throat, with all logic telling her *No, wait*, Remy places her hands on the counter. "I'll do it."

Beni starts walking away, behind the bar, and Remy's heart drops. But the woman goes to open a side door to let Remy in. "Come here. Take the book. It's all yours."

Before Beni or Mr. Yoshino can say another word, Remy races behind the counter, clambers up the ladder, and grabs the book. It's hefty; her hands tremble as she sets it on the counter.

Beni leans over and flips to a page in archaic Japanese, tapping it with one long finger. "It might not work."

Remy's brain whirs as she works to read and translate the Japanese directions.

"True love?" Remy replies, not daring to tear her eyes away from the page. "It wins, every time. Even if my memories get wiped, even if he'll never love me back, those days we spent were everything *in* that moment, and that's what matters. I want to keep that, but even if it's gone, that's okay. I loved every second of those days. I loved all of him in those days. Even if it took forever to realize, he loved me, too."

A moment of silence, then—

Beni's sharp "I told you so!" to Mr. Yoshino and their ensuing bickering melt away into background static. Remy doesn't have time to think about the past, not right now. She doesn't have time to worry about all the paths of the future. Remy's just going to walk on the path she's going to pick for herself.

"This is going to require a hell of a lot of refined magic dust," she mutters to herself.

But, for once, she's in luck.

A SOULMATE ACROSS THE AGES

Think of a memory of true love, of a relationship that can withstand the test of time.

With a pair of magical rose-tinted glasses, summon those feelings; collect the raw dust and draw it into the vial with 50 cc of pure water.

Which memory should she choose?

Then, Remy remembers the plane ride here, their heads bundled together. She remembers their laughter over beating level 5,517 and the way they'd devoured tiny, airplane-food-sized Häagen-Dazs cups as their reward, their lips sticky-sweet.

She knew she was in love before, but it wasn't until that moment that she'd thought she'd lost him, standing in the Shibuya intersection, that she realized just how *much* she loves Cam. And that feeling only compounded with the fortune, with hearing that she'd never have a soulmate, that she'd never be The One for Cam.

Her love for him at that moment was beautiful, even if it may be ending soon. But maybe if she makes this love potion right, then the next couple that stumbles along this potion might be able to fall in love with that same heart-wrenchingly beautiful feeling that Remy felt whenever she looked at Cam, and Cam had just turned to look at her.

Cam is home; the safe harbor to keep her heart, the best friend that challenged her to be more, to explore, to taste, to touch, to *feel*.

She slides on her old, beat-up glasses, though she doesn't need them to see what she's known all along. Her hopes and dreams shimmer bright as snow, sparkling with every heartfelt hope and joy and sorrow—because, yes, love is real and sometimes it's bittersweet; a lover isn't always perfect.

The crystal Beni has set in front of her attracts the sparks of raw magic like a magnet. When she carefully gathers it in her hands and pours it into a glass bottle partially filled with water, she gives it a swirl, and it's like a snow globe. But there's no time to be enchanted; she dusts her fingers off. "What's next?"

"This." Beni pours her potion into a rose-tinted glass, shaped in a heart, like the soulmate elixir Remy and Cam first took. The one she's made is still pale, and hasn't aged in the way the potion that they drank had. Surprisingly, there's already quite a bit of liquid inside. Mr. Yoshino scribbles a label and pastes it on with a bit of charmed sticky dust.

"Where'd the rest of the potion come from?" Remy asks.

"It's the part that Cam made," Beni says, turning the label around to face her. *A Love Potion Across the Ages; Created by Cameron Yasuda and Remy Kobata.* "He was here right before you. In fact, you just missed him."

Remy can't breathe. "But . . . why . . ."

The older woman sets out two vials, pours half of the antidote into each, and tops it off with a dash of the love potion Remy had just helped to make.

"These are yours. The antidote you created with each other, and the love potions you made on your own. This is the only way I can think of to stretch out the antidote you made so that there's enough for both of your memories to come back."

Tears spring to Remy's eyes, and she reaches out.

Beni shakes her head, pulling the vials away. "Wait."

"I need to find him now!" Remy cries out. If she . . . If Cam might still be able to fall in love with her . . . The hand on the clock on the wall shifts: 11:47 P.M.

She's almost out of time.

"This is only the ignition, per se," Beni responds. "A starter to an extinguished fire. This potion may help, yet it's not going to be enough on its own. *You* must find a way to break this curse."

Her heart aches and aches. She thought she'd had a solution, but it has just as quickly become a variant, like one of Cam's alchemy experiments that she doesn't understand.

"Remy." It's Mr. Yoshino.

She looks up from staring at her shaking hands curled around the two vials, the fingers that want to hold the Cam who knows and remembers her.

"Your chance to set this right is very limited." Mr. Yoshino raises an eyebrow. "You, and each of us, are constantly changing people. We are the same people, but we are never the same as before. You choose every day who you love. And, as you know, we . . . we do want you to be in love with your friend, for reasons you now understand."

Remy shoots back, "You twisted my fate—"

Beni holds up her hand. "If not for this, would you have truly taken action? Or would you have been the same person you were before you had heard the fortune?"

"It would've worked out . . ." Remy falters. *Someday. Maybe.*

"Here." Beni slides something over the bar. It's a handwritten note. Cam's writing, she realizes faintly.

Remy,

Please meet me at Ebisu Station?

—Cam

Ebisu Station. Why does that sound so familiar? It's next to Yebisu Gardens, which she remembers being some place for lights . . . or something like that. She can't quite remember. Prickles sweep across her skin.

But there is one thing she can remember: *Cam. Cam is there.*

The clock on the wall ticks; time is running out.

"This way." Mr. Yoshino gestures to a side exit. This door looks more like a torii gate, the kind at the entrances to shrines, carved around the wood frame.

She pushes the door open, but it doesn't lead to the road. Instead, she steps into a train; the other riders have their heads tucked into books or their cell phones, and they don't seem to notice her sudden appearance.

How— What—

A chime rings as the train rolls to a stop.

"We have arrived at Ebisu Station," calls the overhead announcement.

Beni and Mr. Yoshino casted pure magic. But there's no time for Remy to stop and wonder—if she's going to make this right, she needs to act, *now*.

Remy

C am is standing on the platform when Remy bursts out of the train car. He's wrapped up in his heavy peacoat and scarf, and his forehead is pinched looking for her.

"You're . . . you're here," she whispers.

God, she just wants to soak in the sight of him: his hair a messy fringe, the thickness of that lower lip that she wants to take into her mouth, the panes of his jaw that she wants to run her hands over. Maybe—hopefully—there will be time for that later, and for a whole lot more.

But, for now, there's this: "Want to go with me?" Remy holds her hand out and she's hoping like hell Cam will take it. Her heart is in her throat. "I—I won't remember you for much longer."

"Let's go." Cam's eyes are dark. His hand closes around hers, burning hot against the winter chill, hot as the blood pumping fast through her beating heart.

"Let's go," Remy echoes. The clock on her phone is ticking. 11:49. Eleven minutes. Is that enough to make him fall in love with her? This past *week* hasn't been enough.

But maybe depth isn't measured by time, but by memories.

"I'm . . . I'm going to tell you the way I see you," Remy says. "Before you forget me."

Cam takes one step closer to her, and then they begin walking side by side.

It's not fast enough; they won't get there fast enough, but Remy needs him to understand, understand everything, understand the parts of her heart she never, *ever* will tell anyone but him.

"You were never sure of yourself," Remy says. "But, honestly, neither was I. But with you, when I was with you, I knew wherever we'd go together was enough. It didn't matter if we were walking in circles or just lying on the couch playing Candy Crush. When you wanted to take your chemistry classes so badly, I wanted to learn what the hell entropy means, too."

She checks her phone again: 11:51. "Dammit. We're going to have to go faster . . ." She tugs him into a run.

"I like our memories," Cam says, simply. "It *feels* like me. It feels right."

So, Remy plunges in.

"Back in middle school, ohmygosh, I can't believe I'm telling you this." Remy sweats from sheer and utter embarrassment. "Remember when I switched into my PE shorts at lunchtime and you were worried I was cold?"

"That sounds kind of familiar . . ."

"It was my first period!" Remy laughs. "I had to change out of my jeans. You kept asking me if I was cold, if I wanted to swap my shorts with your sweatpants and all I wanted to do was melt into the ground!"

Cam's cheeks burn red. "I—I . . . I'm sorry I noticed your pants!"

They both burst into laughter, even as their sides ache from running.

"No, no," Remy says. "That's not what I'm saying. I'm . . . well, thank you for noticing me! And my pants! And, well, everything!"

After another burst of laughter—pants! They used to worry about *pants*—Cam says, "The me you remember is better than the me that I remember."

Remy stumbles, pulling Cam to a stop with her. They're not at the top of the hill yet. The strings of lights still flicker, on and on through the dark distance. It's like each of the memories that Remy cherishes and can't bear to forget. The second that these moments disappear will feel like she's in darkness, sinking without the surface in sight.

"Cam." Her voice cracks, and she wishes she could blame it on the cold, but that'd be a complete lie. "Cam, we did so many damn stupid things together. So many stupid-wonderful days that I just don't ever want to forget."

Remy breathes in deep. "There's nothing, *nothing* better than being messy and strange and weird with you, Cam."

Something cold brushes against Remy's cheek. Cam runs a finger against her skin, sending icy cold yet hot shivers along her spine.

"Snow," he whispers. "The weather forecast was right."

They're out of time.

Remy begins running again, pulling Cam along with her. "Keep going!"

They burst forward, powering up the hill, and they make it up, even as Remy's lungs burn.

And then they're standing at the top. Down the gentle slope, trees gleaming with strings of lights line the path. From farther away, sky-scrapers frame the view, adding to the luminance. It's glimmering and gorgeous. This is the path she's always wanted to take with Cam . . . yet in a few seconds, she'll forget why she even cared about this place.

She stares at him. "Do you remember—anything?"

"All these memories . . . when you explain them, it fits into place like I *know* it's been in my mind all along," he says. "When I try to recall more . . . it's all fuzzy, like I've forgotten to put in my contacts and I can't see right."

11:59.

Her memory is stuttering out; there are parts of Cam that she *should* know, but the distinct shape and feel and touch, it's all seeping away.

This is it. This is everything before it becomes nothing at all.

Then, Cam says, soft as snow, "I do know this: I'm sorry. I'm really sorry. I finally realized why I took the soulmate elixir. It wasn't for in-tellectual curiosity or some stupid lie like that. I've been hiding all my damn life. I've been too scared that I'll end up like my dad, bitter and angry and alone, that I've become that without ever doing *anything*. I've become *just* like Dad, always stuck in Memory Lane, always stuck in a time that isn't the present. I can apply for another alchemy license. I can try to get into MIT or wherever I want to go another year."

"Then . . ." she whispers. "Why did you take the soulmate elixir?"

"Because you're the one thing I can't ever lose. It was for us to fall in love. But, back then, I was already in love with you."

Snow swirls around them, and Remy can barely breathe.

Love. He had been in love with her all along.

"I—I love you, too," Remy says, her voice catching. His eyes flash with emotion, but desperation swells, the opposite of what Remy always thought she'd feel if she ever heard those words from him. "I love you too much to let you go. I can't forget you, Cam. I can't. I'm greedy, I need more time with you. I need to make more ugly cakes and broken Christmas tree cookies, and flat scones and fluffy biscuits and all the sugary things that will make your potions shine."

He breathes in sharply. They're out of time, there will be no *future* for them if they don't change things now—

"Will you take this antidote with me?" Remy asks, holding out the two vials. He nods, taking one from her hand.

The moment they uncap the tops, the scent of freshly made boba and a lingering note of jasmine tea wafts from hers; she wonders what Cam smells.

From all around the city, clocks begin to ring pure and sweet.

Midnight.

She and Cam tip their vials back, and drink.

One, two—

Cam shakes his head, rubbing at his forehead. His memories haven't returned.

Five, six—

She wavers. Today . . . they'd gone to the park together, right? For some sort of concert? Or had they?

Her memories are already slipping away.

Remy wishes each day was neat and tidy like a photo, so she can hold on to them forever, and keep flipping through the past, so she'll never lose a single moment.

Seven—

"Cam, I want to hold on to every damn memory, but I can't." The taste of the sweet antidote, like a mouthful of fresh water, is fading from her lips. Was it not enough? "Even if I don't remember a thing, I hope I remember this feeling of trusting you with my whole heart. Knowing that each new day will have a spark of happiness because I'll spend it with you. I never want to lose the memories of our time together because that means we can have a future. I want us to have a tomorrow, the next week, a new year. That's what you mean to me. More than words. You are everything that mattered in my past, but more than that, you are everything I've ever wanted in my future."

There's no more time to linger in her fears.

She takes a step closer, her eyes searching his. Cam's breath hitches, a quiet stutter. Her resolve is probably written over her face; he doesn't have to have a lifetime of memories of her to know what she intends.

Because their love? Hell, it's beyond sensation; it's beyond clumsy first kisses or pushing up against hidden corners of their high school. It is simply this: a love that rocks her to her core, whether they simply link arms or share sticky-sweet enchanted ice cream or tell each other all their secrets . . . except the secret she kept from him, all these years.

Her love for him burns through her body, even as the cursed potion tries to erase Cam from her blood and brain.

"Cam," she says, "I'd fight the Old Families of Tokyo to get your memories back, I'd make any antidote even if it risked all my memories . . . because, for me, you've always been The One. I *always* want you to be my past, present, and future."

His eyes widen. "Remy . . . I never want you to lose your memories for me."

"But I love you," she says, her heart aching. "Cam, I *love* you. Even if I forget everything about you, I'll remember that I loved someone as much as I loved you, that my future was always better because I knew I wanted to be with you, and that you will always have all of my love."

Her voice doesn't echo, not with the thick snow blanketing the trees and ground. Even the lights are covered and faded away, encased in a world of pure white.

She feels the echoes, the truth of her words with the final gongs—

Eleven, twelve—

It's past midnight.

They stare at each other. White powder falls like they're in a snow globe, and their world has been shaken up.

She stumbles backward, her head throbbing with a strong, insistent pain like a clock is slamming against the walls of her mind. Remy turns and turns, staring up at the city's bright, blinking lights all around them. She wants to capture those lights in her mind, to remind her of him . . .

To remind her of . . .

Who?

Remy frantically searches for memories, that little filing cabinet, but her mind is too scattered. Everything is gone, a void of black and white, white snow. All she can see is Cam in front of her, staring straight back.

But it's Cam.

Cam.

She—she remembers his name. She remembers the feel of his rough-yet-smooth hands. The way he snort-laughs when she tells nerdy jokes. How he grins like he's five again when they play puzzles or spend all their money on crane games.

"Remy." His voice is hoarse yet smooth, like a freshly frothed hojicha latte. She drinks in the sound of his voice, filling her soul with light. "Remember that time when we drove out to the Monterey Bay Aquarium and the seagulls chased you off the streets?"

She can't breathe. "I remember it differently. *You* dropped your popcorn and then tried to rescue it."

"Yeah, but I was trying to throw it away, not feed the sea vultures." He smiles crookedly, sweet and awkward, *her* Cam. "How about that time we made that exploding potion, and blasted Jack's science fair project apart?"

She laughs. "That all-nighter to remake it was *brutal*. We fell asleep, anyway, before we finished."

"I just remember when we were falling asleep, side by side, on my bedroom floor," Cam says quietly, "I wondered what it would be like to kiss you. At that time, I was already way too deep in love."

More memories: sitting in their high school classroom, his fingers tapping nervously against the plasticky desk, waiting for their new seat assignments as they hope they can sit next to each other next quarter, too. Long study sessions where he's trying patiently to teach her calculus, even though she doesn't understand why anyone would want to learn this mental torture. Then that day in middle school where he'd ended up in public speaking and she'd ended up in computer programming, because they'd both tried to choose the class that they thought the other might take, and they'd laughed and laughed until they had waged a Goldsticks War to end up in pottery class together.

She remembers everything. *Everything.*

Memories spill out and they laugh and compare and bring up even more stories. She notices they remember different parts of the past, like they're seeing it through different lenses. Yet, that's perfect. Because what overlaps are their feelings, the pounding in their chests, the way they can't seem to look at the snow around them, coating their shoulders and hair, or the luminous holiday lights all around, twinkling like shooting stars. They can only see each other.

Then she breathes in deep. It's a new year. The past is the *past.*

All they see is each other. When they have each other, they don't need to recall the past that led them here, or the future that's far away. They're made only of this current moment and the next handful of tiny, perfect, precious *nows*, unforgettable and so beautifully real.

"Remy." His voice cracks. His eyes are wide and shining brighter than the fairy lights around them. "If nothing's ever meant to be, our love was the one thing I'd always wanted to believe in. I didn't realize it until far too late, until you became a stranger to me."

Her heart is nearly pounding out of her chest.

"I knew I was missing you," he says. "I was missing you and it felt strange, yet I didn't know *what* I was missing. I'd wake up and want to message someone, and I couldn't figure out who it was. It was you; you're always the first person I think of when I wake. And—and—and I've been meaning to do this for ages, now—"

One hand rests on the nape of her neck, sheltering her from the cold. His other hand reaches out, tucking a strand of hair behind her ear, out of her face.

"Remy Kobata," he says softly. "Destroyer of Candy Crush, fellow Goldsticks fighter, my best friend, my soulmate. It's always been you, Remy Kobata, even if our fates get cursed."

Remy whispers back, "You will always be my fate. The fortune and potion taught me that fate can be twisted—for better or worse—by the actions we take on our own. No matter how cursed our love may be, even if I forget you, a thousand times over, I will always love you. I will always choose you."

His throat bobs as he swallows, like he wants to drink in her words. "Can I—"

She grabs him by the lapels of his coat and pulls him closer; her arms slide up his shoulders, along his neck, and through his hair, feeling all of him. His hands curve behind her neck and waist, and their lips brush, tentatively at first, and then she takes a stuttering breath of disbelief; his scent like jasmine tea, honey-sweet, washing over her, and their lips crash, soft and sweet and fiery and everything at once. There's no more winter chill and all she feels is the heat of his body.

He tastes like the winning part of a Goldstick, an early morning hojicha latte sparked with joy. His voice is music, and she could live off his whispers and his nearly silent sighs. Her body burns with waves of heat, forgetting the cold, probably burning off any speck of snow on her, because they're together. No matter what comes their way—charmed *or* cursed—they'll have a best friend, a soulmate, to go through the future together.

EPILOGUE

Cam

Most people pass right on by Cam, too intent on heading to Shibuya Station or going shopping down the street. But he stares up at the café he'd wanted to take Remy on a date to, a full year ago.

He has dreamed of this place, of this moment. The sweet taste of its famous tiramisu Mille Crêpe cake, with sparkling contentment enchantments woven into the powdered cocoa, or the French press coffee with a shot of magical strength.

It feels like there are fireworks popping in his stomach, like bubbly elixirs mixed all up. All the final angry words from his dad are fading away, no louder than the pounding of passersby's footsteps. It's a reminder that he didn't belong at his dad's; the blank white walls of their house were never his home.

He rolls in his beat-up, aqua suitcase, pushing it insistently toward the corner table, right when the waitress opens the door at ten o'clock. When she flits by with a menu, he orders the tiramisu and the coffee, but both lay untouched half an hour later.

He's not hungry. He just wants to see *her*.

The other tables fill up; customers come and go, but they're not who he's here to meet.

A quarter to noon—the actual time they were supposed to show up—a girl hurries inside, bringing in a swirl of snow that sticks to her bangs. Her cheeks are pink; her eyes are bright. The girl clutches a stack of books like they're her prized possessions; she's wearing a vintage-looking pastel dress, and carting a canvas tote bag with the word "TMU" stamped on it.

She looks around, scanning the tables.

Cam barely feels himself rising. He wishes now that he'd drank that coffee filled with strength, because his knees are about to buckle under him.

"Remy." His voice is gravelly, way too serious, way too filled with so many emotions spilling over.

It feels like an hour and a split second all at the same time; he strides over to her—do they hug? What are his arms for, even? He wants to blurt out, *I've missed you, how have you been*—a million things he's been thinking of telling her in person in the year since, but if he opens his mouth now all that will come out is gibberish.

She waves at the table, with a laugh. "Let me put down my mess. I guess I brought a few too many books. I thought I was going to arrive first."

They both slide into their seats, face-to-face. It's so good to see her, *her*. Not a computer screen, where she's made of pixels. Not the Polaroids on his wall, where she seems so small and far away. Remy. The real Remy.

"My plane came in early, and immigration was a breeze." *This* was not what he wanted to tell her. Remy studies him, and he brushes his chin. "What? Did I shave unevenly?"

"I'm being a dork. I . . . I just can't believe it's you." She shakes her head. "And I can't believe it's been a full year since."

With those words, his memory pulls him back to the snowy night, where he was about to lose his best friend, forever. He's damn glad she's here in front of him, now.

Remy's gaze is distant, like she's lost in the past, too. "Jack and Ellie want to throw a party for you tonight. Naomi's ready for you to start in her lab—though she's promised that even her cat is more senior than you."

Cam laughs. "It's only because of Naomi that I heard about TMU's special research scholarship. I owe her and Tsukki a lot. I don't mind at all if he's my senior lab partner."

Remy grins, and her smile fills him with more energy than any cup of coffee ever could. "I can't believe how time has flown. So . . . have you gotten the email?"

He nods. "I . . . I got an email from TMU right before I boarded. I think it's the results. I mean, well, I haven't read it, yet. . . . I was hoping to open it with you."

Remy's fingers reach out—tentatively, slowly—so that her hand is halfway at the center of the table. "You're sure? About moving here—school here?"

Cam used to believe that elixirs, fluid as they were, were more solid and constant than him. Their recipes never changed; when mixed together, they always produced the same results.

Cam, on the other hand, always floundered in the face of his dad's demands: *Work for the shop. Love isn't worth it. Eye on the prize.*

But he's not that same Cam from a year ago.

Gently, softly, he wraps his hands around hers; they're still cold from her walk in, and he tries to give her all the warmth he has, just like the way he has always wanted to give her all of his heart.

His eyes meet hers, and he's no longer sloshing elixir. He knows who he is, and what he wants.

"I'm sure," he says. "About moving here, about TMU. As long as you're okay with it, too."

"That's not even a question. I wanted you to move here a year ago." Then, she pauses. "But your dad . . ."

"Yeah, that was definitely some unfinished business. Tough conversation, but I finally said my part. Jack was right. *I* was right."

Remy chews on her lip. "Did he agree with you?"

"We agreed to disagree," Cam says. "But at least he knows what my plans are, and he knows I'm here if he does want to open up our relationship again. I can't live for my dad's expectations. I want to live for my own expectations and hopes. I told him that I'd realized that I will never leave the people I love behind; and those who truly love me will never forget me, either. After all, because of my mother and especially because of us, I believe in those words with all my heart."

"They never do leave us," she agrees softly. "We both changed a lot over this past year, didn't we?"

"But we ended up here," he says.

She nods and echoes, "We ended up here."

Their fingers lace together; her hands are warm, now. She leans forward, and their foreheads press against each other.

His past is filled with memories as sharp as shards of glass. Before, maybe, he would have wished that he could forget all of that. Or he would wish for a simple future, where he'd never mess up. That life could be perfect, even when he knows it can't. But, with Remy, he can get through whatever comes next. She sees his broken parts, and calls it beautiful. And, as he holds her tight, the pieces of their past and future shimmer like a kaleidoscope of colors. That's what being around her does; she helps him see the real magic in the world—and in himself. When they're together, every part of their future and past is something he cherishes.

Wherever they are—Japan, California, anywhere in between—as long as he's with her, Cam knows he's where he was always meant to be, finally.

Credits

Editor—Tiffany Shelton
Associate Publisher—Eileen Rothschild
Editorial Director—Sara Goodman
Agent—Sarah Landis at Sterling Lord Literistic
Art Director—Kerri Resnick
Cover Illustrator—Maxine Vee
Author Photographer—Julie Vu
Design Team—Gabriel Guma
Managing Editor—Eric Meyer
Production Manager—Lena Shekhter
Production Editors—Carla Benton, Cassie Gutman
Copy Editor—Lani Meyer
Proofreaders—Linda Sawicki, Yunyi Zhang
Marketing Team—Alexis Neuville, Brant Janeway
Publicity Team—John Karle
Contracts Team—Sabrina Boyle, Andrea Morales
Foreign Rights Team—Witt Phillips, Emily Miller
Early Readers—Chelsea Ichaso, Eunice Kim, Sarah Suk, Meredith
    Tate

And thank you to my dear friends and family, who inspire me
every day.